Blahom

A Warrior Goddess
Book 1

April Q. Russell

Copyright © 2022 by April Q. Russell CARU Publishing

All rights reserved.

No part of this book may be reproduced in any form or by any electronic or mechanical means, including information storage and retrieval systems, without written permission from the author, except for the use of brief quotations in a book review.

The Library of Congress has catalogued BLAHOM Book One as follows: Names: Russell, April Q., author.

Title: BLAHOM Book One

Description: Georgia: April Q. Russell, 2022

Identifiers: Subjects| BISAC: FICTION/Literary FICTION/ Fantasy / Urban FICTION/ African American & Black / Women FICTION / Fantasy / Epic

This is a work of fiction. Names, characters, places, and incidents either are the product of the author's imagination or are used fictitiously, and any resemblance to actual person, living or dead, business, companies, events, or locales is entirely coincidental.

If you purchased this book without a cover, you should be aware that his book is stolen property. It was reported as "unsold and destroyed" to the publisher, and neither the author nor the publish has received any payment for this "stripped book."

To my heavenly Father
Thank You for being my Author and Finisher

"There is nothing better for a man, than that he should eat and drink, and that he should make his soul enjoy good in his labor. This also I saw, that it was from the hand of God."
— Ecclesiastes 2:24

Planet Sirius

Prologue

From the moment the sun first rose on planet Sirius, there has been a deep-rooted tension between the two ruling species on the land: the Zaeds or God people and the Delions or technology people.

The epic land they share, though small, is vast and naturally beautiful with plentiful resources. Sirius has majestic mountain ranges so tall that the peaks are often obscured by mists of dense white clouds. The warm, soft, sandy beaches have endless coast lines and are home to colorful birds with large wingspans, soaring through the azure sky and past the most vivid scenery. The clear, blue water is filled with vibrant fish that, while breath-taking, are also delicious to eat. The planet is home to massive, glorious sand dunes and in the far north are picturesque areas where snow falls all year. Even the harshest places to live on Sirius are still paradises of pristine beauty.

The two species sharing the planet are very different. The Zaeds, though fewer in number, have been the superior leaders, ruling over the planet's vast landscape and natural resources. They have a strong sense of spirituality, believing that the Alpha God shared divine gifts with them that give their warriors super powers. They devote their life to honoring the Gift Giver and prioritize that over anything and anyone.

The Delions, ruling over the lesser, more barren parts of Sirius, are a considerably larger population than the Zaeds and have highly advanced technological abilities. They believe that only they themselves, not some god, can create divine gifts, and that their technology will give them the ultimate power – control of the entire planet, and the ability to create life. Their implementation of technology seems to be advancing rapidly as their population has almost doubled in the last twenty years.

Despite their differences, both species follow similar social formalities, only sharing intimacies between close relatives and spouses. Both hold themselves to a strict honor code, set in stone by the leaders. ManCohalith and his wife, Mother Hutra, rule over the Zaeds, while the Delions are ruled by ManMattheius John and his wife, Mother Nadine John. Both leaders value tradition and view the positions of men and women in society as sacred, the men celebrated as warriors, and women honored as leaders carrying cultural traditions forward.

Integral to Zaed spirituality is the phenomenon of Transitioning. When Zaed elite warriors reach a certain age, they train by secluding themselves in harsh conditions for days at a time, physically preparing for the change their body will undergo as their body's DNA is rewritten. Not every Zaed elite warrior lives through the process. For those who survive, their physical abilities and divine gifts are blessed, uniting them with the Alpha God, and making them immensely powerful. The Zaed Transition Unit was becoming more refined in their divine abilities under the leadership of ManCohalith.

* * *

The Delions, determined to combat the Zaeds' divine gifts and prepare for a mass takeover, have spent decades developing a new and dangerous technology. In a secret base camp far from the Zaeds, the Delions have built portal which can transport them light years away to planet Earth. In a blink of an eye, a Delion can be in human flesh, possessing the body of an Earthling. The ability to go to Earth and gain power and control over another planet has long been the supreme plan and conquering through technology is seen as the way of the future for the Delion people.

Despite different beliefs, the two species on planet Sirius have not always been at war. Some say that under ManMattheius' thirty-year rule, many Zaed women have disappeared as part of the Delion agenda to create life. Ten years ago, ManCohalith officially declared that repeated Delion efforts to destroy Zaed women constituted war. As a last straw, the Delions had invaded Zaed-guarded land in an attempt to abduct the young Zaed Goddesses, aged three and seven at the time.

Theories abound as to why the Delion targeted the two Goddess, but none are definitive. Pressure from both species has recently risen after the year-long disappearance of ManCohalith's niece.

Chapter One

Blahom could feel the rhythm of the music pulsating from within her as she made her grand entrance along the pathway cleared for her arrival as the solo performer in tonight's CCDC ceremony. The soloist was always the last dancer to arrive, joining the rest of the ensemble before the dance began.

No one knows exactly what "CCDC" means, but it is often said that the "D" stands for Dietrickt, a dance performed only during Transitioning. It is a phenomenon, anointed with a spiritual elegance that often leaves those in attendance crying, shaken with renewed hope. The Dietrickt dance is performed before a Transitioning soldier undergoes his final trial and again upon his successful completion and return.

Dances at other CCDC festivities are a mix of tributes of thanksgiving for the seasons of life, celebrations of victory on the battlefield, or to honor brave fallen warriors. Festivities are laced with music and food and there are decorations of lights and fabrics representing royalty, honor, and majesty. No other event, job, or responsibility carries precedence over CCDC festivities and they are considered of great importance and are a true staple in the culture of the Zaeds.

CCDC festivals have been deemed sacred and instrumental to tipping the scales in the Zaeds' favor on the battlefield.

Blahom had been the solo performer for most Dietrickt dances for several years. She was blessed with the ability to bring joy through her dance, leaving people happy and light after her performance.

She walked past her admirers with humble confidence, a regal, relatable Goddess with a big heart and a bright smile. The young girls and women of the land looked up to her and, before the increased security statutes were implemented for all Zaed women, Blahom could often be found walking in the town's marketplace, talking, having a brief bite to eat with the commoners, and enjoying socializing and answering questions about dancing.

It was no secret that the Zaed men likewise adored Blahom. Her father had already been presented with many early marriage proposals. Blahom was flattered. Her youthful heart loved fast and hard and had already been broken once.

Blahom's elegant walk along the path radiated her feminine and spiritual power as she approached the performance area and the ensemble of dancers. The crowd was welcoming and cheering her on. She noticed Jhapalle, her most recent love interest, standing where he was sure to catch her eye, a bouquet of fresh flowers in his hands. It had been almost a year since he was caught sneaking out of her room at night. It was a minor infraction, but after the disappearance of her nineteen-year-old female cousin, ManCohalith and Blahom's mother implemented a firm watch order and Blahom and her sister were now always accompanied by their two Lady Mothers.

Blahom smiled at Jhapalle, a brown, smooth-skinned warrior Zaed. She was yearning for his affection. *His kiss on my neck and hand palming my backside ... the electrical charge of daybreak,* Blahom thought to herself. For a moment, her smile slipped. It would be nearly impossible to return to their prior romantic adventures with the team of Lady Mothers always on guard.

Bringing her focus back, Blahom could feel the heightened energy as warriors had returned with exciting news of a Zaed triumph against the Delions and the successful Transitioning of two commanders. The CCDC victory tribute was well underway.

She looked ahead at the ensemble of dancers. *Uggh, where are Lita and Allysia? Why are they not in position?* she thought. Blahom was a perfectionist. When it came time to perform, she wanted everyone polished and ready so the dance could be a blessing to the warriors.

"Come ON, Allysia, we can't keep them waiting!" A young Zaed dancer pulled the arm of another dancer, who was dragging her feet.

"We're not keeping them waiting, Lita, Blahom is still arriving," Allysia whined. "I had to go to the bathroom, and I don't know if I remember all my steps."

"You do remember, stop being childish. Hurry!" Both rushed to get into position with the other dancers who were poised and ready. A slightly older dancer turned to face them, her eyes dark as the midnight sky, and chocolate-brown hair around her face. She raised an eyebrow at the two girls before letting out a small laugh at their tardiness.

"It's not funny, Zya," Lita silently mouthed.

"Somewhat, it is," Zya mouthed back. "But it is time now, so we need to be in prayer and focus."

The music was loud, and the dancers calmed themselves. To the sound of drums, tambourines, and horns, Blahom found her way to the center. She, the Lady Mothers, and the Lady Sisters dance ensemble were ready to perform the honorable Dietrickt dance

completely in sync with one another.

Tonight's Dietrickt dance celebrated the Transitioning of young commanders Thistle and Jakk, the nephews of ManCohalith and Mother Hutra. It had been over two years since the Generals decreed the warriors ready for Transition and to undergo their final trial. The two had returned in triumph.

Blahom led a style of Dietrickt dance that was fast, quick, bright, and upbeat. The tempo picked up speed – allegro to vivace to presto – but always flowing within the dancers. Adorned with golden fabric draped off their strong shoulders, the women moved with grace, elongating their arms and legs in complete unison.

The Lady Mothers and Lady Sisters ranged from thirteen to sixty years old. They were tall and elegant. The Lady Mothers were the most seasoned and sought-after dancers in their communities, regal and beautiful, handpicked by Mother Hutra. The Lady Sisters were the daughters and granddaughters of the Lady Mothers, trained from birth to dance, and what they might lack in poise and experience, they made up for in dancing ability and enthusiasm. Each dancer was a beauty in her own right and well-known in the land.

None, perhaps, were more recognized than the Goddess-ordained daughters of Mother Hutra: Blahom and Katyana.

It had been decades since two Goddess sisters joined the CCDC dance ensemble at the same time. The Lady Sisters' popularity increased, making them more celebrated than many generations before. It was becoming more important to keep the dancers not only safe but also grounded and buffered from the increased admiration.

Mother Hutra managed the dancers well, constantly preaching the purpose of their dancing as divine gifts. She gave gentle reminders that their acclaim was never to overshadow their true calling as a CCDC dancer.

It was halfway through the performance and time for Blahom's solo. In silence, the Goddess stepped forward and knelt on the ground, the ensemble of dancers in a semicircle behind her. Blahom slowly rose, lifting her spine and elongating her neck. The music started; she stood in first position. The music drum hit another beat. The young Goddess slid her perfectly pointed toes out. The drum began beating faster, the rhythm accelerating. Soon, she was gliding through her movements, not missing a beat. She felt sand sift between her toes as the smell of salt water tickled her nose. She felt the anointed rhythm within her. She threw her head up, arched her back and flung out her long, graceful arms to the sky.

The tempo picked up pace once more, and Blahom's wide hips

moved rapidly as sweat beaded down her body, her heart pounding in tune to the beat.

The Zaed community, from the leaders to the battle-weary warriors, watched in awe and felt their spirits restored. United in thanksgiving prayer, they drew strength from each other's presence. Commanders Thistle and Jakk stood front and center as Blahom danced before them and, with ManCohalith's prayers, their inner power was awakened.

The drumbeat stopped, and to Blahom, it felt as if time stood still. She knelt again on the ground with her hands reaching towards the sky, a gesture of thanks to the Alpha God for the divine gifts now bestowed on the two commanders.

As the music stopped, the community showed their appreciation, singing joyously, clapping, and praising. The two commanders were weak from receiving their new powers and shed tears of gratitude.

Flowers were thrown at Blahom's feet. Holding her pose, Blahom felt her chest rise and fall, her soggy clothes clinging to her body. She had pushed herself hard, but even through the sweat and the crowd, Blahom stood, looking truly ethereal. Her brown skin glowed in the sunlight; her thick, sandy-brown hair was braided into an intricate bun. Her dress flowed and billowed with the breeze, the golden fabrics cinched at her waist, and the sleeves hanging from her shoulders, showing off her pronounced collar bone. Around her neck, a precious golden choker that shone in the sun, made from soft fabrics, and adorned with an emerald pendant. Her hands wore purple lace gloves that changed color depending on the dance performance.

As a part of the royal family, Blahom was a Goddess by blood, elegant and virtuous. ManCohalith had prayed many nights during Mother Hutra's pregnancy that if she gave birth to a daughter, the child would be gifted with a beauty as fine as silk fabric and grow in strength to represent the culture and unity of the Zaeds. At birth, Blahom had ice-blue eyes, a color unheard of for her complexion, but as she grew, the blue turned green, and the green began to trim in gold. The Zaeds saw the beauty of her eyes as a gift from the Alpha

God, and a visual representation of the majesty of the land her father ruled, many parts of which she had never seen.

Dancing was Blahom's duty as a Goddess, something that she would never dream of changing. She was learning to enjoy the admiration dancing afforded her, and her growing popularity as she started to blossom out of her teens. And although Mother Hutra made sure she had no time to get into trouble, Blahom caught the eye of many elite male Zaeds, and she was constantly daydreaming of what a love affair could mean.

Thank you for this opportunity to dance for the Zaeds, Blahom silently prayed, slowly panting for breath. *I thank you, Alpha God, for our victory and the hope you allowed me to bring through my dance.*

"Thank you for your performance, Goddess. Shall I be your water boy?" A tall, handsome young Zaed reached out to hand her a glass of water.

Blahom was shocked that Rasheed, the adopted son of her uncle, had made it past the Lady Mothers. She smiled, then looked over her shoulder to see Jhapalle trying to make his way through the crowd to deliver his bouquet of flowers.

Locking eyes on Rasheed she said, "Thank you, however with your ability to reach me so swiftly, you must be much more than a water boy. Maybe you are the son of General Brakkus, my mother's brother and favorite uncle." Blahom smiled at the look on Rasheed's face. "I will accept the water. Thank you."

Rasheed handed her the goblet of water with pride.

"I'd like to thank you for your performance too, Ms. Goddess, but I did not bring water." Blahom broke away from Rasheed's gaze and looked down to see a small child staring up at her. The girl was clearly nervous speaking to the Goddess, her hands fidgeting anxiously. Blahom was torn, yearning to talk to Rasheed, who had been swift enough to bring her water despite the sea of protectives around her, but she was just as surprised at the young girl's ability to reach her. To ease the young girl's nerves, Blahom knelt again.

"It is quite alright, young one," she said.

Blahom

Rasheed had made his small but significant point. He backed away respectfully so Blahom could be left alone with the girl, but not before giving her a look of longing.

"My father died in the last battle, and I'm happy to know that your dance today honored him," the girl said as tears welled in her eyes.

"This is my duty. I am grateful to dance for your father and for all his fallen brothers," Blahom said with a warm comforting smile. The girl smiled back with pain behind her eyes.

"My father was a commoner, but he wished that I would learn to dance and become a Lady Sister dancer one day. I have no idea how to train for dancing, as we are of the Welch tribe, and there are no women who have ever been more than market sellers. My mother is not among the Lady Mothers, even as an honorable helper. Are you able to help me learn to dance, though my father will never to see me?" The girl's voice carried unwavering strength for her age, as she dropped her head, and struggled to hold back tears.

Blahom held the girl's small hand. "I will see to it that you will become one of the best dancers in our land. You will have the best training, and you will show up every day and dance in honor of your father and our Zaeds. Yes, your father is dead now, but be brave in your time of loss. Death is inevitable for us all, and now you must live and grow and make him proud," Blahom's voice was soft but strong, as she echoed words used by her father.

"Goddess, we need to leave. Your parents have left the ceremony early." Lady Mother Clara came forward, interrupting the moment between the two.

"I must go now, brave girl. I will get word to the council of the Welch Tribe for you." Blahom gave the girl a hug before she was ushered away quickly by Lady Mother Clara who helped her up on her horse with one fluid motion. Blahom looked around for Rasheed, but he was nowhere to be found. She sighed with slight disappointment, hoping she would be able to see him alone soon.

"Blahom, you mustn't make promises you cannot keep," Lady

Mother Clara said as she mounted her own horse. A beautiful middle-aged woman with defined arms and an athletic build, it was Lady Mother Clara's responsibility to stay close to Blahom's side since the birth of the young Goddess.

"I will keep my promise. How can we not invite the daughters of fallen warriors to join our ensemble?" Blahom's mind was focused on the girl and how determined she was to keep her word. *If all the Lady Sister dancers are only those of trained Lady Mothers, what is to become of the little girls who are born to women who do not dance?* she thought.

"I understand you, Blahom, but are we to train every Zaed girl in the land? That would be impossible. Everyone has a position, and everyone should hold that position with pride," said Lady Mother Clara.

"Understood, but shall we not teach them the beauty of the gift of dancing? Shall they not be celebrated? Who celebrates a woman selling fresh fruit and the meat cut from a cow?"

Lady Mother Clara raised an eyebrow. "Well, I seem to recall that you do. Or at least you should, every time you eat or drink with joy. Perhaps you will celebrate them more, especially seeing that you are missing out on tonight's feast?"

After a ceremony, Zaeds gathered around rows of table beautifully presented in the center of town. The feast consisted of various arrangements, from fruits that were picked earlier in the morning, freshly caught fish, and Blahom's favorite, perfectly roasted skewered meat.

Blahom was speechless for a moment, feeling deeply apologetic. "The feast?"

"With the best produce and meat the land has to offer, carefully picked and curated by those ... those who don't get celebrated." Lady Mother cleared her throat, her wisdom speaking loud to Blahom. "You must first understand her tribe, and the value they offer to our land and people, so that you are able to celebrate them and then help the young girl celebrate who she is and how to blossom in that, rather than encouraging her to want to be what and who you are."

"Of course. My heart wants only her to be happy." Blahom felt guilty, realizing she knew nothing about the Welch tribe or their craft.

"Well then, help her understand that happiness is finding joy in her journey. Happiness is knowing who she is and excelling in that."

Blahom had received the message and wanted to change the subject. "I did notice the lamb skewers on the menu today. I am appreciative and eating is a joy to me. But it's unlike Mother and Father to leave during a ceremony. Do you know why Lady Mother?"

Lady Mother Clara shook her head. "I do not. All I know is that I am to retrieve you before you take off towards the feast."

Blahom tried to ignore the grumble in her stomach at the thought of all the food she was leaving behind.

"Let's head out. Katyana and Vasco are sure to be with Mother Hutra and ManCohalith. Wouldn't want to keep them waiting." Lady Mother Clara kicked the side of her horse, commanding it to go forward.

"Trot," Blahom said, encouraging her horse to pass up the inspiring greenery nearby.

As they rode back to the city, Blahom's adrenaline was still coming down and her mind was anxious. She knew that her mother and father never left early during a ceremony and she braced herself for the worst. The worst usually meant death after a battle. These days it also seemed to mean another problem for the Zaed women, which often led to strict schedules. Blahom did not want to believe that after the Dietrickt dance there would be news of a close death, but her thoughts chased themselves through her mind. *What if it means Vasco or Father are preparing to go away to fight a war that seems to never end? Is there an alternative to the war? How can we stop the attack on our women?* Blahom had hoped that her cousin would randomly show up again and all this stress and drama would be over, but she knew her thoughts were simple and improbable. Still, she was tired of death and the lockdown rules and cautions.

Getting closer to home, Blahom was missing the feast she had to leave behind. She was also bit annoyed at missing the opportunity to speak with Rasheed, who had often silently flirted when they saw each other at family gatherings. *Maybe our love will be easier than the one I had with Jhapalle. After all, he is family,* she thought. A small smile graced her face as she remembered his offer of a glass of water, clearly trying to show her that he had his mind made up about her and was intentional about every step. The courage and boldness of making his way to her even before the Lady Mothers was attractive to Blahom. Deep inside, Blahom felt that she could love him. She wanted to love him.

Lady Mother Clara picked up the pace in front of her and, tightening her grip on the reins, Blahom pushed forward as she continued her silent prayer from earlier.

I am grateful for my position as a Goddess and dancer. The prayer for love is one that I will forever pray. But my heart hurts for the girl and the look in her eyes. Please help me to understand what the point is with war. Why do you allow war and pain? Why is that a season? I'm not sure why I should pray for love only to have my lover, or my father or brother killed during battle. I ask that you please make this go away? And food, please feed me swiftly tonight. Amen.

Blahom enters performance area

Chapter Two

"Great solo my beautiful sis," Vasco said as Blahom ran through the front door. "Too bad we couldn't stay longer to enjoy the feast." His tone indicated his annoyance, but Vasco leaned down to give Blahom an endearing kiss on the cheek. Clearly, he was uneasy about the situation as well.

Vasco was a Lieutenant and intimidating to most people. His stern square face was hardened from war, his dark skin marred by multiple scars from weapons that had come within spitting distance of ending his life. Some whispered that he was more ruthless in battle even than his own father, his drive to eliminate the Delions coursing through him. Vasco remembered all too well the night the Delions attempted to abduct his sisters a decade ago, and since the disappearance of his cousin Daniella, his hatred towards them and their despised technology had only grown. His broad chest rippled with muscles from years of hard training, and a long scar ran from his shoulder to his large bicep, a souvenir of letting a Delion get too close: it was a mistake he never made again. Despite his scars, Vasco was extremely handsome.

"Yeah, it sucks. I could smell food as I was leaving. My stomach is still rumbling," Blahom said, still anxious at whatever news was awaiting them and trying to take her mind off the situation. "Hopefully there will still be some food left if we're able to get back."

"Is food all you two can talk about?" Katyana, the youngest sister, walked up to her siblings, a half-eaten skewer in her hand.

Katyana was a beautiful young teen Goddess. Despite being much younger, her eyes were sharp and focused. Katyana was indifferent about being what she referred to as a "dancing Goddess." As the youngest, she got away with far more than her elder siblings, even occasionally claiming she "felt ill" to get a pass not to perform in the ceremony. Blahom and Vasco had never been allowed to miss a CCDC ceremony, even if they were sick.

"Oh, shut up. Your tummy feeling, okay?" Blahom asked mimicking a baby voice as Katyana kept munching on the skewer, her arms crossed over her chest.

"It's not my fault the fruit was off this morning," Katyana smirked. "Now this skewer on the other hand is pretty good."

"The two of you, knock it off. We need to focus on meeting Mother and Father and see what's going on." Vasco let out a sigh and tried to shake his nerves. Vasco always seemed to be on edge.

The three siblings and the Lady Mothers entered the Throne Room, where ManCohalith, Mother Hutra, and a couple of dozen family members of the Hutra Dynasty were waiting.

The two leaders radiated strength. ManCohalith was a five-star general in the Zaed army and emanated control, discipline, and warmth. His face hardly moved, always appearing stern, yet loving. He had a comforting grin, but Blahom could count on one hand the number of times she had seen her father smile showing his teeth.

Mother Hutra was powerful in her own right. Her appearance was gentle and soft, with rounded cheeks and a comforting smile. Dressed in ceremonial garb, Mother Hutra was draped in deep purple satin that pooled around her like water. Her dress was slit from her hip down, exposing a muscular but slender leg, sculpted from years of dancing. Every smooth curve of her body emanated femininity.

The siblings knew not to be deceived by their mother's elegance and gracefulness: she was a no-nonsense Zaed woman. Mother Hutra was quick to discipline her children and every soft curve could turn sharp, full lips pursing together while her eyebrows raised, as if daring them to press her further. She did not need to speak for them to know they were in trouble.

Standing next to Mother Hutra was her younger sister, Lorraine. She was a frail yet elegant woman in her late thirties, known for keeping secrets and typically only spoke when interpreting dreams. Despite her quiet demeanor, she was charming and respected. When Lorraine entered the room, eyes immediately were drawn to her. Even ManCohalith wasn't immune to her silent charm.

By Lorraine's side was her daughter Trinity. She was a young toddler with big golden eyes and high cheekbones. Trinity was also quiet, like her mother, and she heavily resembled Blahom even more than Katyana did.

To the left and the right of their parents' thrones stood the top generals of the Zaed warriors and their families. Two of the generals were ManCohalith's brothers and two were Mother Hutra's.

General Velio, the eldest of the generals, and the most experienced in battle, was ManCohalith's middle brother and the two shared a close resemblance. Both had calculating brown eyes and pronounced cheekbones. Their beards were identical, thick and long and speckled with silver hairs. They had an ongoing competition on who had the best beard, each believing that theirs was the most glorious, but to most viewers, there was absolutely no difference at all. Next to General Velio stood his wife and their two sons, Thistle, twenty-four years old, and Jakk, twenty-three. They were new warriors and already well-respected, having recently completed their second battle fighting alongside Vasco on the battlefield.

General Lakin was ManCohalith's youngest brother. It seemed he had more scars than flesh. Despite being annoyed by its itchiness, he had grown out his beard to cover a long, jagged scar that ran across his throat from a Delion attempt to decapitate him. Under his battered appearance, his eyes were gentle. He had a love, maybe even a weakness, for women, and though his scars made him look intimidating, women loved him for it. Standing by his side were three women who had borne him five children, also in attendance. His youngest and eldest children were born to the same woman: twin girls, just learning to talk, and Daniella, his first born, who would be twenty-two this year. Daniella had been missing for over a year and though the General rarely spoke of her, everyone knew he was laser focused on finding her. His youngest son, Colin, a preteen, was close to Katyana's age. His eldest son, Burris, twenty, stood proudly by his side, having just become a warrior and now training and praying for his time to Transition.

On the right of General Lakin was General Brakkus. He was the shortest and loudest of the Generals, and his beard was as big and wild as his personality. A patient man, he was the lead trainer to most of the incoming warriors. He was Mother Hutra's youngest brother, and where she was reserved and calm, he was rambunctious and energetic. His jovial and friendly demeanor made Brakkus the favorite uncle of Blahom and Kat.

Standing next to General Brakkus was his wife Melissa, and their adopted son, Rasheed. In contrast to his short, wild warrior father, Rasheed was tall and tidy, with short brown curls, striking hazel eyes, and an exuberant energy, often smiling when things appeared bleak.

General Murn, the eldest brother of Mother Hutra, was the survivalist of the group. He was always in training mode, and attended meetings straight from the field, with dirt underneath his fingernails, smudges of mud on his body, an no attempt made to camouflage his appearance. While he looked unkempt, he was still proud of his beard, always making sure that it was clean and immaculate.

In the far corner stood Zya, Vasco's girlfriend. She had a slightly curvy stature, her chocolate-brown hair wrapped in an elegant bun,

Blahom

and her dark brown eyes slightly worries. Vasco's eyes darted to her before he looked up at his parents, ready to listen to their news.

"Thank you for your swift arrival," ManCohalith said, his voice like distant thunder, soft yet powerful. ManCohalith and his wife always showed respect to their children, to honor their hard work and diligence as Goddesses and a warrior. They knew each child had a destiny that was much bigger than the parents that birthed them. They understood the responsibility placed on each child was much more than any other their Zaed their age in the land. Both ManCohalith and Mother Hutra poured an equal amount of love and discipline on all three children and treated them as the heirs that they were.

The three siblings stood at attention in front of their parents, Vasco in the center with Blahom to his left and Katyana to his right. ManCohalith and Mother Hutra seemed to tower over them as they sat in their throne chairs.

In the presence of ManCohalith, one felt like an ant in the face of God. Despite his age, he was as fit as his generals and held himself like the authority he was. His back was straight and rigid, like a mountain, not bowing to anything that tried to push him. His deep eyes held wisdom both from the battles won and battles lost.

"I have called you all here because we must discuss a pressing matter," ManCohalith said, getting straight to business. "It involves Mother Hutra's recent dream. It is why she had to leave the ceremony earlier today. Now she wishes to reveal her dream in everyone's presence."

The three siblings stiffened at that. Vasco rolled his eyes.

Blahom's thoughts raced silently. *A dream? Not again. Wait ... lemme think ... did I do anything recently?* Blahom hurried played back the last few weeks and any secret thing she may have done trying to get away from the tribe around her. *I can't think of anything. As much as I wanted to, I have not been able to see Jhapalle. I have had no secret meetups at night. Ha! I've been pretty good; this can't be about me*

A dream from Mother Hutra was always something to respect. It was either a prophecy of the future or a discovery of mischief that her children were up to.

Maybe it's about Vasco and his girlfriend. Is she pregnant? Blahom wanted to take a quick glance at Zya but knew it would be awkward. *Hopefully it's about Kat. Mother dreamed about her faking being sick this morning and now she is going to lay into Kat for shirking her responsibilities as a Goddess,* Blahom playfully thought to herself, remembering the countless times her mother had shamed them for misbehaving. Blahom became aware of Rasheed standing with his father. Her eyes slightly widened, but she attempted to keep composure and prevent herself from looking at Rasheed. *What if she had a dream about Rasheed and me. Did it show a future for us together? What if Mother found out about our hidden flirting?*

All the siblings' minds were buzzing with questions, and once the room was silent for several moments and everyone was at full attention, Mother Hutra spoke.

"My dream was diluted; it is hard to recall what happened in my dream." Mother Hutra squeezed her eyes shut, grasping at what she could remember.

"When it began, I was surrounded by a thick cloud of black smoke. The cloud of smoke swirled around me and was dripping with blood. Then out of the palm of my hands, two balls of white light emerged, lighting my vision. The white lights danced before my eyes but then slowly started to Transition into a deep blue color. Once both balls of lights were radiating blue, they flew into the black smoke."

Eyes still shut, Mother Hutra continued. "I think, I recall at that point the smoke started to become lighter in color. The blood stopped dripping and the thick cloud of black smoke became the same blue color of the balls of light. Once all that occurred, I heard the soft thrumming of drums. That's when I woke up." Mother Hutra opened her eyes.

The hall was silent for a moment, everyone taking in what

Mother Hutra had said. ManCohalith silently clasped his hands together in a prayer for clarity. Lorraine whispered her own prayer for herself, then stepped forward and spoke.

"This is an incredibly magnificent dream, there are a lot of details and each one is significant in interpreting the dream," she said, her voice soft yet unwavering. Each of her words had a weight behind them. "Are we sure that this is being shared in the right company?" She glanced in the direction of Zya, who shut her eyes to be unseen. Because Zya wasn't direct family descent, nor borne any children by any of the Generals, it was unusual for her to be in the presence of the Hutra family dynasty, especially during an urgent private meeting such as this.

Vasco moderated his tone before he spoke, but his eyes betrayed his annoyance. "I invited her, dear Aunt. She has every right to be here, as I am. She will stay."

"Vasco, we will discuss this invitation later. Today we will allow Lady Sister Zya to stay." ManCohalith was sure to have the final word.

Lorraine looked at Mother Hutra, who nodded. Vasco gave his mother a silent look of thanks while Blahom held her breath. It was getting extremely tense.

Lorraine shook the tension off. She prayed, then began.

"Black smoke in a dream is symbolic of hatred while blood symbolizes death. When the two are entwined, it symbolizes war. As for the two balls of white light emanating from your hands ..." Lorraine paused, choosing her words carefully. "A ball of white light is symbolic of good to come. This can be in the form of an idea or a person. Since the light was emerging from the palms of your hands, this is symbolic to something that's extremely close to you.

"These two balls of white light represent your daughters, Blahom and Katyana. What is important to note is how the lights change from white to blue, which is often symbolic of warriors who have Transitioned.

"The balls of blue light entering the thick black smoke are

symbolic of warriors going to battle. The blood ceasing to drip symbolizes the halting of death. The smoke changing from black to the same color of the blue light means a shift away from hatred. The sound of drums is heard in dreams when victory has been achieved." Lorraine turned to look at Blahom and Katyana before she turned back to her sister.

"What this means is for the first time in our history, your daughters – Blahom and Katyana – must train as warriors if we want to defeat the Delions' and stop the attacks on our women."

A shocked silence fell over the room. Blahom's eyes widened, and she frantically looked from her sister to Vasco. Neither face betrayed any expression, but Vasco's hands were balled into fists.

"Warriors?" Vasco blurted out in shock.

ManCohalith put his hand up, attempting to halt any more outbursts from Vasco. He closed his eyes, letting out a sigh.

"But women are not to be warriors, Father!" Vasco insisted, his voice rising. "Her interpretation is ludicrous! They have their duties as Goddesses, they cannot be sent into battle ..."

"Silence!" ManCohalith exclaimed and Vasco quickly held his tongue while everyone else in the room stiffened at their ruler's raised voice.

A long intense silence filled the room. Everyone was still, and all eyes on ManCohalith. Then he spoke.

"Something has been disturbing my spirit for months," ManCohalith said, digesting the prophecy. Unease lay heavy in the room, as Mother Hutra's eyes darted in disbelief from Lorraine to her daughters, and then her husband. Even the Generals looked at each other with shock and concern.

"I must be alone, to pray and think on this matter." With that, ManCohalith briskly walked out of the room and closed the door behind.

Nobody followed or said a word, knowing that all they could do in this situation was stand and wait. Rasheed's eyes were wide with shock, and he quickly glanced at Blahom, who shot him a short glance of terror.

Standing on the balcony, ManCohalith took deep breaths, looking out at the land. He needed to ground himself in the present. He took in the deep blue of the sky. He focused on the greens of the surrounding fields and the darker shadows of the mountains. He slowly moved his palms upwards to face the sky and let his breaths come through his nose, exhaling out of his mouth. He felt the air move through his body.

A storm was already raging in the space being his eyes, and ManCohalith knew this was not the state in which to make important decisions. He knew it was taboo for women to become Zaed warriors, and his own daughters at that. They were Goddesses, and they were meant to represent every aspect of femininity as they grew into womanhood. And, social taboos aside, ManCohalith had seen the horrors of war, and that was not something he relished his daughters experiencing.

ManCohalith shook the thought of his daughters from his mind, trying to focus on his responsibility as a ruler. He was wise enough to know that everything had its time, and it was no longer time for emotions. It was time to trust in faith. He let out a long sigh, releasing tension from his body. He knew that Mother Hutra would not have dreamed this if the Alpha God was not trying to tell them something.

The Delions had sent a clear message that their mission was creation of life and they needed women for their labs. Something was brewing and ManCohalith was aware of the danger. Over the last few months, as the Generals worked to find Daniella, they had discovered more about the technology the Delions were crafting. The reports coming back indicated technology so advanced that it meant a serious annihilation threat to the Zaeds if they were slow to respond. For weeks, ManCohalith had been praying, asking for answers as to how to put a halt to the war, and, in this moment, he was given his answer.

He took another hour to stand, kneel, think, and pray, before he reentered the room, where the others awaited him anxiously. ManCohalith took his seat, and looked around the room, and spoke.

"We need to consider what Alpha God is trying to tell us. We must remember that He does not act, think, or feel in the ways we do, yet his decisions are for the betterment of us all," he said sternly.

"The Delions have been at war with us for decades. They have captured our women and kept them from us. There is a device that empowers them to visit other planets and devise plans to take over. Ten years ago, they stepped onto our soil to take my young Goddesses – a moment I'll never forget! They've learned how to infiltrate our inner walls. They now have our beloved Daniella. General Lakin, I am sure you can agree, that the offense they committed, has unleashed something dangerous in us as fathers and leaders. Something that no one will want to deal with."

Mother Hutra could tell by his forced, even breaths that he was trying not to let his emotions cloud his judgment. His jaws were clenched, not with anger, but unease, and a tear fell down her face. The idea of her daughters training to fight in the war made her stomach twist as she looked at them, their faces full of emotion.

ManCohalith looked at his two daughters and took centered himself again.

"I will not have my daughters seen as weak, and I will not allow the Delions to commit the same treasonous act again. We will have total victory over the Delions, so we will comply with the voice of Alpha God. Starting tomorrow, you both will begin your training to become Zaed warriors, and all will be well."

Chapter Three

"Let me speak with Mother Hutra alone, and we will meet again near the Battle Strategy Hall," ManCohalith said. Rasheed grabbed Trinity's hand, while the rest of the wives and mothers left with their children in tow. Vasco lingered a moment, clearly wanting to stay but his father and mother nodded at him and he followed his sisters out of the Throne Room. The rest of the Dynasty and Lady Mothers gave the three siblings space, waiting in the Dining Hall where food was being served. Zya gave Vasco a last look and he nodded at her to go inside the Hall for the feast.

Blahom smelled the food but at that moment she had lost the will to eat.

"I don't like this," Vasco said, anger tingeing his voice.

"Why? Because you're afraid you'll no longer be the best warrior," Katyana beamed, striking a heroic pose that she saw in plays, clearly not taking the severity of the news seriously. "Soon our people won't be singing songs of the valiant Vasco but of the courageous Katyana."

"You're young and dumb," Vasco grabbed Katyana by the shoulders. "You don't know what the Delions are like. You have never been on the battlefield and watched someone get their neck sliced right in front of you and the blood of the dying splatter on your face. Do you know what a dying Delion's blood tastes like? No, you don't." Vasco saw the fear behind Katyana's eyes, and tried to remain gentle. "The last thing I want is you or Blahom in harm's way."

"Sister?" Katyana needed a bit of space from her angry big brother. "What do you think about us being the first Goddesses to ever be warriors?"

Blahom was silent. *They have my dear cousin and Lady Sister Daniella. She's afraid.*

"Sis, do you want me to get you food?" Katyana asked. "If you're worried about dancing, I wouldn't sweat it. Mother would never let us stop performing," Katyana said with a reassuring smile, gently grasping her sister's hand, and trying to get her attention. "I think she'd become a warrior herself before she'd let us stop dancing."

"Enough with this warrior nonsense, Kat. This is not happening!" exclaimed Vasco.

Blahom wordlessly nodded, still unable to take in all that had transpired.

"Maybe Aunt Lorraine is lying," Vasco said, lowering his voice. "This whole situation is wrong. Neither of you should be made to fight. I can't let that happen." There was weight behind his words.

Blahom felt a numbing terror throughout her body.

"Let me in. You're getting stuck in your head again, Blahom." Blahom was jolted out of her thoughts by Vasco's hand on her shoulder. "Sister, let me in. You need to know that I will see to it that you won't have to fight."

"Lying is a strong word, Vasco." Blahom finally found the words to speak, and Vasco shook his head.

"I don't care. This is absurd. I don't want you or Kat fighting."

The three siblings looked up when the doors to the Throne Room opened and ManCohalith and Mother Hutra walked through.

"Katyana, Vasco, come with me. We will wait at the door of the

Hall. Blahom, stay behind with your father," motioned Mother Hutra.

With that, Blahom was alone with her father. Usually, there was stillness between them. No idle chitchat; only silence and the matter at hand. A peaceable silence, as they took comfort in each other's presence, both content to focus on their thoughts before speaking. They would need that comfort today.

ManCohalith looked at his daughter. She was seventeen years old, practically a woman. She had grown in character, beauty, and strength. She was eloquent – and tall, almost close to his own height and he had to wonder how he missed those years of growth.

Fond memories flooded back. Blahom as a child, catching all the bugs that made their way into her room to release them back outside, not having the heart to kill them. She was always the gentle one, who held life as precious. But ManCohalith knew his darling Blahom had another side. Things came easy to Blahom. She was a fast learner and certainly the curious one, always finding mischief. But she was strong, especially when she focused. He knew the key for Blahom was extreme focus. Distractions were her weakness.

Has she always been that tall? he thought to himself.

"You look just like your mother," he said softly, breaking the silence and breaking into Blahom's thoughts. "There are a lot of noble warriors who would love to wed you." He knew she would not react, and he moved on.

"You don't wish to become a warrior, is that correct?" ManCohalith locked eyes with his daughter.

"That is correct, Father."

"I knew that would be your reaction; that's why we need to find you a suitable warrior to wed." Blahom gave her father a quizzical look. He had never wanted to marry her off quickly, just the opposite, which clearly showed he was grasping at straws. He was protective and wanted her to marry only when ready. ManCohalith caught her confused gaze and took in a deep breath.

"Based on Mother Hutra's dream, the Alpha God is letting us

know that it is vital that both you and Katyana train to become warriors if we want to protect you and put an end to this war on our Zaed women."

"I understand," Blahom said stiffly, trying to hide the sadness from her father. "Vasco thinks that Aunt Lorraine may have misinterpreted the dream." Blahom would not tell her father that Vasco called his aunt a liar. That was a strong word to use and Blahom knew Vasco was out of line.

"You mean Vasco said she lied?" ManCohalith looked his daughter straight in the eye to let her know that nothing got past him. "I know my son, your brother. I know how he feels about his aunt. That is not your load to carry. I will handle him. Aunt Lorraine has never interpreted a dream incorrectly, and I don't think she'd lie and tarnish that record now.

"I hope you know that Mother Hutra and I did not want this to happen. This is your calling. We cannot get in the way of your destiny, especially since there is so much at stake. I'm not sure how it will play out but for now we will have you both train. It will be good for you all to be able to defend yourselves." ManCohalith turned away, trying to gather himself.

"I know, Father," Blahom spoke softly to her father's back. ManCohalith could see hear she had more to say.

Turning to face his daughter, "What all do you know?" he asked, to force her to talk.

Blahom paused and glanced at her father as if to be sure he was ready to hear her reply.

"I know why Vasco does not like Aunt Lorraine. I know you are an honorable and victorious ruler with many flaws." Blahom spoke up but not too loudly. "I know that there is history that may actually taint her gifts of interpretation."

"Thank you for your expression. You have a little wisdom daughter, but certainly much more to learn. You are correct, I am flawed. I have never claimed to be more than a mortal Zaed and it is only through the divine gifts gifted to me that I am able to be a victorious and honorable ruler. You remember that for yourself, Goddess and now warrior. But our flaws do not dictate if we retain the divine gifts or not. Our flaws are put on us as a cloak of humility to the Alpha God. You are incorrect regarding your Aunt Lorraine. Her personal flaws do not corrupt or take away from her divine gifts and her dream interpretation today." ManCohalith paused, making sure Blahom had digested all that he had to say.

"Would you like to ask me anything?" ManCohalith waited.

"No, Father."

"Blahom, the situation with the Delions is serious. There is more you should know. We have reason to believe that the Delions' teleportation device has sent them to planet Earth. A device like that could turn the tides of this war in an instant." ManCohalith gently grasped Blahom's hands, looking her in the eyes.

"I know that you dislike violence, as do we all. Yet I always taught you that, like the seasons, there is a time for everything: for love and for hate; for war and for peace. I need you to be strong. You and your sister have been called to be pioneers and to help bring an end to this. I need you to see yourself as a warrior. A Warrior Goddess. If not, you will fail."

Blahom was stuck in her thoughts – *Where is my cousin?* – but she felt the weight of his words. Was she the key to bringing about the end of the war?

"Then I must train." Blahom used her words to squash the fear in the pit of her stomach. Her eyebrows furrowed together, and she could feel the paint on her face creasing. She was still a radiant Goddess with a duty to the Zaeds.

"I cannot deny peace of mind to the women of Zaed. This war has gone on for far too long. I will do anything to help find Lady Sister Daniella."

"Do not fret daughter. Love will find you. We will prepare you for war so that your future is full of love." ManCohalith gently placed a hand on Blahom's forehead, anointing his daughter with strength and courage. Their conversation was over.

"They are waiting for us," ManCohalith said, and Blahom followed him to join the rest of the royal family. Her legs felt light, and her stomach was bubbling with nerves.

ManCohalith turned the corner where the hallway echoed with voices of Mother Hutra, Katyana, Vasco, Lady Mothers Clara and Chi, General Velio, General Lakin, and their sons, soldiers Thistle, Jakk, Burris, and the youngest Colin, and General Murn. With nothing more to say, Lorraine had left her family moments earlier. Silence fell in ManCohalith's presence.

Blahom walked next to her father as she always did, her back stiff to hide her fear. Mother Hutra knew she was scared and sent her a sweet aura of love.

"Well now, whatever just happened must have been a reassurance to you. Look at my daughter walking taller and radiating a newfound energy that we all can notice." Mother Hutra had a way of encouraging her children at each step of their lives. "Take your sister's hand," she said.

Blahom took Katyana's hand with a new, determined courage.

Vasco watched. He would support the family, but his temper was ranging inside.

"The first thing we are to do is to have you all see what a Battle Strategy Hall looks like. It is here we will make it official. Follow me. This is a moment to memorialize." ManCohalith opened the door and strode in, the rest following.

Katyana and Blahom took in the unfamiliar environment. They had never been allowed into this room, as it had been considered no place for a woman, especially a Goddess. Glancing at the tactical maps and weaponry and papers of reconnaissance missions, Blahom felt the reality of the situation sink in.

All of this will become normal to me in due time, but right now, I feel like a zombie. My stomach is burning. Is there a bathroom?

Blahom turned to look for her brother. She wanted him to know she understood everything. Locking eyes with Vasco, she knew he was livid about the situation, but had no choice but to accept it.

Blahom

Holding Blahom's hand, Katyana was beaming ear to ear. ManCohalith had arrived at the front of the large room. He gazed down at his youngest child and smiled at her with a soft look, proud of her youthful and fiery spirit.

"You are bound for great things." Gently placing a hand on her head, ManCohalith anointed her. "You are young and there are things that won't make sense to you yet. Listen to your sister during this time, for she will be your strongest support." He beckoned Katyana to turn and face Blahom.

ManCohalith turned his attention to the Generals.

"Blahom and Katyana's training will begin tomorrow." ManCohalith looked to General Lakin, nodding to give him permission to step before Blahom and Katyana. With that, the General cleared his throat and began a commencement speech that all Zaed warriors had heard. The sisters' first step to becoming a true Zaed warrior had begun.

Lakin's voice was loud and ceremonious. "Your destiny towards honoring the Zaeds is about to begin, and there is a long journey ahead of you. Training is rigorous, physically, and mentally demanding. Becoming a warrior is something not achieved swiftly and will take years to complete. You are expected to learn a multitude of different skills and tactics that will be valuable for the battleground. The Generals standing before you will guide you in preparation for training in weaponry, hand-to-hand combat, fighting on horseback, archery, survival skills, battle strategies, and how to maintain a warship."

Looking to ManCohalith, General Laken stopped before moving on. "Will the Goddess aim to Transition, sir?" ManCohalith nodded, "Please give them the full speech."

General Lakin continued. "After your successful training, and if the Generals see fit, you will undergo your Transitioning experience. This is where your divine gifts will be born. This is also where many warriors have died well before entering the battlefield. Death comes out of ...," General Lakin, paused in the middle of the sentence, it was obvious he thought about his beloved first-born Daniella.

He gathered himself and continued. "Death comes out of disobedience to listening to the new awakening voice that will speak to you during Transition. There will be no one around. This is the ultimate test to listen to the voice, remember what you have been taught and comply. Failure to do so has and will cause your demise. If you survive the Transition, you are expected to achieve and maintain peak physical condition," he paused again, looking hard at both the girls, "beyond just ceremonial dancing."

As General Lakin continued with his speech, Blahom's body was in the room, but her mind was someplace else entirely. Her stomach was bubbling with anxiousness. Vasco used to come home looking like a corpse. He had a wound that covered half his face; he couldn't see out of his left eye for weeks. *Is this what we are to become? I'm not going to last through this. Where is the bathroom?* She swayed on her feet. Mother Hutra, noticing, interrupted General Lakin, and tried to ground her daughter back into the moment.

"While your training is important, you are still first and foremost, Goddesses," she said. "You both will continue to practice the Dietrickt dance. We will not risk you losing your power of femininity while training." She shot a pointed look at General Lakin, most likely for referring to their dancing so flippantly. She knew that was not part of the traditional speech.

"Blahom are you ok?"

"Excuse me, Mother, I must go to the bathroom." Blahom's eyes pleaded with her mother.

"Lady Mother Clara, please escort her to the bathroom," said Mother Hutra.

"Forgive Mother Hutra, but I have never been in this room, and I am unfamiliar with these chambers," Lady Mother Clara said, flustered.

"It is really ok, Mother. I believe I can take myself to the bathroom if Father or Vasco will quickly point me in the right direction." Blahom was not waiting for permission and started walking briskly.

"It's over there and to the right behind the wall," Vasco pointed with irritation at this whole fiasco.

Katyana felt a small weight lift from her shoulders. She took solace in the idea that she would still be able to dance. She might now always like it, but she knew it was a place for her.

"Yes, Mother Hutra, we all know how important the Dietrickt dance is. My daughter Daniella was a Lady Sister dancer under you. I wouldn't dare have thought about making her or my darling nieces' throat-slicing murderous Zaed warriors, infringing on their femininity," General Lakin said, understanding that with all the emotion tied into the situation, it would be a long road ahead. He was clear not to argue with his brother's wife for interrupting his speech.

"I appreciate your candid humor, but if it weren't for our dancing, we'd have no tradition, the warriors would not be renewed in strength and no battles would be won. Should I remind you of that, Lakin? You all would be dead without the femininity that you mock."

"And I don't disagree with you, yet, even with the dancing, my daughter does not stand here today. I pray she has not met her fate with death," General Lakin responded and turned his attention back to the Katyana and then ManCohalith.

Mother Hutra was quiet. She knew she had ignored his feeling regarding his missing daughter in her own concern about her daughters.

"Alrighty then," General Brakkus stepped in to ease the tension and sadness in the room. "We understand that today is a different day than most. There's no need to continue with a commencement talk, sir. Tomorrow, I will instruct them in the basics of hand-to-hand combat."

"Ha! Shouldn't we wait for the new warrior-in-training to return from the bathroom?' Vasco asked sarcastically.

"We will," said ManCohalith.

The room was quiet again. The new soldiers were taking everything in and the wait felt like eternity.

"Shall I go get her? Lady Mother Clara asked.

"No, she is capable of returning alone," Mother Hutra said.

Blahom came walking back briskly and stood back face-to-face with Kat.

"Please face forward daughters," ManCohalith said and nodded to General Lakin to continue.

"General Brakkus expects to see you in the training arena at sunrise." Lakin handed both girls their warrior training uniforms.

"Yes, General," Katyana said quickly.

"Yes, General." Blahom hoped her voice sounded as enthusiastic as her sister's.

"We will take the uniforms and make them fit for a Goddess." Mother Hutra motioned to Lady Mother Clara and Lady Mother Chi. "Take Blahom and Katyana to the bath house and bring them food. My sweet Blahom has not eaten today, and we must feed her." Mother Hutra was in full mother bear mode, and everyone understood.

"The food is already waiting there," ManCohalith said, looking at his concerned wife and trying to offer her some comfort. "I will briefly join the others in the Dining Hall."

The bath house was a warm, serene, and inviting place within the castle. Lulling music played and masseuses were ready to unwind knots and tensions from both civilians and battle-wearied warriors. The perfect place for two young women after such an unexpected day.

Blahom loved the bath house after dancing. It was a treat gifted by her mother for all the dancers after a successful CCDC ceremony. She was a little annoyed that Katyana got the pleasure of a bath house massage today having missed dancing in today's ceremony. *Kat always manages to get rewarded for her lies*, Blahom thought.

Blahom ran to the spread that had been just prepared, a fresh take on the day's ceremonial feast. She glanced at the table and for the found a new appreciation for the food, the fruit, and those who prepared it. She thought of the young Zaed girl from the Welch tribe. She thought about the death of the young girl's father and how heartbroken the young girl was. She remembered vividly the lesson that Mother Clara had taught her earlier.

What am I going to eat first? I can't waste my hungry. My stomach is rumbling at an all-time high. Blahom grabbed a skewer. *Thank you for this food. I am more grateful than ever for the market sellers and those who prepared the food and blessed the land and my belly.*

Blahom bit down, vowing to chew slowly and enjoy the savory moment of the first bite. She wanted to eat in silence and clear her mind. Silence was always possible in the bath house, but a clear mind would be nearly impossible because today had yielded lesson after lesson after lesson and her head was full. She ate and glanced at her sister who was eating again, likewise at a loss for words.

"Shall we get you on the table?" Lady Mother Clara asked Blahom. Working on a tight muscle in Blahom's leg, the masseuse felt the young Goddess's tension begin to fade. Despite the heavenly treatment, Blahom's mind couldn't shake the events of the day.

How do I go from killing my Dietrickt dance performance today to being asked to kill a Delion? This is crazy. Is this real? Could Vasco be right about Aunt Lorraine?

Chapter Four

"How dare you lie to put my sisters in danger!" Vasco exclaimed as he faced Lorraine, Trinity, Rasheed, and his aunt Melissa outside the Dining Hall. The group stiffened at the anger in Vasco's voice. Zya trailed behind her man, struggling to match his pace.

"Vasco, my loyal nephew, you should go. It has been a long evening for us all. Let me walk with you to your room?" Rasheed's mom was one of Vasco's favorite aunts and loved him dearly.

Leaning over to kiss his aunt on the cheek for her sweet gesture, Vasco made himself clear. "No, Aunt, I do not need to be put away like a child. I'd like to stay here and confront my mother's sister about her lies."

"I have not called you a child, but you are acting like a mad man. The entire land knows that you are a protector and a warrior, as do I. At this moment, you have the right to be upset about the new proclamation, and I will not deny that of you. Do you understand?" His aunt was patiently trying to get through to her nephew as she saw the flames raging from him.

"Aunt, forgive me if I offend you, but war is an offensive matter and people will do anything for power. I cannot listen to you at this moment until the lies are addressed by Lorraine."

"Excuse me, Mother," Rasheed stepped forward. "You are not on the battlefield at this moment, cousin." He moved his mom behind him.

"I have spoken no lies. The dream pains me as much as it pains you," Lorraine spoke gently.

"What pain are you in, Lorraine? I see no pain for the disruption that you have caused this evening. The disruption you have caused for years. This is just what you wanted!" Vasco was not letting up, clearly drunk with fury.

"Vasco," Rasheed stepped closer, placing a hand on his cousin's shoulder. "This is a lot for all of us. We all love the Goddesses. You're angry, and we understand, but it's not Aunt Lorraine's fault."

"Do not touch me!" Vasco retorted, throwing his cousin's hand off his shoulder. "You don't know what she's done! She is a liar, and this is where it stops!"

"Vasco, please," Zya placed a hand on his back. "Return to your room, this is enough." Her eyes were pleading with Vasco as she looked at Rasheed, but both men ignored her.

"Lying is a strong word, cousin. Dream interpreters never misread a dream, let alone lie about it. That's unheard of, and you know it." Rasheed was determined to calm his cousin, but to no avail.

"There's plenty of reasons for her to lie! Isn't that right, Lorraine?" Vasco's eyes bore into his aunt's, waiting for her to respond.

"Watch your words and tone, dear nephew. I'll say it again: I would never lie about interpreting a dream." Lorraine stared back at her nephew, remaining calm despite his ignorance.

"Why not? You have plenty to gain for getting my sisters out of the way!"

"Vasco!" Zya was shocked that he would say such a thing in the face of his aunt. She knew he had a strong temper, but she'd never seen him like this.

"Vasco, you should leave at once," Melissa had a firmer tone, anxious to reach her nephew.

"Excuse me? May I remind you who I am?!" Lorraine had reached her limit; her voice was raised. "I am a Zaed-called dream interpreter, a position I would never jeopardize with petty lies. Just as important, I am your aunt. I have changed your diapers and babied you when your mother needed moments to herself. I have helped raise Katyana and Blahom since they were infants. I would never wish for any harm to come to your sisters!"

"Is that what you tell my father when the two of you are alone?"

"I don't know what you're talking about," Lorraine said, grabbing Trinity's hand, and preparing to walk away.

Vasco laughed. "You claim you're not a liar, yet here you are lying to me right now. You know exactly what I'm talking about! You have no husband! You court no one! Just admit you want to be my mother! Admit that you wish for Trinity to take the place of my sisters – so much so that you are willing to fabricate a dream, just to have my sisters destroyed. You know damn well, that if anything happens to those two, that will destroy my mother."

"Your father would be extremely disappointed if he heard you speak the voice of death on your family," Lorraine stepped close to Vasco. "He loves your mother and all his children. Life, love, romance, and betrayal are something we all must face and grow through. This isn't some saga play where we all want to kill each other. Your young, male, naive ego is getting in the way. I am in no way able to handle the position that my sister has as his wife. She is gifted beyond measure, and not I, nor any other woman, can take her crown. I encourage you to have more faith in your mother." Lorraine's eyes were locked on Vasco, careful not to back down.

"Mom, please escort Aunt Lorraine, Trinity, and Zya away. Trinity is tired and should be taken to rest. This is nothing that a young child should hear."

Lorraine held eye contact with her nephew for a moment before

Blahom

she walked away with Trinity, who had tears in her eyes. Melissa gestured towards Zya, but she refused.

"I'm not leaving him." Zya was standing her ground, her eyes mere slits as she stared at Rasheed.

"Zya, beloved, go." Vasco's tone was low, serious.

"But ..."

"GO!" Vasco raised his tone, startling Zya. Rasheed closed his eyes as Zya hurries away, tears starting to well up.

"You were out of line, Vasco." Rasheed's voice was low.

"Am I out of line? I suggest you start to think about Blahom's well-being as your own if I am ever to give you, my blessing. I see how you look at her, and trust me, a Goddess such as Blahom needs someone who can protect her. She needs a warrior, not a water boy."

Rasheed took a deep breath, tired of his cousin's emotional antics. "This has nothing to do with me and Blahom. Her well-being is secure with me, so I suggest you worry about the business of your unborn child to an unwed mother. You need to direct your energy and concern towards your own affairs." Rasheed stared into his cousin's eyes, ready for any challenge Vasco wanted to push his way.

Vasco looked at Rasheed, his anger slowly dissipating.

"I am a Lieutenant, Rasheed. You are not. We are trained to recognize the enemy, even within our own camp. We are trained to show no mercy to the old or young. Stay out of my business with my aunt, and I may stay out of yours." The two walked off, going their separate ways.

* * *

"Are you afraid of coming face to face with a Delion?" Katyana asked as they were getting ready for bed. The sisters shared a bedroom, common among female siblings. Katyana sat on her bed, dressed in her nightshirt, while Blahom was in the bathroom. A child-like innocence permeated the room. With no Lady Mothers, no generals, and no parents, they could just be sisters.

"I don't think 'afraid' is the word I'd use, but I think most Zaeds have to find courage when coming face to face with a Delion." Blahom scrubbed her face with a warm cloth, trying to remove any residual paint.

"What is the word then? 'Scared'?"

Are we really about to do this? Katyana thought. *Start training? Mother seemed very afraid for us, and Father ... I don't know what Father was feeling. Should I be angry, like Vasco? Or afraid? Please, Alpha God, give me something to hold onto.* Katyana waited to hear her big sister's response.

"No." Blahom placed the washcloth down and sat on her bed. "I think nervous is the best word."

"Yeah, you were nervous when your stomach was rumbling in the middle of the General Lankin's commencement speech," Katyana laughed. "You took an awful long time, you know."

Katyana moved from her own bed to sit on Blahom's, eager to continue the conversation of the day's events. "But why nervous?"

"Well ... now that we're going to become warriors, I know it's inevitable that I'll eventually be face-to-face with a Delion. I guess I'm just nervous for that day to come."

A soft silence fell between the sisters, neither aware of the other's feelings. *I'm terrified,* thought Blahom, *but I can't let Katyana know. I must be strong, for her. I hope she's okay. I know she wasn't showing her true emotions today. How does she feel about Mother's dream? Does she doubt it, as Vasco does? I've never doubted Aunt Lorraine's interpretation.* She gave a deep sigh. *Could it really be what she's saying? Daniella is still missing.*

"I'm nervous too," Kat whispered, her earlier bravado all but gone. The air felt heavy, and Blahom strove to change the subject.

"Do you remember Lieutenant Kov? Rasheed told me he was captured by the Delions and escaped and now he's acting strange. I don't think he'll ever be the same again."

Katyana leaned forward, intently listening. "What do you think the Delions did to him?"

Blahom

"Maybe they're just terrifying, but rumor has it they were able to capture him after entrancing him."

"What do you mean that the Delions entranced him?"

"Brother says they have a weapon that puts you in a trance and makes you see a false vision of what you desire most."

"Really? Out of all weapons to create, that sounds so lame," Kat said wrinkling her nose.

Blahom smirked at her sister. "That device could make you see the most handsome warrior prince who would dote on your every need. He would ask for your hand in marriage and give you everything that you could desire in life, no Lady Mothers around," Blahom laughed, teasing her sister, reciting a fairytale-like dream. Katyana did not laugh back.

"What I want most in the world is to slaughter all Delions. They can't use their weapons on me when all I want is them dead. I hate them."

Blahom was taken aback by Katyana's intensity. Kat was only three at the time of the attempted abduction of the Goddesses, and Blahom herself could only remember the aftermath, though, sadness welled up in her as she remembered the constant nightmares her sister suffered in the years after. And now their cousin had vanished, something else to blame on the Delions. Still, Blahom hadn't known the extent of Kat's anger.

"Let's get some sleep. We have a big day tomorrow," Blahom held Katyana's hand tightly. Katyana smiled, squeezing her big sister's hand in return.

"I thought you liked Lady Mother Clara?" Katyana went back to an earlier comment.

"I don't like her, I adore her. Of course, I love my Lady Mother. There are just times when I need to be able to expand or explore without her or anyone around," Blahom said, but just wanted to go to sleep.

"I get it. You want time to kiss Jhapalle. Or is it Rasheed?"

"Goodnight, Katyana, we have an early day tomorrow." Blahom rolled over and wrapped herself in her warm blanket.

"Goodnight, sister."

* * *

Katyana and Blahom entered the training arena, where General Brakkus informed them that day one of training was learning a technique similar to boxing. Both Lady Mother Clara and Katyana's Lady Mother, Chi, were watching on the sidelines. General Lakin had hoped to train the Goddesses as any other warrior, but ManCohalith refused and was clear that his daughters would never be unaccompanied even during training.

"Right jab, right uppercut, left jab, left uppercut," commanded General Brakkus and both Katyana and Blahom threw punches in command. Brakkus was in full General mode and was not the jovial uncle they had come to adore.

Blahom's arms ached as they went through motion after motion. With each movement, she punched with less precision, as if the weight of her own arms was too much to bear.

Lady Mother Clara's watched in shock. Goddesses had never been trained as warriors and here Blahom was, on the first steps of a path to the battlefield. Chi watched Katyana likewise, her body tensing as the girl threw punch after punch.

"She's too young," Lady Mother Chi uttered softly, unintentionally speaking her thoughts out loud. Lady Mother Clara agreed but didn't respond.

"Lady Mothers, please remain quiet. You are here to observe, not comment or speak." Surprised that General Brakkus heard the comment, the two got a bootcamp lesson of their own.

After a couple of hours, General Brakkus sent the two siblings to grab water from the Lady Mothers. But there was to be no break.

"Back to the bags, ladies," General Brakkus called them back to

Blahom

practice on a makeshift punching bag filled with sharp hay, before they had a moment to sit.

Quivering from exhaustion from the first hours of the punching formations, Blahom felt her arms worn and weary. *What the hell? I won't be doing this every day. This is ridiculous!* She delivered her first punch to the bag with a grunt, feeling the power of the hit travel up her arm. She quickly hissed in pain and pulled back her hand.

"You'll get used to the sensation of pain," General Brakkus said with a small smile. Looking at his nieces reminded him of the pain of his first niece, likely dead. *Perhaps training would have saved her*, he thought to himself. "But nice form. Keep at it."

The change from punching air to punching something solid brought a newfound energy, but Blahom's excitement evaporated as the punching bag's needle-like composition stung her hand. The thrill was gone and all that was left was fatigued muscles and drips of blood dotting her knuckles. She whimpered, gingerly holding her hand.

"Watch your thumb placement," General Brakkus warned. "If you tuck in your thumb, you might break it, don't want that." Blahom shuddered at the thought of breaking any of her fingers, let alone her thumb.

Only four hits into the punching bag training, General Brakkus called a halt.

"Alright, we don't need a blood bath today," he said with a morbid humor unusual for him. "You two are dismissed. I expect both of you here tomorrow. Same time."

Blahom's body slumped, her regal posture disappearing as her knees started to buckle. Lady Mother Clara was by her side with more water, and rummaged through her bag, quickly pulling out healing ointment and bandages. "Drink."

Blahom's shaking hands struggled to get the water in her mouth. "Thank you," she panted. Lady Mother Clara gingerly applied ointment to Blahom's hand. Blahom forced herself to breathe through the dull sting of the ointment, and Lady Mother Clara moved on to bandaging her abused knuckles. Blahom looked over, relieved that Lady Mother Chi was providing Katyana with water and bandaging her equally abused hands, the purple bruises contrasting dramatically against Kat's pale skin.

"Now that you are dismissed, let's head back inside to the Dining Hall. You need more water and some food to rebuild your strength," said Lady Mother Clara.

Fatigued and weary, Blahom wordlessly nodded, slowly following the Lady Mother. Barely able to keep her eyes open, a bone-weary Katyana followed close behind, using Lady Mother Chi as a crutch.

Waiting for them inside the castle in a room adjacent to the training arena was a worried Mother Hutra and a concerned ManCohalith. The powerful rulers, were mere parents at this moment, knew how strenuous day one training would be, and that it would only get more difficult. Vasco had argued with his father about skipping his own training to be there for his sisters, but ManCohalith would not budge.

Once the doors opened and they saw their children, Mother Hutra gasped at their limp, overworked bodies while ManCohalith stiffened. Small dots of blood were already bleeding through the bandages the Lady Mothers applied and the girls' demeanor was far from that of regal Goddesses.

"The smallest of streams can carve into the largest of mountains, but these events take time and patience," ManCohalith said, grabbing both of his girl's chins and looking into their eyes, hoping his words gave them strength. His words were also to remind himself that his daughters' knuckles would harden, and their arms would grow stronger as time progressed, as his had. "You both did well today."

Mother Hutra ran over to her children, gently grabbing their hands and examining the bandages and blood. She tenderly kissed their knuckles and then wrapped her arms around her daughters in an embrace they felt too weak to return. With her children nestled in her bosom, Mother Hutra looked over their shoulders and glared at General Brakkus and her husband. It was only day one and blood had been drawn. Pulling away, Mother Hutra gave her children a warm smile, trying to hide her guilt and anger.

"Come. We have plenty of food prepared for you both."

The long hallway through the fortress leading to the Dining Hall was filled with silence, occasionally broken by pained grunts and beleaguered sighs from the two Goddesses.

Chapter Five

Blahom gasped as the air was knocked out of her. Her mouth was dry and tasted vaguely of copper from biting her tongue hard enough to draw blood. She stared up at the morning sky, wheezing.

This had become their new life. Training outside in the arena at sunrise.

Ughhh ... that hurts, she thought bitterly, all energy drained from her body. Her view of the sky was blocked by Katyana looking down at her and appearing smug as ever.

"For all that dancing you do, you certainly aren't quick on your feet," her sister smirked, then extended a hand to help Blahom up.

Truth was, although they still trained as dancers, the dancing was starting to take a back seat to their new calling. The schedule was warrior training, bathing, class, and food, then dance rehearsal. Then back to nighttime strategy training. The night sessions had replaced the free dance time allotted to all the dancers to voluntarily practice together or alone. They were missing the friends they often saw during the evening dance gatherings.

"Not all of us wake up and wish to start throwing punches,

knocking their sister through the eyes, and getting a busted lip in return. No, fighting you isn't intuitive for me, Kat."

Blahom knew that she would use her power differently if she were fighting an actual Delion, but using her strength to overpower her sister felt unnatural. Knowing that years of dancing made her the stronger of the two, Blahom had to restrain herself during their sparring practices. The last thing she wanted was to hurt Kat. It had been weeks since day one training, and though becoming stronger, Blahom was still trying to adjust mentally while Katyana seemed to be finding her groove.

Blahom grabbed Katyana's hand and stood up, still wheezing from the air being knocked out of her.

"Strange, we tend to like it. You know you're the weird one out of Vasco and me."

"Weird you say?" Blahom was clearly pissed off, irritated and over her little sister. "What's weird is that you think it's alright to be running your mouth like that. Go for my ankles again and your ass will be in the dirt." Blahom hated fighting and even more hated fighting her sister, but her patience was wearing thin.

"Awww, are you upset because I keep attacking your weakness?" Katyana said, void of emotions. "Is that not the point of war, sister?"

"Katyana, you're such a child and obviously don't carry the mental capacity to deal with this. I should speak to Mother about your antics."

"Are you going to run to Mom, or run to your water boy lover? Let's see how he'd fare in battle."

Blahom felt betrayed that Kat seemed eager and willing to batter her. Time and time again, she resisted too much aggression during practice, hoping to avoid more unsightly bruising.

"You're an idiot. Rasheed just may be my lover one day. You shouldn't be jealous. I pray the same for you. Although I'm not sure who will marry a goddess who has no insight of when or where to apply or release pressure. Now that I'm realizing my sister is a liar and will make it a point to twist reality, I must remember this day and treat you accordingly." Blahom did not have it in her to fight Kat, but she knew her words could be almost just as impactful as Kat's hit to her ankle.

Feeling bad, Katyana gave her big sister a look of humility and handed Blahom a flask of cold water. "I'm sorry," Kat said sincerely.

Still on alert, Blahom accepted her apology and wanted to let it go. "ManCohalith should be here soon to check on our progress. We still must practice the sparring lesson General Brakkus gave us before he arrives," she said bitterly.

General Brakkus had elevated their training to involve bo-staff weapons. The bruises on their legs from their last bo-staff practice were not yet healed, Blahom's camouflaged by her dark skin while Kat's stood out for all to see. The weapon wasn't as sharp nor as deadly as a sword, but it still packed a punch when swung hard. Blahom took pride in her shapely legs, an attribute that many knew her for. Jhapalle had often complimented them in their private moments, but now her smooth legs were becoming more and more marred by unsightly welts and bruises.

"The Lady Mothers are not here, and we are training alone. If you don't want to, we don't have to practice with the bo-staffs today," Katyana said.

The Lady Mothers had escorted the two to the morning training arena and were sent word by Mother Hutra to come to her briefly for a pressing matter. Blahom was surprised that she and Kat were alone. The Lady Mothers should've been back by now.

Blahom let out a long sigh, wanting nothing more than to agree with Kat and skip the bo-staff training for the day. She was tired and unenthused about her new life, but she imagined the look of disappointment if ManCohalith arrived and saw that they weren't training, and guilt welled up. General Brakkus had taken to leaving the training agenda for the day and trusting the girls to train without him. It was her duty to stay the course and not allow anyone to distract her until she had another clear path, so whether she liked it or not, she was going to carry it out.

"No, we were told to do weapons practice today. We can't ignore orders."

Grabbing the two bo-staffs lying on the sidelines of the field, Blahom tossed one over to her sister. They both were becoming used to the heavy weight. Tilting the staff to the side in a diagonal defensive stance, Blahom was ready to block any move that might come her way. She focused on tightening her grip on the bottom portion of the staff, knowing that Kat loved striking low.

"I know you don't care about dancing, Kat, but I do. Let that be the last time you go for my ankles and jeopardize my dancing." Blahom gave her sister a final warning, her eyes cold.

"Yeah, yeah, I heard you earlier," Katyana shrugged.

Like at the start of a dance, the two Goddess got into their new learned warrior positions, their stances tense, feet planted firmly, hands raised ready to both block and attack. They stared at each other, cunning eyes trying to anticipate who would make the first move.

Katyana's eagerness led her to drive her staff forward, and Blahom, becoming an expert at defense, blocked the attack. Katyana dealt quick blow after blow against Blahom's staff, Blahom blocking and dodging, her eyes focusing on her sister's foot movements. Kat was fighting in a pattern and, like dancing, she had repetition in several movements. Blahom, following Kat's rhythm, used that pattern to anticipate and counter the attacks.

Without warning, Katyana switched up. Instead of an attack coming from the lower left, she swung her bo-staff quickly from the upper right. Jumping backwards, Blahom's eyes widened in shock as everything played out in slow motion. She felt the gust of wind from Kat's bo-staff on her face, nearly grazing her skin. An underhanded move like that could have cost Blahom a tooth. Her keen defensive intuition saved her from a hard blow against her temple and she felt a momently swell of pride. Then relief burned into hot anger. Her eyes narrowed as she stared at her sister, incensed.

First ankle shots, now face shots? She is underestimating me and I'm about to show her.

Frozen for a moment, Katyana noticed the look in her sister's eyes. Tightening her grip on her bo-staff, she raised it in the air, and charged fast. Blahom dodged, blindsiding Kat with an agonizing jab to her side. Kat staggered. Blahom instinctively landed one more jab to the other side for good measure. Any mixed emotions were gone.

With that hit, the fight changed. Katyana's pain, shame, and anger erupted and her cutthroat nature flared and her eyes shone with the need for revenge. Blahom paused, thinking to them both some space. She knew she needed to center herself and she wanted her sister to calm down, and to learn her lesson.

Rather than pull back, Kat's instincts screamed at her to retaliate. Pushing through the pain radiating up her side, she charged at Blahom, swiftly jabbing her staff towards her sister's delicate ankles, trying to force her down. Blahom escaped the jabs but Kat continued her attacks, only escalating her sister's fury. Enraged, Blahom drove her staff towards her little sister's shoulder. Plunging to the side, Katyana blocked several attacks, trying to force her sister back to fighting defensively, but Blahom relentlessly went after her. Each swing of the staff increased the intensity and the air rang with the sounds of clanging wood. Both sisters fought as if they were in the heat of battle, continuing to meet each other's swift movements time and time again. Their chests heaved and their exhaustion grew, but their fighting raged on, fueled by emotions they no longer controlled.

Fury pumped through Blahom's veins, and for the first time she drove her staff at Kat's ankles, at that moment no caring if the hit shattered bone. Katyana jumped, dodging the blow and raised her own staff to strike. Blahom, caught Kat's staff with a firm steady hand, ripped it out of her sister's fingers, and threw it yards away. She swung her staff, driving it into Kat's ribs, sending the young Goddess to the ground.

Kat let out a scream of pain, but it fell on deaf ears. The time to try to step away and calm down had passed. Raising her staff in the

Blahom

air, Blahom aimed another blow. Kat's wide eyes watered with fear. A small tear trailed down her cheek and Blahom snapped out of her anger, terrified at her own actions.

As quickly as the tears came, they left, and the sly younger sister smirked and grabbed a fistful of loose dirt on the ground, flinging it directly into Blahom's face. The green-eyed Goddess screamed in agony as her eyes burned. Katyana drove a well-practiced punch into Blahom's gut, snatched the staff from her hand, and delivered a blow to her side that landed a weak Blahom flat on her back.

"Looks to me like I won," Katyana mercilessly said to Blahom, standing over her.

"What the hell is wrong with you? You went for a face shot!" Blahom exclaimed, wiping her eyes and trying to look up from the ground.

Blahom and Kat's fight during training

Something shifted in Katyana's eyes. She was cold. "General Velio says there's no rules on the battlefield. A Delion will never hesitate to take an opportunity to slit our throats." Katyana turned her back and walked away. She paused, turning around and looking down at her sister again.

"Kill them before they kill you." Kat left the training arena, her parting words sending a shiver up Blahom's spine.

Adrenaline high, and not paying attention Katyana bumped into Lady Mother Chi who had returned with Lady Mother Clara.

"Where are you going?" Lady Mother Chi grabbed Katyana by the arm.

"She is a horrible sister and I'm no longer able to be next to her," Kat said frozen, with her head dropped but eyes looking up.

"This warrior training has turned my baby sister into a mad woman," Blahom blurted out. "I must talk to my mother at once. She is too young to handle what has been put before her. I don't need Vasco or anyone else to put a stop to this. I will see fit."

Blahom picked herself up off the ground and took her stance as the elder sister, more regal, more polished and, at this moment, seemingly more in control.

"You two will not fight outside of the training that is presented. Lady Mother Chi and I returned to you much later than anticipated. For that we apologize. However, discord is spreading throughout our land and it is causing severe consequences. We have been with your mother, comforting her after your brother's slander against her sister after the dream was revealed. The two of you brawling is not news her heart nor health can take right now. Both of you will exit as the Goddess you are and will have no more communication until the dust settles." Lady Mother Clara had spoken and Blahom and Kat listened and obeyed. As far as they were concerned, neither the dancing nor training required them to speak. The room they shared was large enough that each could move around without having to make eye contact. Blahom was happy for the solitude, something she yearned for before the fight.

Dance rehearsal was in the morning. Kat had her first solo performance coming up and Blahom was fully prepared not to help her. *How can I go to Jhapalle?* she thought, craving a break from the ensuing chaos. Blahom looked at the bedroom window, the one she had escaped through many times. She looked at Kat who was falling asleep, suspicious that Kat ratted her late-night rendezvous out to their mother, and if she had not done so before she surely would now. Annoyed and bothered, Blahom turned over and tried to go to sleep.

Katyana winced as Lady Mother Chi painted makeup across the bruise on her cheek. It had been five days since her out-of-control sparring match with Blahom and her body, especially her ribs, ached with every movement.

Her pale skin made it difficult for Lady Mother Chi to fully conceal the bruises, but the Lady Mother was patient. After an hour, her bruises were covered, and Katyana took a deep breath. Lady

Blahom

Mother Chi applied silver makeup, painted as three evenly shaped stars to signify that even in the darkness there was light.

Katyana remembered how Blahom would praise her, saying that she looked like a star dancing on the sands of the beach. Looking in the mirror, Katyana grinned at her reflection. The extra training had increased her appetite. She was eating more and filling out more. As Lady Mother Chi finished applying Kat's makeup, she felt more regal than ever. Kat felt each bruise as a symbol of adulthood, and tonight for the first time, she felt like a true star.

Her lips shone in the sunlight coming in through the bedroom window. Kat was adorned in her traditional heavily printed ceremonial gown. The turquoise prints contrasted beautifully against the silver silk fabrics that hugged her hips. Large bracelets decorated her tiny delicate wrists, clinking against each other.

For the past few days, Blahom was only speaking to her sister if it were completely unavoidable. Kat was used getting ready together, but since the fight, Blahom had distanced herself down the hall with Lady Mother Clara. Katyana pursed her lips and gave herself a little shake. She refused to acknowledge her role in her sister's absence, but deep down it gnawed at her.

"I can't think of that now," Kat grumbled to herself. She needed to focus. She had the solo lead in tonight's ceremony.

Lady Mother Chi raised an eyebrow as she heard Kat grumbling and a twinge of guilt tugged at her heart. She and Lady Mother Clara rarely let the Goddesses out of their sight. However, the nasty public argument between Vasco and Lorraine was causing distress to the entire family and affecting Mother Hutra's heart. Trying to help, the Lady Mothers left the sisters to be at Mother Hutra's side, deciding that the two Goddesses could train on their own briefly. Neither had imagined that in quelling one family tension, another would begin to boil.

"Is your makeup to your liking?" she inquired.

"Yes. It's perfect," Katyana responded tersely.

Katyana walked out of the room, Lady Mother Chi close behind.

The beach was not far walk, but it was enough time for Kat's mind to wander, and it turned with regret to memories of her sister's comforting and confident voice. Trying to shake of the impending guilt, Kat refocused with each regal step she took, and wondered how much she would shine tonight during her solo.

"Have you a list of questions ready for when you see General Velio tonight?" Lady Mother Chi inquired, interrupting Kat's thoughts. She knew her charge well and recognized that Kat would want to speak with the war-seasoned General.

"Of course, I do, Lady Mother Chi. Once the dance is finished, he is the first person I will talk to."

Lady Mother Chi smiled but held her tongue when she thought about asking if Katyana would also speak to Blahom.

Chapter Six

Excited Zaeds gathered on the cliffs and roads surrounding the beach for the CCDC ceremony. The musicians arrived first, taking their positions on the side of the performance space, clad in fabrics the color of their instrument, their hands painted with musical notes and symbols. The Zaeds had been cheering and shouting since Blahom and the ensemble of dancers arrived, taking their positions as well.

Stepping onto the beach, Katyana immediately commanded attention as she made her way through the sea of Zaeds young and old. The wind blew through her curly dark blonde hair. A smile graced her lips as she felt the energy shift and all eyes on her. The fervor of the crowd increased and the Zaeds applauded and sang in reverence, fueling Katyana's pride. This was truly her night. She arrived at the performance space and walked towards her parents and bowed to them both, showing respect to the rulers.

"Remember this is about the blessing to the people, not how perfect or imperfect you are," ManCohalith said, and Katyana nodded.

"Yes, Father. Always," she said.

"Feel the music within you, daughter, and let it heal you," Mother Hutra said.

"I will, Mother."

Katyana's Solo Performance

Kat took her position with the other ensemble dancers. She noticed Blahom several feet away but avoided eye contact.

It was time. The music lifted, and so did the arms and faces of the dancers to the night sky. They moved across the sand as one. Kat, Blahom, and the ensemble of dancers with bare feet were going through the carefully rehearsed choreography of the Dietrickt dance. Katyana continued through the dance, twirling gracefully, crossing her friend Lita and her sister. She expected to meet Blahom's eyes as in rehearsal, but Blahom spared Kat no glance. Agitation distracted Kat from her timing, and for half a beat, she fell out of step, stumbled, and dropped to her knees, though she quickly got back into rhythm. Blahom, noticing the fall, was happy her sister recovered and did not let herself get distracted during the performance.

Kat was mad at herself for her hiccup. The daughter of a warrior, her instincts to rectify her mistakes and dominate brewed in her. She would make up for it in the solo performance.

The music changed and the flutes were echoing and blending into the waves of the ocean, Katyana's cue that it was time for her solo. She began, flowing as gracefully as the ocean. Her arms rising above her head and around her body. She lifted her leg, holding it in the air. Kat looked strong. The training and new confidence had given her a new presence as a "dancing" Goddess. The ensemble of dancers and Blahom looked on in awe, enamored by the power of Katyana's performance.

The orchestra shifted tempo and Kat picked up the pace of her movements, leaping and spinning in the air, in a move Blahom had shown her many times. She arched her back while flinging her arms up towards the sky and her stance brought her perfectly aligned body together and demonstrated talent and growth. She had come into her own.

You learned something. Nicely done, Kat, Blahom thought to herself.

Once Katyana had finished her performance, palms facing upward to the night sky, she could hear the audience singing. The rest of the ensemble joined back in and, in unison, all the women ended on their final pose. Glancing over her shoulder at Blahom, Katyana hoped to catch her sister's eye, only to see that Blahom continued to give her the cold shoulder.

A horn sounded, signaling that the dance had concluded and it was time for the feast and all the Zaeds applauded and sang. Kat relaxed from her end pose and her eyes spotted General Velio in the audience. The dancers dispersed and she looked for Blahom, with no luck. Blahom had already blended into the crowd, nowhere in sight.

Katyana ran straight for General Velio. Lady Mother Chi quickly joined her side.

"Katyana." Stopping the young Goddess in her tracks was Lieutenant Kov. A thin man, not nearly as bulky as most Zaed warriors, but sharp on the battlefield. Everyone, including Kat and Lady Mother Chi, had heard how he had been captured and tortured by the Delions. He hadn't been himself ever since.

"Good evening, ladies."

"Good evening, Lieutenant Kov," said the Goddess and Lady Mother Chi with a nod.

"I wanted to give you deep thanks for your ceremony tonight. You performed wonderfully," he said, and Katyana nodded, anxious to finish up so she could talk to General Velio.

"It is my duty," Katyana answered shortly, trying to sidestep the Lieutenant, but Lieutenant Kov wasn't done.

"And I also want to thank you for your service," he smiled. "I worry though, how dance rehearsals have been since you've started warrior training?"

"My sister and I are balancing the two just fine," Katyana shrugged, looking away every several seconds to make sure that she could still see General Velio.

"Still, at thirteen, you are being trained similar to how we mighty Zaed warriors have been, correct?" The questions caught Kat off guard. "We are being trained as warriors. No differently than you were,"

Lieutenant Kov nodded. "Is that so? Have they been training you in hand-to-hand combat?"

"Yes." Kat responded with annoyance.

"Have you progressed to using weapons yet?"

"Yes, to bo-staffs," Kat answered quickly remembering Blahom's conversation about Lieutenant Kov acting strange since he was captured. Lady Mother Chi was on full alert of the interrogation to the young girl.

"With your weight, do you find it difficult to hold a proper sword? It certainly is strenuous work. That is, unless they have not been training you as strictly as they should be." Lieutenant Kov continued to pry. Lady Mother Chi took a step between the Lieutenant and Katyana.

"She is being trained just as any Zaed warrior. She also does not owe you any more answers about her training. That is something only she needs to be concerned with," Lady Mother Chi said sternly.

Lieutenant Kov quickly took a step back.

"I didn't mean to offend the young Goddess. I apologize, my filter isn't quite how it has been ever since I was captured," he said, his voice tinged with pain.

"Thank you for your service," Lady Mother Chi said respectfully. She turned to Katyana, pushing the young Goddess away from the Lieutenant. "Didn't you wish to speak to General Velio?"

"Please, don't let me ..." Lieutenant Kov's voice drowned into the crowd as the two women had already started walking. Moments like these were why Kat loved Lady Mother Chi. Katyana started to walk at full speed towards General Velio, but she spotted Blahom out of the corner of her eye, laughing with Lita and Allysia. Slowing down for a moment, Kat was torn on what to do: should she forgive Blahom, or keep the petty feud going? She thought for a split second before scrunching up her nose, and, her energy refocused, ran towards General Velio.

"General Velio!" she called, and the General turned around and looked down at her.

"Good evening, young Goddess. Blessed performance today," he smiled politely.

"Thank you," Katyana grinned. "I have a few questions for you, if you have the time."

"Of course, I have time for one of my favorite Goddesses."

Katyana didn't need any more of an invitation and launched into her first question. Lady Mother Chi watched, amused by the Goddess' curiosity.

"Do Delions have any specific weaknesses?" she launched immediately into her first question.

"The Delions are like us. They feel, they love, they laugh, they cry. Some have extra-long fingers but I'm not sure if that is a weakness or a strength." General Velio chuckled. "Their weakness is that they are dependent on their technology, and we are dependent on a much higher, omniscient power. If anything were to happen to their devices, then their power would weaken. They have no divine gifts to lean upon. Without their technology, a Delion is useless, just as we are useless with the Alpha God," General Velio responded. "The Alpha God cannot be destroyed, but their devices can be dismantled in minutes." Katyana nodded, repeating his answer in her head so she would remember it.

"What is something that should always be in the back of my head when I'm on the battlefield?" she inquired and General Velio laughed.

"You ask as if you're needed on the battlefield tomorrow," General Velio said, through his chuckles.

"We don't know when the next Delion attack could be. Their

technology keeps advancing. I want to be ready for anything," Katyana answered with earnest eagerness.

"Alright then. Something that should always be in the back of your mind during the heat of a battle is your flank."

"My flank?" she repeated.

"Yes, your flank," he nodded. "Most of the time when we lose a battle, it is because Delions have been able to come up from behind and surround us. Always keep your enemy and your forces in front of you. Do you understand?"

"Yes, General Velio," Katyana nodded, committing his words to memory.

"Do you have more questions for me, young Goddess?" he inquired.

"Yes, I do." Katyana took a deep breath. She had been struggling with this question since her fight with Blahom. "You told me earlier that on the battlefield it's kill or be killed. Is there never a time to show mercy?"

General Velio studied Katyana's serious face and stroked his beard.

"That is an interesting question. War is brutal. In this war with the Delions, there is no place for mercy on the battlefield."

"I understand," Katyana felt a small smile tugging at her lips, feeling justified in her fight with Blahom.

"You and your sister are having some conflict, correct?"

Kat's eyes widened in shock that the General knew about the fight and Lady Mother Chi smirked, happy that he was bringing up what she wanted to say earlier. Katyana started to speak, but held her breath, unsure if she wanted to admit it out loud.

"Divide and conquer is always a tactic of the enemy forces," General Velio said, and Kat was at full attention again. "You need to trust your allies." General Velio's face hardened, and he looked Katyana sternly in the eye.

"In battle, your life is in the hands of your comrades. Any rift can lead to death of not just you but everyone around you. Just as tonight

Blahom

during your dance the tension between you and your sister was a distraction. It caused you to make a mistake. We noticed. Just as a Delion will notice. If there is any hope of winning this war, both you and your sister need to stay in one accord. If you break the bond, distractions, mistakes, and distress will only continue to happen. As a result, ruin and destruction will come upon everything we hold dear. Showing no mercy should be reserved for the battlefield alone. You must always show compassion and forgiveness to your allies."

"Yes, General Velio," Katyana said quietly, surprised and humbled by how perceptive the General was.

"There are other matters I must attend to with Lieutenant Kov. I hope the rest of your evening is pleasant." He nodded to Katyana, then at Lady Mother Chi.

"Thank you and goodnight," Kat and Lady Mother Chi said in unison. With a final nod, General Velio strode off back into the crowd.

Kat was pensive, repeating the words from the General in her mind. She was grappling with the idea of swallowing her pride to mend the rift between her and her sister. Several feet away, Blahom was still talking and laughing with their friends and Rasheed had joined the group. Blahom spared her sister one glance, then looked away. Fury burned in the pit of Kat's stomach.

Lady Mother Chi noticed the frown etched into Kat's face as her eyes locked on Blahom in the crowd. Wanting to reach out and remind Katyana of the conversation they just had with the General, Lady Mother Chi gently placed her hand on Kat's shoulder. The look on Kat's face didn't change and Lady Mother Chi felt her heart sink. There was nothing she could say that would sway Katyana's feelings. Even General Velio's words were now swallowed up by the ocean of Kat's emotions.

"Let's go get some rest," Lady Mother Chi insisted.

Katyana headed away from the festivities, determined to avoid her sister altogether.

Days turned into weeks and weeks into months and the tension between the two sisters remained. Blahom found no time to escape and satisfy her urges with any of the male Zaeds who were doting on her. She was frustrated and, despite hardly speaking a word to her sister, she didn't miss a beat training to become a warrior and maintaining her duties as a Goddess.

The strain between the Goddesses was obvious to those around them, and the feeling of unease permeated the dancers during rehearsals. Blahom and Katyana were unbothered by the popularity of their conflict. Watching the rift between the sisters continue to widen, Mother Hutra, ManCohalith, and the Generals grew concerned. The Zaeds watched, anticipating that one of the Goddesses would break the feud and apologize, but the sisters were stubborn, neither willing to bend and reconcile.

* * *

Katyana and Blahom were in their room, silently getting ready for the day. The tension was thick between them, all words now seemed to lead to further feuding.

"You talk too much. It's quite annoying. Stop talking to me," were Blahom's last words weeks ago to Katyana, who was sure to grant her sister her wish.

Blahom waited impatiently for Lady Mother Clara to finish helping her get into her warrior training attire so she could leave the awkward silence of the room and finish her hair and moisture butter application down the hall. While it wasn't easy for her to transfer her heavy garments to another room, hair and skin products were a different situation.

A knock on the door broke through the silence and the sisters' mother walked into the room.

"Good morning daughters."

"Good morning, Mother Hutra," the Goddesses said in unison, both immediately were on edge. Mother Hutra only visited in the mornings if she had something important to discuss.

Blahom

"Still not talking?" Mother Hutra stared at her two daughters, looking to Blahom first and then to Katyana. Both were silent, unable to respond to their mother with an answer she wanted to hear. Mother Hutra shook her head in exasperation.

"First the public fighting between Vasco and Lorraine and now you." She locked eyes with each of her daughters. "I have noticed that neither of you seem to care, but your family and the Zaeds do. You are Goddesses and the Zaeds look to you for unity and healing. What the two of you have been carrying on with has been the antithesis of that. This problem you have with one another needed to be resolved months ago." Mother Hutra's voice was stern and both sisters squirmed with guilt. "I don't know what started this and frankly I don't care as long as it ends. You both need each other, and this petty fight is ridiculous. You may be achieving your goals and performing your duties, but you foolishly struggle with pride and even a peasant knows that is a weakness. Soon the two of you will have nothing but one another to rely on."

Mother Hutra took a deep breath. "I haven't come here to only scold you. I am here to tell you that your life is about to change. I had a long conversation with General Murn yesterday," Mother Hutra said, annoyance clear in her voice. "It is time for your excursion out of the safety of the training arena. For the next two days, you will be with General Murn, dedicated to intense on location warrior training."

"Two days?" Blahom was startled. *This can't seriously be happening!*

The two Goddesses had been training with General Brakkus, but General Murn would be a different experience. While both Generals were stern and tough, Brakkus still had compassion. He understood when the two Goddesses needed a break and never berated them. General Murn, meanwhile, was known for how little compassion he showed his trainees. There were rumors that Murn could be more ruthless than a Delion. He had made trainees cry, and even more, made them howl in pain. That was simply General Murn's teaching style. Since a child, Blahom knew General Murn as the uncle, stoic and tough, and couldn't remember the last time she had seen him smile.

"Finally, we're being treated like the warriors we are!" hailed Katyana.

"You are a warrior in training. You are a Goddess. Don't forget that you are that first," Mother Hutra's voice was stern.

Mother Hutra's attention turned to Lady Mother Clara and Lady Mother Chi.

"Both of you know what I expect. Don't let General Murn bully you out of your duties. He can be cruel, but I need you two to be unwavering with him when it comes to my daughters."

"Yes, Mother Hutra," the Lady Mothers responded, digesting the idea that they would be subject to two days of training with General Murn. With a final nod to the Lady Mothers and a look of unease at her daughters, Mother Hutra left the room.

Chapter Seven

The two sisters and their Lady Mothers quickly headed to the Battle Strategy Hall to meet with General Murn, who was standing at attention, waiting for them. He was stiff-necked and serious, and while there were hard lines on his face, not even one came from laughter.

"I see you two are joining us," General Murn grunted when he saw Lady Mother Clara and Lady Mother Chi. The Generals had spoken amongst themselves for months against Lady Mothers in attendance during the Goddesses training.

"Mother Hutra made it clear. We go where the Goddesses go," Lady Mother Clara said. Her eyes stared at Murn unwavering, as if daring him to try to disobey the will of Mother Hutra.

"Of course, and I am sure that you will not interfere with their training as ManCohalith has made it clear that I am to prepare them for battle," said General Murn, a hint of smugness in his tone. While Mother Hutra was not to be disobeyed neither was the will of ManCohalith.

Pivoting his attention to the Goddesses, General Murn spoke, and the room echoed with his cold and harsh voice.

"The next two days of training will not be enjoyable." Both sisters stared at him, ready for whatever he was about to explain.

"During war, there will be times when you will experience the most extreme conditions, no matter your location. There will be days that are so cold you risk losing fingers and toes while your body goes numb. There will be conditions that are stifling with unbearable heat that your skin will bubble and ooze from the sun and you'll want nothing more than to submerge yourself in parasite-riddled water just to cool off. You will deal with the nature of the world around you, whether you're in the deepest parts of the forest for weeks at a time or fighting for your life on a naval ship amid a monsoon. Nature can be more unforgiving than the most dangerous of Delions, and you will have to know how to react."

He threw two packs of supplies to Katyana and Blahom. The packs were heavy and hit the girls' breasts, making the stagger under the weight. Blahom choked back a curse; being more developed, the sting and throb of her breast lingered on.

"We are going to travel into the forest for two days and see what kind of survivalists you are."

Despite the change of pace, Blahom and Katyana shouldered their packs and followed General Murn into the forest. Lady Mother Chi and Lady Mother Clara followed closely behind, carrying their own, perhaps slightly lighter packs.

Down long, cobbled roads, past houses and farms, the area became less and less populated. They hadn't even reached the forest and Blahom's feet ached from the hike. The forest was located far beyond their main hub. The dense treeline was like its own type of wall, and it sent a chill up Blahom's spine. She never would have thought that the forest could look so intimidating.

General Murn looked up. From the quick prayer he gained a sense of renewed confidence, his back straightened, and he stuck out his chest, striding into the forest as if he did it every day. Like helpless children, the group put their faith in his leadership and followed behind without hesitation.

Blahom

"If either of you have any questions, wait on my command to ask."

"Yes, General Murn," Katyana and Blahom said in unison.

"You too, Lady Mothers." General Murn gave Lady Mother Clara and Chi a long hard look, but they squished up their faces and did not respond. There was an obvious silent power struggle them.

Walking through the dense forest, a yellow colorway caught Blahom's eye.

"That's the Melby fungus," General Murn told them, pointing to the small yellow bulbs on several rotting trees on the forest floor. "Unfortunately, it isn't edible, but it is an indicator that there is underground water. Great place to start."

General Murn pulled a small shovel from his pack and handed it to Blahom.

"Where you see the fungus, push away the rotting wood," he instructed, "so you can get to the ground. Then start digging."

Digging was easier said than done. This wasn't the powder-like sand of the beaches near their home. This was dense and claylike and each jab into the ground seemed to push back against the shovel, as if the dirt was fighting back, refusing to yield to her advances.

Both Lady Mothers looked on, clearly wanting to help but not daring intervene.

Ughh ... this is hard. Is Kat next? Hope so. Maybe I can fling some of this dirt on her. Blahom's arms ached as she dug deeper and deeper, blisters starting to bubble on her hands. Shoveling was not a swift task.

The ground was wet, but compact. It felt like an eternity before Blahom finally shoveled away a lump of dirt that revealing cloudy water.

"The water is muddy, but it is still drinkable because the moss is usually able to filter the impurities," explained General Murn, taking the shovel back from Blahom, to her relief.

Still not wanting to let go of the anger from their ongoing fight,

Katyana would not look at her sister, turning away and pretending to be enthralled with the new environment.

"You, the tiny one." General Murn grabbed Katyana's shoulder and forced her to turn around. "What do you think this is? A little dance recital? There's no daydreaming while you're on the battlefield, especially while your comrades are doing hard work. Space out like that and you die." He shoved Katyana to the ground.

"Both of you, take a drink. The little brat first." Lady Mother Chi bit back her tongue, wanting to lash out at the General. Blahom and Katyana hesitated, looking down at the murky water. "That's an order! You think you're going to have fancy water just handed to you on the battlefield?" General Murn shouted, looking at both the Goddesses expectantly.

I'm the only one who can call her a brat. Blahom instinctively became protective of her sister. Dipping her head down, her nose caught a whiff of a rancid sour smell, and as she brought the thick brown water to her face she gagged. Her stomach roiled and she turned her head away and vomited.

Filtered water, my ass!

Lady Mother Clara took a step towards Blahom, ready to comfort the young Goddess. General Murn stuck out his arm, commanding her to stay put. She shot him a glare, but remained in place, looking on helplessly while Blahom wretched.

Katyana mustered up her courage and took a gulp of the water, wanting to prove the General wrong. Her face scrunched up, barely swallowing, she coughed, almost gagged, then quickly spit it out.

"You won't be spitting out water when you've been hiding in the trees for a week with only muddy putrid water to drink." General Murn handed an empty metal flask over to Katyana. "Collect some water for camp later tonight. We will boil and clean it up a bit."

Filling up the flask to the brim, Katyana corked the bottle and the group continued onward. The Lady Mothers realized that that was the first of many lessons over the two days and the Goddesses had only just begun.

The forest now was a constant mix of undeveloped land with rocks, tree roots and thorn bushes slowing them down and threatening to trip them up. As they marched up a steep incline, Blahom felt the air beginning to thin. The muggy heat made sweat cling to every inch of her body. She was thankful that the uniform had short sleeves, but that barely felt like enough to cool her down. She could feel blisters starting to form on the back of her heels and feet where her boots rubbed uncomfortably. Each step felt as if she was fighting the mud and the undergrowth and still they climbed higher.

Exhausted, Blahom noticed the General was far ahead and took a moment to rest, leaning against a nearby tree. Katyana, feeling her own exhaustion, looked over at her sister in envy, wondering if she could find her own tree without the General turning back and noticing.

Blahom took in a deep breath, but on her exhale, she knew immediately that something was horribly wrong.

"Something is blistering on your arm!" Lady Mother Clara yelled out, noticing from afar. The General whipped around immediately.

Making an awful popping sound, the amber-colored sap on Blahom's arm started to bubble against her flesh. Screaming in agony, she tried to brush the sap off, but only succeeded in getting it on her hand, making it foam and burn.

Lady Mother Clara sprinted towards Blahom, her heart pounding in panic at the young Goddess's pain. Putting his hand out, General Murn stopped Lady Mother Clara from coming closer. It took everything Lady Mother Clara had not to shove the General's arm away, but she reminded herself that he was in command.

"Okay, do something then!" Lady Mother Clara shouted at General Murn. He ignored her.

"This is why you don't touch anything," he chided, appearing more bothered by Blahom's screams than her pain. "Shut up. Keep screaming like that and you'll attract predators. You want one of your Lady Mothers to be swept away and devoured all because you couldn't handle a little pain?"

Blahom bit down on her bottom lip, her screams becoming pained whimpers, and she could taste the copper flavor of her blood.

This hurts but I can't let that control what I do. Ugh, this hurts so bad! Okay Blahom ... Positive thoughts. You need positive thoughts. You will be ok. This doesn't hurt.

Quickly, General Murn pulled leaves off the tree Blahom leaned against, then placed them on the sap on her arm, letting them stick to her skin. As he worked, Blahom tried to remain still, panting in pain. Her heart pounded loudly in her chest, echoing in her ears. Forcing herself to steady her breath, the burning sensation slowly subsided the longer the leaves sat on her skin.

"Does it still burn?" Murn's question held no concern.

"Yes, a little," Blahom whispered.

Murn quickly ripped the leaves off from Blahom's skin, peeling away sap and several layers of her flesh.

To her horror, Blahom looked down and saw the harsh raw red skin exposed, watching the blood drip down her arm. Katyana stood at attention and her eyes widened at the sight of her sister's destroyed skin. She pulled her gaze away from Blahom and looked over at Lady Mother Chi.

"Do something," Katyana whispered. With a more reserved voice, Lady Mother Chi spoke up.

"Please General, let me ..." Murn raised his hand, indicating to Lady Mother Chi not to speak.

"It's just a little second-degree burn. I just treated her. What more do you want? A hug and a kiss?"

Lady Mother Clara stared at Blahom, who was now standing erect, her shoulders back, taking deep breaths. Blood was dripping down her arm, but the young Goddess appeared to pay that no mind. Lady Mother Clara could see behind the pain in Blahom's eyes, a new sense of courage and strength were being born.

General Murn then pointed at the amber sap oozing from the tree.

"This tree is a Hant tree, and it creates sap. Hant sap is acidic and will burn the flesh of whatever it encounters. I'm sure you'll remember that from now on, won't you?" he chuckled and started walking, continuing the lesson. "The only way to neutralize the burn is to put the Hant tree's leaves on the sap. The leaves secrete a base oil that negates the acidic properties."

Why the hell wasn't this said before we started this outing? Blahom thought bitterly.

Lady Mother Clara couldn't stand seeing Blahom bleeding.

"Please General Murn, let me treat ..."

"My job is to train the Goddesses, not to baby them," General Murn said coldly. "I will allow for Blahom's wounds to be treated once we have set up camp. For now, we will keep moving. We still have ground to cover."

Lady Mother Clara and Lady Mother Chi shared a glance, both seething with anger at how General Murn was handling the girl. However, they knew that the intensity of this training was at ManCo-halith's command. After seeing the spark of strength in Blahom's eyes, Lady Mother Clara wondered if babying Blahom truly did hinder the young Goddess, rather than help.

"Then we will follow your lead," Lady Mother Clara said, as she continued following behind the General.

With his back turned to them, General Murn picked up his pace.

"Katyana, Blahom, keep up! Lady Mothers, feel free to go at your own dainty pace, but you two should be no more than ten steps behind me," General Murn waved them forward and the two Goddesses were quick to obey.

"Yes, General Murn," they said, breaking into a light jog. Easily maintaining the stride the General had set, the Lady Mothers felt slighted. General Murn was fully aware of the Lady Mothers' physical prowess and their strength. They knew this would be a long two days for everyone.

Hours without a word spoken, the group pushed on, traveling uphill through rocky terrain and muddy soil. Knowing that the day was ending, Lady Mothers Chi and Clara were relentless, enduring the exhausting trek to prove to the General that they were not weak, hoping that their strength could be drawn on by the Goddesses, as they noticed Blahom and Kat struggling to keep up. The entire training excursion was on Zaed soil, awe-inspiring soil that neither Blahom nor Kat had seen before, but as they continued uphill, the soggy soil turned to plentiful, green grass, and the sounds of the goldcrest could be heard. Blahom noticed the Transition of the land, and her curiosity started to grow despite the pain.

General Murn stepped onto a downed tree that crossed the rushing water to the other side of a stream, and the Lady Mothers quickly followed behind him, leading to a space between the trees that opened to reveal the beautiful landscape of towering cliffs and sparkling aqua-blue water.

Blahom and Kat gasped at the environment they called home, the continuing aches in both of their legs seemingly melting. The surrounding sounds of the forest were accompanied by crashing waters of the falls nearby, the landscape lush and green. The setting sun washed over the land, a bright shadow that covered the girls in warmth and a deep red glow. Although the trek thus far was brutal, Blahom couldn't help but take in the awe-inspiring nature around her.

This majestic land belongs to us, the Zaeds. It's something that I was born to protect, just as Vasco and Father, and his father.

Blahom frowned. *Wait. The reason for this war is because of this coveted land, and that's pathetic! Why can't we just share since there is so much of it? The fact that so many have died over a land, technology, or who believes what makes no sense!*

"Keep moving!" General Murn's gruff voice snapped Blahom out of her thoughts, and she continued to walk, longingly taking one last glimpse at the landscape, before the trees swallowed it up.

They trudged on. Movement caught Blahom's eye. A familiar creature camouflaged in the grass crossed their path and General Murn continued onward, almost stepping on the venomous creature.

Blahom

A Celen snake! A bite from that and you can die in minutes! Blahom's mind raced.

"Watch out, General Murn!" Blahom said, trying to warn him, quickly pointing to the snake. The General paused then nodded.

Bending down to the snake, Murn picked it up confidently behind the back of its head. Writhing and contorting its body, the snake hissed, trying to break free.

"General, have you lost your mind?" Lady Mother Clara remembered not to yell but there was panic in her voice.

Turning to smirk at the Lady Mothers and Goddesses, General Murn put his arm towards the snake's mouth, and the serpent bit down savagely, fangs sinking into the flesh of his forearm. Blood oozed; the snake pumped venom; Murn chuckled.

Putting her hand over her mouth to keep from screaming in terror, Lady Mother Chi stared at General Murn and Blahom and Katyana were frozen in place. Lady Mother Clara began digging through her medical pack, trying to find something to help cure the venom.

"Watch carefully," General Murn grunted, garnering everyone's attention, pulling the snake away causing more blood to seep from his arm. Throwing the snake into a bush, General Murn watched it quickly slither away to safety.

Looking at Blahom and Katyana, he brought his wound to his lips and sucked at the broken skin, spitting out a clear liquid and he kept sucking until he was spitting out nothing but blood.

"I have been bitten by those damn devils more times than I can count," said General Murn, chuckling, blood dribbling down his lips.

Katyana let out a gasp and Blahom felt herself take a step back from the General. It took everything within Lady Mother Chi not to vomit at the sight of him. His uncharacteristic grin and bloody face reminded the Goddesses of a cannibalistic monster in a scary story Vasco would tell.

Enjoying their shocked faces, General Murn continued. "That is what you will have to do if you are ever bitten. Immediately start sucking out the venom and spit it out. You will continue to do this until you are spitting out your own blood, being certain that all the clear venom is out of your body."

What the hell is wrong with Murn? I remember Vasco saying something about sucking out venom, but he never said anything like this. Blahom stared at the grin on the General's face in bafflement. *Is my uncle crazy? Is he really smiling? Yeah. He's crazy.*

"What happens if you're bitten in a place you can't reach?" Katyana said in a timid voice, now worried and afraid.

"You better have some good people around you willing to help. If not, you're dead."

General Murn's words sunk in to Blahom. Now everything became real. There was no possibility of escaping their destiny and General Murn was preparing them for the harsh reality. She and Kat will be fighting enemies. She and Kat will become warriors. The need to survive crashed down over Blahom at full force. *Kat and I have been fighting for months, but there's no time to be mad when our survival is at risk.*

"Come, we have to keep going and find a place to stay the night." General Murn marched on.

As they continued onwards, Katyana picked up her pace despite her weariness to keep in stride next to Blahom. Lady Mother Clara walked easily while Lady Mother Chi gently coached Kat on how to persevere through her muscle aches. General Murn remained several paces ahead.

"My skin itches like crazy," Katyana muttered, nails scratching roughly against her arm.

"Itches?" Blahom whispered, her full attention now on her little sister.

"Keep up!" General Murn barked, not turning around to look at the group.

Both Lady Mother's stiffened at Katyana's statement. Stepping forward to Katyana, Lady Mother Chi was surprised when Lady Mother Clara grabbed her hand and shook her head.

Blahom

"We are not to intervene. Let's not baby them," Lady Mother Clara said in a low, quiet voice. Lady Mother Chi paused. She had never considered that she was babying Kat, but recalled now having experienced her own hardships that made her stronger. Katyana needed to experience hardship as well if she was ever going to survive on the battlefield. Lady Mother Chi continued walking near Katyana but made no move to examine her arm.

"It won't go away," Katyana's voice raised slightly, trying to stay calm while she continued clawing at her skin in panic.

Blahom noticed the Lady Mothers whispering. The shifting dynamics unnerved her. Realizing that the Lady Mothers were not going to push against General Murn on her sister's behalf, she ran towards him. Blahom stopped in front of the General, halting him in his path.

"General Murn, we must stop right now," Blahom said sternly, bringing the entire group including Murn to a standstill. He looked at the women with a hardened glare.

Running back to Katyana's side, and examining where her sister was relentlessly scratching, Blahom's eyes widened in shock. Katyana's skin on her forearm was writhing, as if her skin was an eggshell and something was trying to break free. The sight made Blahom's stomach churn.

"General Murn," Blahom's voice wavered as she looked over at the General with concern.

"What?" he asked nonchalantly.

"Kat's skin is moving," Blahom's voice was wavering despite her efforts to sound calm, not wanting to further alarm her sister.

Guilt washed over the Lady Mothers. They locked eyes with General Murn, silently asking for direction. Would they be babying the Goddesses if they were to intervene? Or was this a serious medical emergency that needed their caring hands? General Murn looked away from the two, offering no answer.

Walking over in no particular hurry to Katyana, General Murn glanced at her arm. He shrugged his shoulders indifferently.

"It's just the Lillit Mite. They're only dangerous after around eight hours, plenty of time for us to treat her after we set up camp."

"Eight hours? Why not just treat her now?" Blahom pleaded, trying to control her anger at how unconcerned the General appeared.

"Because we need to set up camp first. We can't just stop for any little inconvenience. Your sister has unfortunately got a parasite. They'll crawl into your skin trying to make a home. They usually do this to dead animals, but they'll occasionally burrow into live creatures. They live in the long grass we've been walking through and Kat was just unlucky to come in contact with them. We have ample time to treat her. We don't have time to get stuck out here and slaughtered by wildlife all over a little bug."

Katyana's face paled and she scratched at her skin more furiously.

"Scratch all you want. It won't do much." General Murn walked on. "Keep moving. Both of you. We got two hours."

Kat kept running her fingernails over her forearm until the blood began to run.

"Dear Katyana, you need to stop," Lady Mother Chi said with worry.

"I can't." Katyana replied continuously scratching at her arm.

"General Murn," Lady Mother Chi called out, halting the group once again. "I understand that we are to not intervene but look at her arm. At least allow us to treat her with a salve to stop her itching."

General Murn was silent for a moment. He saw the trauma on Kat's face. He also knew that compared to everything that was about to get thrown at the Goddesses, this was nothing.

"Treat her with lotion if you like. It will alleviate the scratching, but it won't fix the mite problem."

"Thank you," Lady Mother Chi quickly approached Katyana and pulled out lotion from her bag, applying a large amount onto the young Goddess' skin.

General Murn turned and started walking again. Deep down, he hated every moment of the training. He hated having to treat his nieces like warriors. He hated having to be cruel and harsh just as he was towards his usual male Zaed trainees. He hated Mother Hutra's dream and he hated having to comply with it. Remembering the Zaed men he had seen slaughtered on the battlefield, he would do anything to keep that from happening to the young Goddesses.

"Stay close. We still have further to go." Blahom and Katyana followed obediently while both Lady Mothers walked behind the Goddesses.

The minutes dragged into hours as the group trudged onward and the sun began to dip lower in the sky. General Murn lifted his hand, signaling the group to stop.

"That landscape over there should make for a good place to set up camp," General Murn pointed to where the trees sparsely grew. "We will need to cross this river. Don't let your packs get wet."

Staring at the wide murky river, the four women were unsure how to make it to the other side.

"Stop stalling. The water is shallow."

Wanting to set up camp as soon as possible, Katyana walked into the stream after General Murn and Lady Mother Chi followed suit, holding her pack over her head.

Not wanting to have to dry her pants later, Blahom held back a few seconds to roll them up and Lady Mother Clara waited patiently behind her.

Stepping into the frigid, weedy water at the river's edge, Blahom's boots were immediately soaked, and a chill ran down her spine. The water was shallow, but the current was strong. Struggling to stay upright, Blahom focused on balancing with the weight of her pack and racing quickly towards the bank on the other side.

Once they crossed the river, General Murn nodded in approval at the surrounding area.

"This flat land makes for a good place to set up camp. First things first, we have to make a fire. Surviving in the wilderness is almost impossible without fire," explained General Murn. The Lady Mothers made a move to help, but the General stopped them.

"Shall I remind you again that this is a task for the Goddesses? You are not to interfere."

"Yes, General Murn."

Turning to grab branches that littered the forest floor, Blahom felt something wriggle on her leg. Looking down, she saw a large slippery leech attached to her calf. *Dammit I can't catch a break. It must have come from the river!*

General Murn was making his way towards her once again looking more annoyed than concerned.

"It's just a leech. All these beautiful bugs seem to love you ladies out here. You want a leech sucking on your leg or would you rather get picked off by some predator in the dark? Nightfall is coming and fire is the only thing that keeps creatures that see us as a snack at bay. Gather firewood quickly and once we get it going, we can burn the leech off."

Blahom joined Katyana and gathered firewood from the surrounding area. Moving quickly, both wanted to be rid of the creatures plaguing them. Once they had a large pile of sticks and logs gathered, the sun had begun to set, and a chill permeated the air. Starting his own fire as an example and illuminating the camp, General Murn showed the two Goddesses several different fire-starting techniques. Each was responsible for starting their own fires.

Katyana was quickly able to get a flame going, warming her wet feet in front of it. Struggling to focus, Blahom tried to work faster, rubbing the sticks frantically together, forgetting the technique General Murn had just taught them. She wanted nothing more than to detach the leech sucking contently at her blood.

"You're rushing the process," General Murn said, pointing at the agitated motions of Blahom's hands. "You need to be calmer."

"Calm?" Blahom heard herself say what she was thinking out loud and quickly reeled herself in. She tried once again and once again failed.

"You need to stay calm under pressure or you're going to die the moment you step foot on the battlefield," General Murn said harshly,

Blahom

breathing down her neck, adding additional pressure to her to start the fire. "Strike your flint less frantically and make sure your kindling has room to breathe."

Several strikes later, Blahom was finally able to get a flame going.

"It's something to practice," he said, when he noticed Blahom frowning. "It took me years to be able to start a fire."

General Murn grabbed a stick and handed it to Blahom. "Light that, then put the fire to the leech. Make sure not to burn those dancer legs." General Murn chuckled and Lady Mother Clara cringed.

Blahom hesitated for a moment, unsure about putting fire so close to her body. But the sight of the creature feasting on her blood made her ignore her fears. She quickly placed the burning stick to the leech, and it immediately detached. With his large hand, General Murn snatched the creature and threw it into the fire. It hissed and crackled within the flames, blood oozing from it. The sight made Blahom's stomach churn knowing that some of the blood was her own.

Lady Mother Clara was relieved seeing the leech detach from Blahom's leg.

General Murn then turned his attention to Katyana, who was palming her forearm where the parasite was still located, her face contorted in a disgusted and anxious frown.

"Now you, little lady, have gotten yourself into an entanglement. Getting rid of your little friends isn't going to be as easy as your sister's." Grabbing a pot, the General filled it with the water that Katyana collected earlier. Placing the pot into the fire, everyone watched as it took only a few minutes for the water to come to a boil.

"Stick your arm out," General Murn instructed. Before General Murn had fully finished his sentence both Lady Mothers had rushed over and were standing in front of the girl while Blahom was at her sister's side.

"Do you intend to scald her arm? Do you intend to leave her deformed?" Breaking the silence security code, Lady Mother Chi screamed, never more appalled in her life. "What is wrong with you?"

General Murn remained calm. "Nothing. We are going to pour this on her arm. Don't be naive and think that I don't understand the situation." His voice was stern but level.

"And you are naive to think that I am just going to idly sit by while you pour scalding hot water on a child!" Lady Mother Chi clapped back.

"My intentions are not to burn her, at least not more than necessary. If we all share that intention, then everyone needs to assist."

"So, we are all to be a part of this demented act?" asked Lady Mother Clara backing up Lady Mother Chi.

"The benefit of getting the mite out of her skin justifies the burn," said General Murn calmly.

"Benefit?" Lady Mother Chi was seething with rage. "How does creating third degree burns benefit anyone?"

"Because burn wounds will be easier to heal than eaten away flesh."

"No! Absolutely not!" Lady Mother Chi was out of control. Blahom watched as she held Katyana, who was sobbing.

They had never seen this fire, defiance, and fury from Lady Mother Chi or any Lady Mother. No Lady Mother ever had a reason to rebel against the commands of a General. To the young Goddesses, she was inspiring but fanatical.

General Murn stared intently at Lady Mother Chi. "I understand that you're devoted to the young Goddess and that this situation is horrifying. However, I implore you to listen to me." Katyana was scratching in pain.

The calm in his voice and the concern in his eyes silenced Lady Mother Chi, but she was still on edge.

"If we don't remove the mites from Katyana's skin, they will continue to eat away at her flesh. They will also start laying eggs, which will result in more creatures eating her flesh from the inside out. Their feces can cause infections, which will infect her blood and spread throughout her body, killing her. I believe a controlled burn is worth trying to forgo this outcome."

"There are ways at the fortress to treat her other than a burn. We will head back now!" Lady Mother Chi insisted.

"Did you forget how long it took us to get here? And to traverse the forest in the middle of the night with just a torch is begging for a disaster to happen," General Murn said.

"Then we leave first thing in the morning."

"By that time, we risk her blood being poisoned by the mites. Do you want your precious little Goddess to die from sepsis?"

"Then why didn't we turn back when this first happened?" Blahom was furious. "You're going to burn my sister for what? A stupid lesson!?"

"We didn't turn back because in war, turning back isn't an option."

"This isn't war, this is training!"

"It is my duty as a General to make your training as close to what war is like as possible. Which means no turning around and that you might leave with a scar or two. ManCohalith has trusted me with this training. I would hope that you all would honor his trust in me."

"My Father wouldn't stand for this."

"Then you don't know your father." General Murn's words cut through all the night air. Blahom stood in front of him, her anger still swirling within her, but she was left without any further rebuttal.

Not budging, General Murn went on with his plan. "In order to do this, we do this as a group. Blahom, you are going to hold onto Katyana's hand to make sure she doesn't move too much during the initial shock of the burn so that the water doesn't burn more skin than necessary."

General Murn turned his attention to the Lady Mothers. "Lady Mother Clara, you are going to grab a cloth and have it ready to immediately soak up the water once it is poured. Once you remove the cloth, Lady Mother Chi will be ready with healing salve and gauze to apply to the burn. This will mitigate the scarring and the pain."

The group settled, but remained uneasy. The General locked eyes with Katyana. "Katyana, this is the fastest way to kill the mites. They can't survive being boiled. Now that everyone is ready, can I trust you not to scream and give away our position?"

Katyana was shaking but nodded her head.

"I will not scream," she said. Lady Mother Chi stepped through and hand Katyana a thick cloth.

"Here, bite on this, honey," she said gently. She glared at the General, daring him to scold her.

"Good, now, everyone, focus."

Blahom held 'er sister's arm out while the Lady Mothers grabbed their supplies, anticipating the moment the boiling water was poured.

General Murn looked at Katyana and the young Goddess nodded her head with bravery in her eyes. Furrowing her brows, she held her breath in anticipation.

With everyone in position, General Murn grasped the pot and poured the water carefully onto her forearm. Katyana shook violently in pain as tears rolled down her cheeks. The delicate skin blistered. Refusing to scream, she bit down hard on the cloth. Blahom held onto Katyana tightly, fighting back her own tears, wishing that she was in her little sister's place. The Lady Mothers were swift with their duties, and the ordeal lasted only seconds.

Once all was done, Blahom continued holding her sister. She wanted nothing more than for them to go home.

Night fell quickly and despite the trauma, work still needed to be done to set up the camp. Darkness brought the cold and more predators, so fire and a strong shelter were vital.

Running on sheer adrenaline, Blahom and Katyana got to work. Katyana's movements were slow, and she hardly picked up a single stick, but no one was going to scold her after all she went through. General Murn didn't stop the Lady Mothers from grabbing firewood, knowing that no more lessons were needed for the day. Having to boil the skin of a Goddess took a mental toll on everyone, himself included.

Within an hour, the campsite was complete. Blahom and Katyana sat on the ground while the Lady Mothers rummaged through their bags, preparing salves and grabbing bandages. Neither of the sisters moved, both staring at the fire trying to ignore the pain radiating throughout their bodies. Fatigue from their strict dancing routines was a walk in the park compared to the intensity of this day.

Gathering their supplies, the two Lady Mothers gave way to their maternal instincts, and they turned to the battered and exhausted girls. Lady Mother Chi gave Katyana a strong hug, stroking the girl's hair, and then began treating her wounds. She examined the Goddess's forearm with a close eye. The damaged gooey skin was still fresh from the boiling water, and the burn all together was about the width of three fingers. If they hadn't followed General Murn's plan, the burn would have been much worse.

Lady Mother Chi took out a bottle of strong alcohol, pouring several drops over the wound to disinfect it. Biting down on her lip, Katyana suppressed her screams of pain, breaking the Lady Mother's heart. Noticing the cold wind blowing on the exposed flesh, the Lady Mother ached at the thought of her charge's pain. She covered the wound in healing salve and wrapped it loosely to mitigate dirt and germs getting to the damaged skin.

"You were so strong today," she said to Katyana.

"Incredibly so," agreed Lady Mother Clara. "You both were," looking at Blahom with kind loving eyes as she tended to her wound. "You were made to be strong, and you proved that today." Her words had their own power, bolstering Blahom's spirits slightly, despite her pain.

Lady Mother Clara unlaced Blahom's boots, sliding them off carefully, trying not to further aggravate the blisters covering the young Goddess' foot. She worked quickly, pouring the alcohol on the blisters then quickly applying the healing salve. Blahom breathed heavily in pain, feeling the disinfectant burning the open wounds.

Lady Mother Clara then turned her attention to Blahom's ankle, which the girl had twisted on the rocks in the river.

"It is clearly swollen and aggravated. You showed so much strength hiking through the terrain today," she continued. Lady Mother Clara could see the events of the day were weighing heavily on Blahom just as they had weighed heavily on her. Blahom was silent, her mind far away.

"What are you feeling right now?" Lady Mother Clara asked, now sitting next to the young Goddess, her voice soft and gentle. Blahom looked up at her, eyes glistening with tears that threatened to spill over.

"I know training is harsh, but I should have been better at it. Father told me to look after Katyana and I failed. I should have ended this fight like Mother said. I should have been able to keep the parasite from getting to Kat. I feel like I'm not ready to become a warrior and this day proved it, and Kat was the one who suffered. If I wasn't being so stupid, Kat wouldn't have that burn mark for the rest of her life."

Blahom's voice wavered as she spoke, her eyes staring at the ground, shaking her head in frustration. Cupping Blahom's cheek with her slender hand, the Lady Mother tilted Blahom's head up and locked eyes with her.

"This is training, Blahom. You are not supposed to be ready for this. These types of experiences are supposed to test you. Furthermore, it isn't your fault that Kat got hurt. The fact that you and your sister are still breathing with no broken bones means you both did well."

Blahom stared at Lady Mother Clara's face, glowing in the warm light of the fire. Her heart swelled, grateful that Lady Mother Clara was by her side at this moment, as she had been so often in the past.

"Thank you for being here," Blahom said, leaning into Lady Mother Clara, who wrapped her in her arms.

"There is no place that I would rather be." Lady Mother Clara gently stroked Blahom's hair as the young Goddess relaxed into that warm feeling of comfort.

The soft lullaby of Lady Mother Chi singing to Katyana filled the air of the camp. The bugs of the forest chirped while the firewood crackled, broken down by hot embers. General Murn had propped himself up against a tree, back turned to everyone and staring out into the dark forest, watching vigilantly for any sign of danger.

"Your son is a warrior, isn't he?" Blahom asked.

Lady Mother Clara stiffened for a moment, surprised by the question, but then resumed stroking Blahom's hair.

"Yes, he is."

"Did he train under General Murn?"

"All warriors train under him after General Brakkus." Lady Mother Clara frowned. "After my son came home from his first forest excursion, he was shattered like a glass ornament on a stone floor, fragmented and scattered every which way. He had broken his arm, three of his fingers, and dislocated a shoulder." Blahom sat up, looking at Lady Mother Clara with pity.

"Worse than the broken bones, was his broken spirit. I remember him returning and looking different. There was something behind his eyes ..." Lady Mother Clara trailed off, shaking her head. "Like I said, Blahom. You've done well today."

Blahom saw the pain in the woman's eyes and took that moment to hug Lady Mother Clara again.

"Come, my dear, let's head into the shelter that you and your sister built. You need to rest, and it looks like little Kat is already asleep," Lady Mother Clara said, glancing over to see Lady Mother Chi guiding a half-asleep Kat to her sleeping bag in the shelter.

Blahom followed Lady Mother Chi and Kat into their makeshift shelter. It wasn't the sturdiest or prettiest shelter, but covered by a heavy tarp, it kept the cool night air out. Curling up, Blahom sunk into her sleeping bag.

"Goodnight Goddess. Let sleep wash away the pain of the day," whispered Lady Mother Clara as she gently kissed Blahom's forehead. Before Lady Mother Clara could follow Lady Mother Chi back outside, Blahom drifted into a deep sleep.

Waking up early in the morning, Blahom relished the journey home. No one spoke during their trek back. The sisters kept their eyes forward, hyper aware of the environment and weather around them as they trudged on, not wanting to repeat any mistakes from the day before. The sun was high in the sky when cobbled roads came within eyeshot, and Blahom's mind wanted to sprint for the doorway, but her body felt like it had been trampled by a stampede of horses. At the sight of her home, tears pricked the corners of her eyes.

The group passed through the city gates, relieved to return to the warmth of their home. It was a quiet, early afternoon and most Zaeds were occupied with work or school, but those out and about were quick to notice the battered group, briefly staring and then quickly looking away. They were familiar with warriors returning from brutal forest excursions, but seeing two Goddesses coated in dirt with caked mud underneath their fingernails was unexpected. The girls' hands were covered in dried blood and Blahom had a pronounced limp while Katyana's burned arm was heavily bandaged. It had been rumored that the Goddesses were training, but this was the first time it was truly confirmed. A flurry of whispers hummed throughout the city.

Chapter Eight

Mother Hutra waited for her daughters at the castle steps. She wrapped them in her arms, eyes scanning every cut, bruise, nick, and scrape that marred her daughters' skin. Her heart constricted with guilt. Leaning and sobbing into their mother's embrace, Blahom and Katyana felt their energy drain. This was their first time away from their mother, and the stress of experience came crashing down on them. Mother Hutra fought back her own tears.

"My sweet beautiful strong Goddesses," she whispered, kissing the tops of their heads. Clutching her girls, Mother Hutra looked piercingly at General Murn.

"It was just two days and one night, they're fine." General Murn shrugged his shoulders and Mother Hutra's eyes narrowed. She reluctantly let go of her daughters, and took a step towards General Murn.

"Don't tell me that they're fine. They'll be more than fine, they're my daughters. What the hell happened out there?"

"You know damn well what happened. You remember Vasco's first forest excursion." General Murn had little patience for Mother Hutra's maternal rage. "With their precious little Lady Mothers, they received unheard of special treatment. Treatment that Vasco or any other warrior never had or will have! Most by this point are handling being in the forest alone for weeks at a time, but these two, honestly, they wouldn't last a day out there on their own. Your children will be dead if they keep training at this pace!"

Mother Hutra's body tensed, and she stared at General Murn with rage.

"Lady Mother Clara, Lady Mother Chi. Please take Blahom and Katyana to the bathhouse." Mother Hutra's tone had venom behind it; venom few people ever saw. The Lady Mothers quickly ushered the two sisters indoors.

Alone with General Murn, Mother Hutra spoke. "Don't you ever mention death in front of them."

"At this rate you'd be lucky if they survived their Transition, Catalena."

"Who do you think you are talking to? Did you forget that I have Transitioned?" Mother Hutra's voice held a wrath that could intimidate the strongest of Zaed warriors. She resorted to a statement that she seldom used. "You are not to ever address me as Catalena. You are speaking with the wife of ManCohalith, the ruler of the Zaeds. A title that I earned. Know your place."

General Murn clenched his jaw. "Understood, Mother Hutra," he said with a head bow.

"And never forget that."

Mother Hutra had turned away when General Murn spoke. "Don't confuse my concern for your children, my nieces, with cruelty."

Mother Hutra paused for a moment, then turned to look at her brother. He stared at her with his usual stoic face, but she knew his eyes well, and saw their deep concern. Still, she held her ground. "I know what is to come for my children and I will have them prepare as I deem fit." Mother Hutra turned her back to her brother, closing the doors behind her, and hurried to her daughters.

Blahom

She entered the steamy bath house just as the two tubs were almost filled with warm water. Light streamed in through the windows, shining on her daughters and illuminating the injuries that they had sustained.

"Lady Mother Chi, Lady Mother Clara. Thank you for accompanying the Goddesses on their forest excursion. Take the rest of the day to rest, and my deepest appreciation to you both. I wish to spend time alone with my daughters."

"Yes, Mother Hutra." Mother Hutra engulfed them in a warm embrace and turned back to her children.

Mother Hutra gently took Blahom's hand, helping her keep her balance as she stepped into the tub. Reaching next for Katyana's hand, Mother Hutra saw the burn on her daughter's arm for the first time. She held back her reaction and instead gently took the hand of her daughter's other arm. She felt Katyana clutch onto her.

"It will be alright. Your wounds will be healed."

The Goddesses sunk into their tubs, hissing in discomfort before exhaling sighs of relief. Neither spoke; they were too exhausted. Their eyes focused on the ceiling of the room, replaying the events of the past day in their minds.

Mother Hutra lathered up a cloth with a fragrant soap and started gently washing Katyana's arms, being careful not to touch the burn.

"You are both so strong," she said. She wasn't used to seeing her vibrant daughters so silent. Her own mind was still on her conversation with General Murn. *Could Murn Be right?* she wondered. *Are my daughters not strong enough to survive the Transition? Maybe I have been too protective of them ... Stop it, Catalena. You're strong, and your daughters are too!* She tried to harden herself, but she knew the truth. *Or maybe ... maybe it's time to tell them the full truth and help them gain strength.*

"I don't think I've ever told the two of you exactly why I was the only woman to ever Transition." Mother Hutra held her breath, noticing the glance her two daughters exchanged before turning to her. *This is it. There's no turning back now, and they must know. I can't continue to run from my past any longer.*

Walking over to a closet, she pulled out the tea kettle that had been gifted to her after she had given birth to Vasco. The kettle boiled quickly on the brazier and carefully she poured three cups of steaming tea, slowly mixing some honey into the girls' tea so it was to their liking. *Am I truly about to do this? I haven't thought about this in a long time, but when I look at my daughters ....* Sipping her tea, Mother Hutra shot a quick, worried glance at her daughters before she took a deep breath. *I can't continue to shelter them; they must know.*

"In my youth, I made mistakes. Those mistakes brough my loyalty to the Zaeds into question. A mandate was put into effect, and I was made to Transition because I had to prove myself." Mother Hutra sipped on her tea, trying to find the right words. "When I was a little older than you," her eyes went to Katyana then to Blahom, "and a little younger than you, I was collecting berries in a field on the outskirts of the city and saw some Delion boys around my age goofing around. In those days, we knew that our species were at odds, but there was not nearly the tension and the separation that we have now, nor the hatred that we have instilled in our children against the other." Mother Hutra looked sad and disappointed. "The Zaeds were always spiritually led, and the Delions were technology driven, but we knew we had an obligation to try to get along living on the same planet."

With a brief flash of a flirty smile she continued her story. "There was one handsome boy who was very focused, tinkering on a control that was flying a makeshift drone. I was mesmerized by how his long fingers worked on the remote and his keen eyes. Even though he was so focused, he took a moment to look away from what he was doing to notice me. He smirked and asked if I liked his machine. I replied yes and I had never seen such a thing in my life. That's the day I met and fell in love with ManMattheius. And he loved me in return."

"ManMattheius!" Blahom exclaimed in shock.

Blahom

"You mean the ruler of the Delions?" Katyana was floored, the two breaking the silence.

"He wasn't the ruler of the Delions at the time. He was just a child, and so was I. Our love was a simple and a pure one. We would sneak and talk and share secrets. But tensions were already running high between us because of his friends' spreading rumors. One day we took a dip together in the nearby lake, performing a makeshift ritual and made a vow to love each other. Perhaps as any young love does." Mother Hutra let out a small chuckle, questioning her state of mind at the time. "We were found by his friends and ultimately, we knew our love for each other would be forbidden by our elders. Shortly thereafter, the war started again and our relationship was seen as treasonous and I was vilified and hated."

"So, you were made to Transition to prove that you no longer loved him?" Blahom said, bewildered.

"Yes. Years later, I was still despised by nearly everyone. I loved your father and he wanted to marry me even though he had heard the rumors. He was heir to the throne and other beautiful women who never had any dealings with a Delion wanted to be his wife. His Father, the ManCohalith at the time, wasn't going to let a young woman with my history marry his son so easily."

"A mandate was put into effect that if a woman had previous dealings with a Delion and the heir asked for her hand in marriage, that woman must prove her worthiness by undergoing Transitioning, something no woman had done before." Mother Hutra closed her eyes for a moment as she remembered how scared she was to take up such an honorable position. She'd seen the warriors after going through their training, and she'd fear that the same would happen to her. *I'm telling them for their own good*, she reminded herself. *It is only right, but I was so scared for myself and anxious for how ManCohalith would embrace my love after the Transition was complete.*

"Your father added a statute to that mandate: If a woman was courageous enough to undergo Transitioning and come out alive, she was granted the right to accept the heir's hand in marriage and, after she became his wife, no one was to speak of her past again. Transitioning was the most painful experience of my life. I screamed and cried. It felt like my insides were being scorched by flames because during Transitioning your entire essence is being destroyed and rebuilt. I didn't have the physical training of a warrior. No one cared. My mother was terrified and furious that I would go through with this. Your grandfather had died many years before, so my brothers tried to stand against it, but that had little say-so in my life. After all they were my brothers not my father."

Mother Hutra took in a deep breath. Recalling and telling the story was draining, but she was determined to tell it as honestly as she could.

"I did have mental fortitude from the harsh lessons instilled in me by my father well before he passed on. Praying and fortitude helped me to stay alive. There were so many moments where I wanted to give in and let death put me out of my agonizing pain. But I had to remind myself that the most magnificent of diamonds are forged through pressure and scalding heat. I was going to emerge as the wife of the next ruler, and I wasn't going to let anything stand in my way when it came to being with your father. You both are a testament to my success and to this day, nobody has attempted to use my past against me."

Mother Hutra looked at Blahom and Katyana and took a fortifying sip of her tea. *Murn may be right. I don't want to be weak, but my daughters are my weakness. I'm their mother. I won't let my daughters have the same helplessness that I did, and Murn won't mistake my motherly nature for vulnerability. I'm doing what's best for my children, Blahom and Katyana ...*

Mother Hutra took a shaky breath. "You two are mirroring my life. I want you to understand that Transitioning wasn't easy then and it is not going to be easy now." She smiled at her daughters. "I know you two will survive and become more powerful than anyone will possibly be able to comprehend. You are Goddesses and just as pure gold, even the hottest of flames will never be able to destroy you."

Blahom

Mother Hutra poured her daughters another cup of tea and then started to wash Blahom's hair, softly singing an old soothing hymn. *"Sweet, sweet loves, my sweet, sweet loves ..."*

As she sang, her mind wandered into memories of her Transition and the agonizing pain that led to her gift; to prophecies that had to be spoken. *"You are loved you should know you are loved."*

As she sang, she felt a cold pit forming in her stomach remembering the death of her mother-in-law, who had been there for her Transition with loving words of wisdom and advice. *"I can feel your knees sinking ..."*

Guilt welled up in Mother Hutra's voice and she continued to sing, trying not to cry. *"One of these moments and it won't be long. You will look for me and I will be gone."*

Her mind flashed back. She was twenty years old, curled up in bed next to her new husband and the comfort of his presence lulled her sleep; into a dream. In her dream was ManCohalith's mother, lying on a bed with her son holding her hand and weeping.

"Oh, one of these mornings ..." She sang on with half a mind, reflecting on the memory of her first prophetic dream. She remembered not being able to look away as the blood oozed from the corner of her mother-in-law's mouth. She remembered how in her dream the blood trickled down the side of her mother-in-law's face and onto the white pillow beneath her head. One final breath and ManCohalith's mother's hand went limp.

"You will look for me and I will be gone. But you are never alone."

Mother Hutra remembered how her mother-in-law's death woke her and she knew even then that the dream had meaning, but she couldn't bring herself to share it with ManCohalith.

Her song was a familiar one to the girls who always enjoyed their mother's own rendition of the popular hymn. Slowly, the melody of the song wilted away on Mother Hutra's lips, her sweet notes coming to a halt as her mind was completely in the past.

"Mother?" Mother Hutra snapped out of her memory, gazing

down at Blahom. "Are you alright? You stopped singing." The Goddesses were looking at her with concern.

"ManCohalith's mother, your grandmother, was the only one who showed me love in those days before I married ManCohalith. She saw me for my strength and respected me. She was the one who told me not to let the power of my past be for others, but for it to be my own."

Mother Hutra paused, then said in a small whisper. "There's something that I haven't told either of you before. It's about the last few days that I had with your grandmother on your father's side."

This piqued the interest of the girls, who had never met their grandmother but heard countless stories.

"I was twenty years old, and in a medical room because I was burning up with fever. I didn't know why I was so sick. Your grandmother was there for me. She told me it was because I was keeping something bottled up and it was eating away at me. If I didn't release whatever I was holding onto, I would die." Mother Hutra added some hot water to both of her daughters' tubs.

My first vision ... the one that changed my life and broke me down all in one. I couldn't bear to see the death of my Mother-In-Law in my dream come to fruition ... but the girls must know. Every gift will grant them privileges, responsibilities, and sacrifices. It's a double-edged sword. They will learn to take the good with the bad.

The girls waited with rapt attention for their mother to continue.

Mother Hutra was silent for a moment, unsure if she could tell the rest. Tears welled up in the corners of her eyes.

"Mother," Blahom said gently, reaching a handout to comfort her mother. "You don't have to tell us if it's causing you hurt."

"No," Mother Hutra said with a deep breath, regaining her composure. "You both deserve to know this, and it is time that I tell you." She wiped away the tears from her eyes and continued.

"Dreaming has always been a way of the Zaed culture. But who was I to be a dreamer? I had a past that would be frowned upon. No one would believe me. I was terrified, unsure, but through prayer I mustered up the courage to tell her that I had dreamed of her death and your father would be holding onto her when she drew her last breath. Unphased, she gently rubbed my cheeks and gave me a motherly smile and said how happy she was that the color returned to my face." Mother Hutra paused to let all that she had said sink in for her daughters.

She continued. "Please listen and do not miss this: once I revealed the truth, I immediately felt the fire within me extinguish and the weight of the secret rise from the pit of my stomach."

"But ... did she not understand that you told her she was going to die?" Katyana inquired.

"I asked her the same thing, but she was a wise woman. She reminded us that death came to us all and she was comforted to know her son would be by her side when she passed on."

Silence hung in the air for several moments.

"Ten days was all we had. There was nothing I could do to prevent her death. Her lungs were always weak, and they finally gave out." Mother Hutra looked at both of her beloved daughters. "She passed exactly how I dreamt it, with your father holding onto her."

"Do you blame yourself?" Blahom inquired. "For having your prophecy?"

"Initially, yes, I did. It took me several years to realize that her death wasn't my fault. There are times when I feel guilty even now," Mother Hutra said softly. "Still, had it not been for the dream, your father would have been leading a group of warriors into a battle. Because of my prophecy, he stayed to comfort his mother. The warriors he was supposed to lead were ambushed and slaughtered. They had no chance, and had he been there, he would have died too. In having your father stay back to be with his mother, his life was saved."

Mother Hutra sipped her tea, smiling gently.

"Your grandmother empowered me by teaching me that day to tell her my dream." Mother Hutra looked at her daughters. "What I am going to tell you next is because I want to empower you by exposing the past. If you embrace your past, you can never have your power taken from you." Mother Hutra's full attention was on Katyana.

"There is something you must know, my child. Something I want you to hear from me rather than anyone else." *This is the hardest thing I've ever had to say, but it's been kept from her for too long,* Mother Hutra thought, her heart pounding. *I've kept it from her for too long, and she deserves to know the full extent of ... of herself.*

Katyana stared back at her mother in anticipation. Mother Hutra took both her hands and in her own. "Katyana, you are my daughter, but I did not birth you. You are not my blood."

Katyana's mouth hung open in disbelief and she struggled to find the words to speak. Blahom held back tears, unable to comprehend what Katyana was going through. Vasco and Blahom had spoken in private about it, but she had known it was not her secret to reveal.

I hope Katyana understands. She's always had a mother, I'm her mother. This doesn't make her different, and I will make sure that she sees this.

"Then ... if not your daughter ... who am I?" Kat's voice was small and weak.

"You are my daughter, Katyana Hutra." Mother Hutra's hands cupped Katyana's face. "I've raised you as my own and nothing will change that. Your father is still ManCohalith. Your mother was someone who tempted him and unfortunately died in childbirth."

"But ... Father would never ..." Katyana stumbled over her words and Mother Hutra shook her head.

"I love your father. He is a strong and courageous leader. However, he still has an appetite for women and women still love him. Even my own sister." Mother Hutra dropped her head and took her hand away from Katyana's face.

"Trinity is ...?"

"Yes. Trinity is your half-sister." Katyana sunk back into the tub, her mind reeling from what she had just learned.

Blahom felt guilt well up in her stomach seeing her sister grapple

Blahom

with this new information. Blahom hadn't known about her mother's love for a Delion in her youth, but she knew about Kat's parentage and Trinity. She and Vasco whispered about Trinity but never spoke a word about Kat's birth. She remembered having to deal with that information and how hard it was to understand and forgive her father.

"I have forgiven your aunt, now I am asking the same of you both. I'm not telling you this to hurt you. I'm telling you both this so that you are aware of your complete past and nobody can ever use that against you." Mother Hutra cupped Katyana's cheek again. "Katyana, you will forever be my daughter. Not even you could change that if you wanted to."

Tears were streaking down Katyana's face, but she nodded, leaning her hand into her mother's warm palm.

Mother Hutra looked at both of her daughters with admiration. *These are the daughters I raised and taught. They WILL survive their Transition, and they won't let their past hinder them; it has only made them stronger today, so that they will go forward in this life with grace and bravery.*

"As Goddesses, you were meant to do more than CCDC ceremonies and the Dietrickt dance. My gift of dreaming has accelerated your destinies, but as your mother I never want to let you go. I have no doubt that you both will do great things with your divine gifts and gain strength while being able to balance and overcome whatever sacrifices you will need to make along the way."

Chapter Nine

Vasco paced around his bedroom while Zya sat on the bed, anxiously watching. His heart pounded in his chest as he anticipated this upcoming meeting with the Generals.

"Beloved, you must be calm," Zya said. "You cannot be this riled up meeting with the Generals."

She stood up and placed her hand on Vasco's chest, stopping his movements. His breathing was heavy as he glanced at his love. "I don't care, they are unable to see the problem at hand, and are instead choosing to train a thirteen- and seventeen-year-old female in the art of war." His tone was aggravated, but he tried to stay calm in the presence of Zya.

"Is it not a good thing that your sisters are being taught by some of the greatest warriors we have?" Zya asked softly, running her fingers along his scar.

Vasco took Zya's hands and held them in his. "We are at war," he said sternly. "My sisters are not a priority. This war that we've been fighting since I was an infant is priority. These Zaed warriors are priority!"

"Shush," Zya tried to calm him, but he let go of her hands, his voice steadily rising.

"No! Those are my sisters! My baby sisters, who are being trained to fight like men and kill like men, when they shouldn't be able to fathom the horrors I've seen!"

Zya winced, and put her hand to her stomach, scared by the rising anger in his voice, and Vasco's anger melted. "I'm sorry," he said, his voice soft as he reached out for her and leaned down to kiss her tiny belly and then her forehead. "I love you, Zya. I don't mean to scare you; I'm just upset with how everything is going."

"Then you need to address it, and not get emotional in the process. Tell them they are needed to focus on the warriors who are on the battlefield, and you can be responsible for training your sisters."

Vasco gave a small smile. "How did I end up with someone as beautiful and wise as you?"

Zya playfully shrugged. "I don't know, you got lucky."

Vasco chuckled as he gave Zya a kiss, and gently kissed her stomach again. "I will be back later."

"And I will wait for you."

Vasco made his way to the Throne Room, lost in his own thoughts. *With no Generals on the battlefield, we're bound to be overthrown quickly by the Delions if they notice our point of weakness,* he thought. *I need to help Daniella. I need to help my sisters' become warriors, before they are sent on the battlefield.*

He paused for a moment, his mind all over the place. *Wait, I do not want them on the field. They're women, children at that! But I don't want the Delions to overtake us.* He thought of Zya being abducted, or dead, and he pushed that thought away.

The doors to the Throne Room were tall and heavy, engraved with markings and detailed in gold accents. Vasco pushed open the doors and strode in, as the Generals looked at him in surprise and disappointment. The doors closed behind him, but not before Katyana, who had gotten dressed for training early and was aimlessly wandering the halls, peeked around a corner, intrigued as to why her brother had interrupted a meeting of the Generals.

When the Throne Room's doors were closed, it always meant that an important matter was being discussed and there were to be no interruptions. Katyana understood this rule well, but she thought now, *There are no rules in war, and I'm sick of secrets.*

The yelling was loud enough Katyana could hear the muffled voices of the generals. She placed her ear to the door and concentrated until she could make out their words almost perfectly.

"I am fully capable of teaching them on my own," Katyana heard Vasco say. Her heart swelled with pride hearing how confident he sounded.

"We have been over this already and the training will be under me and General Brakkus. You are a Lieutenant Vasco," said General Murn. Katyana bridled at the sound of his voice. She wanted no part of him since the forest excursion.

"Yes, but why would we leave our top Generals with two trainees when we have of thousands of Zaed Warriors without proper guidance and authority?" Vasco challenged. "Without our Generals, the battlefield is left wide open for the Delions to attack, and we still face an unknown device that allows them to transport themselves and take the Goddesses and other Zaed women. The war did not stop and end with Mother Hutra's dream. We should not be taking chances now!"

"Bull-headed or not, your son has a point, ManCohalith," Brakkus' gruff voice interjected.

It was quiet for a moment, and Katyana worried that they were talking too low for her to hear. She then heard Vasco speak again.

"Have I not proven myself capable enough to be a valuable instructor?"

"My concern is your emotions," said General Murn. "These are your sisters. Training them means that you need to set your emotions aside and be uncompromising with them. I know that is challenging and you will not be able to accomplish that on your own."

Vasco's voice hardened. "Says who? I have looked a Delion in the

Blahom

eye while he pleaded for his life. He begged me to spare him, that his wife just gave birth to twins, and he had yet to see them. I was still able to stab him through his heart. I have what it takes to train my sisters for battle. I'm a man and not a boy. I will be treated as such. Do not make me prove that with what I know and what I can do. General Murn, you may consider that an emotional threat if you like."

Once again silence filled the room and Kat felt as if Vasco's statement had hollowed out her heart. She couldn't imagine her brother having to ignore the cries of mercy. *What more does Vasco know? How many secrets does my family have?* Kat thought bitterly, recalling the recent truths her mother told her. Forcing herself not to dwell on Vasco's words, she continued to listen through the door.

"So be it," said ManCohalith. "Today, you are to train your sisters while General Brakkus prepares himself and the other warriors for battle." Suppressing a cheer, Kat chuckled quietly to herself, before she focused again on the conversation on the other side of the door.

"May I please have a word, ManCohalith ..." General Murn began, but the ruler did not let him finish.

"I see your concern, General Murn. Still, let us have faith in my son. I am eager to see his progress with training his sisters." Katyana heard footsteps from inside the room and pushed herself away from the door, sprinting down the hall, past a corner, and bursting into her bedroom.

"Blahom! You'll never guess what!" Kat exclaimed, huffing heavily, out of breath.

"What is it?" Blahom didn't mask the irritation in her voice, her precious minutes of solitude dashed by Kat thundering into the room shouting.

"I was listening through the door of the Throne Room and..."

"Katyana," Blahom cut her sister off as she finished sliding on the boots of her training uniform. "You know that we aren't supposed to eavesdrop on the Throne Room. Honestly, you're too old for stuff like that."

Katyana shot her a mischievous smile.

"No, I'm just not supposed to get caught eavesdropping on the Throne Room," she smirked. "Anyway, Father told Vasco that he is to train us today!"

"Seriously?" Blahom did not try to keep the excitement out of her voice.

"I heard Father say it himself!" Katyana beamed.

"Well good. It's been months since the dream, and we became warriors. The three of us haven't been able to get together like we used to and I'm sure he has plenty to tell us." Blahom smiled, trying to think of the last time the three of them spent time together alone.

"You better be quick then. You know how much Vasco hates tardiness." The two sisters hastily finished getting ready and headed towards the training arena.

Vasco had already been in the arena, waiting for them, his face stern as ever.

"You two were within seconds of being late," he said, and it took everything Blahom had to not blatantly roll her eyes at him.

"I was dressed early and was waiting on my fellow comrade," Katyana said quick to rat out her sister.

"So that is the loyalty you have for your sister? I see we have taught you nothing," Vasco said.

"We are promptly on time, Lieutenant Vasco." Sarcasm bled into Blahom's voice when she used his title. She wished to save Kat from her "lieutenant" brother's scolding. She hesitated when she saw her brother's serious expression, the one he only wore when he was in warrior mode.

"If you're on time on the battlefield, you're dead. If you're early to the battlefield, then you have the advantage of accessing the field and where their possible weaknesses may be." Vasco's tone was majestic and regal, and his deep baritone voice echoed in the room.

Blahom had to stifle a laugh at how strange Vasco's voice sounded. "When did you start sounding like Father?"

"I always sounded like Father."

"Uh huh." Blahom's response said otherwise.

Blahom

Katyana, unmoved by Vasco's sage words of wisdom, cut to the chase: "So, what are you going to teach us today, Lieutenant Vasco?"

"Follow me. For your training today, we are headed to the sea."

The three siblings began hour-long hike south on foot to the shore, passing fisherman's quarters and the marketplace, until they could see the sandy rocky path that led down to the bank. Further to their left was a smooth, longer route leading to the dock where the fishermen's boats and the naval ships were docked. Vasco, determined to take the quicker route, led his sisters along the windy, slippery, rockbound path towards the edge of the shore, to an older-model naval ship.

Blahom was waiting for her brother's rigid exterior to crack and reveal the brother she could laugh and gossip with. The last time they spoke, Vasco had told her that he thought Zya may be with child, and she was dying to know for sure. Kat was also waiting for a shift in their brother, trying to make small talk only to get barked at to take in the quiet. Vasco, clearly preoccupied in his thoughts, remained silent and tense and marched forward with Katyana and Blahom traveling behind.

Soon enough, Katyana's expression turned sour, and she marched on in silence. With her sister sullen and her brother in warrior mode, Blahom drifted into her mind, thinking instead of where she would rather be. Oftentimes she had watched Vasco hold his lover's hand and walk with her through the halls. He was a fierce warrior, yet he had found someone to love. Blahom was in the process of becoming a warrior herself, but she had no clue where Vasco found the time for his partner. Her day was so scheduled and rigid that the idea of finding someone to love became more and more appealing while simultaneously more out of reach. Picturing herself in the arms of a muscular and caring Zaed man, Blahom allowed herself to fantasize about what could be. She wanted to be with someone who she could vent to and who understood her and could make all her worries disappear. Rasheed being a family member understood her best. She thought on Jhapalle and other men with whom she'd had brief encounters. She smiled thinking about how gentle most had been with her. She sighed in content, wanting to live in her daydream.

Soon enough, they reached the older naval ship, its metal worn and rusted by the harsh waves of the sea. However, Zaed vessels were known for their sturdiness, so while it was an older vessel, it would last another hundred years.

"A naval ship?" Katyana looked up at the ship in awe.

"This is what brings us to the sea?" Blahom asked.

"Indeed, it is. You won't be able to frolic around in the sand today, ladies," Vasco said and Blahom, already irritated with her brother's dry humor, rolled her eyes.

"If you haven't noticed, we haven't frolicked in three weeks since our forest excursion," irritation dripped in Blahom's voice. "Kat and I worked our asses off, and not even you get to belittle that." Blahom was becoming tired of their training being undermined.

"I will be teaching you the basics of how to work on a ship," Vasco said, hardly acknowledging Blahom's words. Katyana ran onto the ship excitedly, Blahom and Vasco behind.

The three walked through the narrow steel corridors until they reached a stifling room in the center of the vessel.

"This is the boiler room. It's the main room that powers the ship. Without it, it would be useless. Think of it as the heart of the ship."

"Is this just gonna be a tour of the ship? Sounds pretty boring to me," huffed Katyana. "Since you're our brother, are you not allowed to make things more exciting? Blahom and I went trekking through the forest with stupid General Murn and now we're just touring naval ships like this is some sort of field trip? Some boring training this turned out to be." It was clear that Kat wanted to spend time with her brother and instead was stuck with a rigid general.

Vasco crossed his arms and shot his sister a chilling glare. "Boring? Don't worry, since you don't want to be bored, I'll give you something to do." Vasco reached into a nearby closet and handed Katyana a brush and bucket. It was obvious that he had not come to play.

"Since the boiler room is the heart of the vessel, you need to keep it healthy. Make sure to scrub every inch of it while I continue to show Blahom around the ship."

"Really? That's not fair," Katyana whined. Because of the age difference Vasco had always made a clear distinction between the two sisters.

"Serves you right. That's karma for this morning's antics," Blahom said and then pointed to the water faucet. "Better fill up that bucket."

Katyana glared at her sister and Vasco shot her an unapologetic look.

"Did you expect training to be fair? You said yourself that you had gone through the forest excursion. Was anything that you went through there fair?" Katyana's eyebrows knotted together in frustration.

"No, but ..."

"And this whole situation with you and Blahom having to become warriors. Is that fair?" Vasco pressed and Katyana angrily looked down at the ground.

"No," she muttered.

"Then you should know damn well that nothing about this situation is fair, so don't complain about it to me. Now, fill up that bucket and do as you're told," Vasco commanded.

Katyana froze for a moment. Vasco had never yelled at her in such a way before and her eyes went from the floor, to Vasco, then to Blahom. Her heart sank. Vasco wasn't yelling at Blahom, only at her. She recalled her mother's admission. Surely it was because he viewed Blahom as a full sibling while she was only half. Angrily and reluctantly, Katyana went to the water spigot to fill up the bucket.

Vasco tilted his head to the side, gesturing to Blahom to follow him out of the room. They walked down the corridors of the ship, and once out of earshot of Katyana, Vasco whispered, "I need to talk to you."

Blahom looked at her brother's serious face as they made their way up the stairs to the top deck. The ship let out a small creak, slightly startling Blahom, but Vasco paid it no mind.

Despite wanting to spend time with Vasco again, Blahom was beginning to wish that she could just be left alone. She understood how he spoke to Kat, but she did feel he was too harsh with her. Why was he was so strict now? Before, being alone with her brother had been like an adventure where she was free from the ever-prying eyes of the Lady Mothers and her own Mother. *I crave that old companionship,* she thought. *and if I can't have that, at least let me have some time to myself. Is that a sin?* With everything going on, it felt that way.

Arriving at the control room, Vasco closed the heavy metal door behind them, and they stood still for a moment, each aware it had been a long time since their last one-on-one talk.

"I will not let you and Katyana become warriors," Vasco said firmly, breaking the silence. "I promised you both that I would not let you fight, and I still intend to keep that promise."

Feeling more at ease with her brother, Blahom dropped his title.

"Vasco, I'd love not to be a warrior, but Katyana and I are already almost one year into training. It's clear that it is our destiny to become warriors whether you or I like it or not. Mother Hutra's dream ..."

"The dream was interpreted wrong," Vasco interrupted. "I think that dream was a warning for us, and I know why."

"Oh, so you interpret dreams now?"

There was a mischievous glint in Vasco's eye. It was a look that Blahom knew always came right before they got into trouble. "I thought you were going to spill the news about you becoming a new father," she said. "But I see this is about something different. What is it that you're planning, brother?"

"We have found out more about the transportation device that the Delions are working on."

Blahom's eyes widened. "Like what?"

"We know that they are traveling to and from another planet, probably Earth."

Blahom

"Yes, Father told me," Blahom said, sure to let Vasco know she was not as clueless as he painted her to be. "What can you tell me that I have not heard from our training, or among the Lady Sisters?"

Ignoring his sisters posturing, Vasco stayed focused on the conversation at hand. "They appear to be carrying resources through their teleportation device. Our assumption is that they have already set up a base on the planet and have taken Daniella and possibly others. We believe they are trying to increase their strength with resources from this other planet to retaliate against us."

"So, you think that the dream was a warning about that?"

"Yes. I also know how to end this war while ensuring that you and Katyana don't fight. I want to find our cousin. I'm going to need your help."

Blahom raised her eyebrows and Vasco smiled at her as if his plan was already a success. The ship let out a louder creak, and Vasco glanced quickly around.

"Thanks, but no thanks, Vasco. I know you don't want Kat and me to have to fight, but sorry, you aren't a dream interpreter, and besides I'm all out of favors," Blahom laughed.

"Listen to me, Blahom. I was able to gather some information on the Delions whereabouts. There are two separate camps. One is large and located closer to the beach north of us. The other is smaller and further north, against the mountains. That encampment is where the teleportation device is located."

"Ok, I agree that's big."

"I'm going to propose a plan to Father. I'll send a group of men to attack the camp near the beach. While the Delions are distracted with that main attack, I'll take a group of men up the mountain and steal the teleportation device, finally ending this war."

"Okay, I understand, but how am I supposed to help in all of this?"

"You need to talk me up to Mother."

"Talk you up? What the hell does that mean?"

"You know what I mean. And I'm serious here," said Vasco, his tone reverting slightly back to warrior versus brother mode.

"Why? You already know you're her favorite son."

"Ha ha, not funny, I'm her only son. Can you be serious and show me some respect Blahom? For the warrior I have become. Like the warrior you and Kat are training to be. You have no clue what I have seen or dealt with. So, if I ask you to talk me up to Mother, do not dismiss it with some little girl joke. I need you to talk to her about how capable I am. Talk to her about how I should have more leadership roles. I need Father to go for my plan. It took a good amount of convincing on my part to train you and Katyana alone today and it is clear that General Murn doesn't want me to surpass him. If you talk to Mother, she is bound to talk to ManCohalith and make him more likely to give his blessing to my plan." Blahom appreciated her brother's willingness to be respected. She was feeling the same way. But she knew he was exaggerating to think he would ever pass General Murn.

"So, you just need me to talk you up to Mother?"

"Yes, that's what I just said," nodded Vasco.

"And then you'll win this war?" Blahom wasn't convinced.

"Yes. I'll seize the teleportation device and the war is as good as won. Sirius will finally be at peace, and I don't have to watch my sisters die."

"Okay. Enough! This is not about me not respecting you, brother. This is about bullshit since day one. Everyday there's a new curve ball tossed to me. Forgive me for being over it." exclaimed Blahom.

"Ha! Welcome to war. It's not nearly as structured as dancing. I say that with no disrespect to my sister. I only want to keep you alert and in the moment. This is no joke." Vasco gave Blahom a look of love and admiration. He knew she was struggling with the new calling, and it fueled him to keep close to his plan.

"I'll do whatever I can to help," Blahom said. "I'll talk about how great today was to Mother, and she'll be bound to discuss how much she feels you're ready to lead. Please don't ask me to do much more. I'm at my wits end. Plus, I need you to do something for me."

"What is it sister?" Vasco looked concerned.

"I need you to tell Father and Mother that I deserve time alone. I am practically a woman, and I am stuck with my baby sister and Lady Mothers hovering over me all day. It is not making me strong. It is weakening me. Please tell them I am doing outstanding in training and should be rewarded." Her voice quivered with emotion. Vasco grabbed her hand.

"I will do that, sister. Thank you, Blahom. Father will give my plan his blessing." Vasco reached out and gave her a strong hug. "Besides, I need you around because you will soon become an aunt." Blahom's eyes lit up.

"That is to stay between us. Kat cannot know yet. I must make Rya an honest woman before much longer. Perhaps at the next CCDC ceremony," Vasco said with a small smile.

"Vasco this is wonderful news. But the Zaeds will persecute her if you do not marry her. That is a plan you should think about," Blahom looked concerned.

"You don't listen. I just gave you, my plan. It will happen at the next CCDC ceremony. Now, come on. I think we've made Sister suffer in the boiler room long enough."

"You think? She was eavesdropping during your meeting with the other generals in the Throne Room this morning . She has become quite rebellious. We fight quite often now." Blahom paused, thinking back to the brutal fight that left them not speaking for weeks. "Maybe a few more minutes of scrubbing would do her good."

Vasco laughed, "She's definitely one of us."

His statement made Blahom pause.

"Vasco," her voice dropped to a more serious tone. "Katyana knows about not being fully blood related to us. Mother Hutra told her after the forest excursion. She won't admit it, but she is angry and hurt about the news of Mother not birthing her. I can see it in her eyes." Vasco slowly nodded his head.

"She's old enough to know the truth, but she's our baby sister. Half blood ties or full blood ties."

"And Trinity? She is our sister, brother."

Vasco frowned. "Trinity is a different case altogether."

"Is she? Can you pick and choose which sister you accept?" Blahom's question stopped Vasco.

"Yes, I can, and I have. Aunt Lorraine betrayed Mother and therefore she means nothing to me nor her bastard child. There was no deliberate betrayal from Katyana's mother. She was an unwed woman and free to do as she wanted. She had no ties to Mother. There is a clear difference in the nature of the offence, sister." Vasco turned around without and opened the door to the corridor.

"You are wrong, brother, and evil has set in your heart. Do not put out things that you do not wish to get back." Blahom followed her brother back towards the boiler room to retrieve their sister and finish their training on the ship. *This is my trial*, she thought, *always trying to keep the family together. Can't they see that this anger and bitterness is spreading like a cancer that could tear us all apart?*

"Did you two have fun?" Katyana, her voice biting and perturbed, was not willing to forgive her time in the boiler room and was still upset by Vasco's harsh words.

"Let's not play games. None of this is fun. Everyone standing here knows this. Now, I'm going to teach you more about the ship," Vasco said, trying to brush aside what he and Blahom had just spoken of.

"Well, if we are not to play games, then stop it with the secrets. I know you two were talking because that is what we do. I'm a warrior in training now too. I deserve to know whatever it was you two said," Katyana said firmly.

"You want to know what we were talking about? Fine," Vasco shrugged with ease. "We were talking about Aunt Lorraine. I still don't trust her for putting you two in danger." Blahom knew that

Vasco hated lying to Katyana, but a half-truth was better than a whole lie.

"Well, I don't trust her because she slept with our father. The same as my mother did." The room was silent for a moment. "Let's not play games." Katyana stared them in the eye and didn't say anything else.

"Very well Katyana. Let us stay focused. You will learn to leave people, conversations, and emotions behind that don't belong on the battlefield." Vasco broke eye contact and moved on.

Blahom could feel Vasco's anxious energy as he taught her and Katyana about the old Zaed vessel. As they walked throughout the ship once more, the creaking grew louder, and the ship, while stagnant, started to shift slightly, as if it would break suddenly. As Blahom grew more anxious with the ship's grim creaking, she grew more anxious with her brother and sister. She knew that Katyana would never be the same and it pained her. But if Vasco was correct, then the war would end, and perhaps everything would return to how things were. She loved the idea of stopping this ridiculous training and getting back to dancing.

In the midst of the chaos, she comforted her own soul with solemn thoughts of finding time to fall in love. Her mind flashed to Rasheed's face. She imagined his kind smile and strong arms, then pushed the image away and tried to focus on the task at hand.

Everything hinged on this simple plan of Vasco's working. Blahom's mind was buzzing with the new information.

Chapter Ten

While Vasco was out with his sisters on the naval vessel, ManCohalith was holding an emergency meeting in the Throne Room for the other Generals, Lieutenants and a few soldiers. General Brakkus, standing closest to ManCohalith, was anxious to hear the news after having to push back his preparations for the upcoming battle.

ManCohalith looked out at his men. His back was stiff and straight, if his throne, designed specifically for him, was the most uncomfortable seat to be in. His only movement was his fingertips lightly drumming on the armchair of his throne. His face was completely blank, near unreadable.

The wind outside was picking up.

The officers stood at attention in front of ManCohalith. General Brakkus' was concerned, knowing that if his preparations for an upcoming battle were being pushed back, then this was a dire matter. Rasheed stood apart from his father and the other Generals, carefully placed among the younger, less-seasoned warriors including Thistle, Jakk, and Burriss.

Rasheed was unsure why he was invited to the Throne Room,

but his father insisted that he come as something important was in the air and this was no time to be hiding from the war. Despite being on the battlefield a few times, Rasheed was not fond of fighting, and did his best to avoid it, but he knew he could do so no longer, under the circumstances. Anxiety started in the pit of his stomach, as he looked at his father's face and noticed the tell-tale signs of concern, and he wanted nothing more than to rush out and help prepare for battle. However, he put on a strong face, knowing that was the only acceptable thing he could do.

All the warriors were dressed in battle attire, weapons attached to their belts and sturdy armor covering their skin. Each had a minimum of two swords strapped on, and their metal armor was near impenetrable. Both Rasheed's birth father and adopted father were warriors, so Rasheed had inherited plenty of weaponry. He had his two swords on his hip, three daggers strapped to his chest, and another dagger concealed in his boot. The warriors were heavily fortified and armed, yet still a tension permeated the air, as if a battle were to emerge within the Throne Room itself.

Rasheed looked around the room, and noticed that while his father was called back, Vasco was not. *If Vasco wasn't called back, then this announcement, or news, isn't for his ears*, Rasheed thought. *I hope my Blahom is all right. I miss her. I haven't seen her in weeks. I truly hope she doesn't have to fight; she doesn't belong on the battlefield. Maybe I should speak with Vasco...*

Rasheed wasn't the only one feeling Vasco's absence, though nobody, not even General Murn, would question ManCohalith's decision outright. The trusted that when their ruler decided to do something, there was a reason, but, of course, this did not stop the whispers.

ManCohalith's too clouded in his judgment, General Murn thought, glancing around at the other Generals. *He needs to let go of his emotions regarding his daughters and remind himself that there's a war going on.*

I hope Blahom and Katyana don't have to fight, General Brakkus thought, watching ManCohalith sit on his throne in contemplation. *Too much hardship has occurred already, and if we were to lose the Goddesses ... I don't know what would become of ManCohalith, Mother Hutra ... and Rasheed.* General Brakkus shot a disappointed glance at his son, who was clearly unaware of the seriousness of the situation.

Everyone's thoughts were interrupted when ManCohalith stood and raised his hand, silencing everyone. No one spoke. The wind whistled on.

"Several months back, there was a crisis when Delion forces started infecting warriors on the battlefield with mold," ManCohalith's voice boomed throughout the Throne Room. "The mold was highly contagious, and quickly spread like sap on a Hant tree. Zaeds began getting sick – vomiting, coughing until blood gurgled in their mouths, and within three days they were dead. We lost over 500 Zaeds."

There was silence in the room as the men listened to their leader. From without, the whistling of the wind grew louder until it could be heard beating on the windows.

"Just as clouds gather together as a hurricane builds, I've brought you all here today for a very serious matter," ManCohalith said. "There has been word from some of our informants about the Delions' teleportation device."

"Do we have any leads on where the device is being housed?" inquired Lieutenant Kov.

ManCohalith allowed an awkwardly long pause, during which Rasheed's heart pounded in panic. He assumed that the Zaeds were making headway in the search for the location of the teleportation device. Did the fact that ManCohalith didn't readily answer the question mean they were further behind in the war?

"We do," ManCohalith said, breaking his silence, and Rasheed let out a small sigh of relief. "There are more important things to be discussed today, though, more pressing than the device." ManCohalith stared down at the men in front of him, as everyone in the room stiffened. What could be more pressing than the teleportation device that simultaneously didn't require Lieutenant Vasco's presence?

"Our beloved Lady Sister Daniella is still missing. The Delions' technological advances are a blatant threat to us. There are numerous devices that are being tested that we are completely in the dark about."

The wind outside gusted against the windows of the Throne Room, causing the panes of glass to rattle. ManCohalith drew in a deep breath, trying to suppress his outrage. His voice did not waver.

"I have been told that the Delions are also training highly elite warriors to counter my daughters. They clearly have revelations about the Goddesses that have yet to be revealed to us." In his anger, ManCohalith spoke humbly, knowing that even in his strength, there was weakness. The Delions possessed a canny level of intelligence and they knew something the Zaeds did not. ManCohalith believed this was the sense of humor of the Alpha God to remind him the only way to have the upper hand was to call on gifts and revelations.

Most of the men in the room remained silent at the mention of the Goddesses. This was concerning news, but most of the warriors thought it unlikely the Delions were assembling an elite force to counter the Goddesses – two weak girls, after all. Rasheed knew better; he had never thought of any of his cousins as week.

Blahom is one of the strongest women I know, Rasheed thought, his heart pounding in concern. *She has a big heart, which is nothing to be ashamed of. She's also intuitive and loving. I must get to her. Where is she ... Stop this! You gotta focus on ManCohalith.* Rasheed brought his attention back to the room and deliberately unclenched the fists he had made at the thought of the Delions' elite warriors targeting her. Time to stay strong and calm.

"How would they even know about the Goddess' training?" General Murn asked. ManCohalith didn't say a word. General Murn tried to make sense of what ManCohalith's announcement and his frustrating refusal to elaborate. He planned on training the

Goddesses to the best of his abilities because the last thing he wanted was for them to die the moment they were sent into battle. How were they supposed to stand a chance with an elite group of warriors targeting them?

An aura of unease permeated the room, and the men were quiet, waiting for their leader to say something.

The wind outside sent leaves spiraling through the air.

ManCohalith turned his attention to Lieutenant Kov and spoke. "Now, Lieutenant Kov, you were temporarily captured by the Delion forces in the last battle."

Lieutenant Kov took a step forward and Rasheed and the other warriors looked on, puzzled. What did Lieutenant Kov have to do with ManCohalith's previous statement?

"That is correct, ManCohalith. However, I managed to escape," his voice unwavering, "and with some vital information."

"Indeed, you did," nodded ManCohalith calmly. "Your information did lead to a victory in a minor battle. However, that was all it was. A minor battle." Before Lieutenant Kov could say anything, ManCohalith looked over at his generals.

"General Velio, has Lieutenant Kov been acting oddly since his return?"

"I suppose he has," nodded General Velio. Out of all of the Generals, Velio best kept an eye on the well-being of the warriors. "There have been whispers among his soldiers of him forgetting their names and refusing some of his favorite drinks. However, being captured by the Delions, I assumed his strange behavior was due to shock."

Lieutenant Kov took another step forward, his eyes looking haunted as if he had seen a phantom, and said in a heart-wrenching voice, "ManCohalith, ever since the Delions captured me, I can hardly sleep at night. Every sound, every creak in the floorboard, makes me believe that a Delion is only feet away from me, ready to begin their torment. I was tortured and find things that I once held dear to mean nothing to me. I am a shell of the man I once was." His voice then changed to that of concern. "I hope to ease your concern for your daughters as I can assure you that the Delions are not training special male forces to fight two young girls." There was so much weariness in the Lieutenant's voice that Rasheed felt pity for such a warrior's light being tarnished by the Delions.

ManCohalith stared at the man in front of him and General Murn started to fidget with the handle of his sword. Something wasn't right. Rasheed sensed the tension as well, his stomach tightening into knots. He didn't know why, but it was clear that ManCohalith did not share his pity of Lieutenant Kov. The warriors stared at Lieutenant Kov, knowing that something about their fellow warrior was in question. If ManCohalith suspected one of his warriors of misconduct, then there had to be a good reason.

The wind outside picked up even more, as if a tornado was gaining momentum.

"Please then, demonstrate your divine gift." ManCohalith commanded, as if the Lieutenant had never spoken, and Lieutenant Kov stared at the Ruler.

"My gift?"

"Yes, the one you were blessed with during your Transition," said ManCohalith, totally focused and in control of his emotions. Rasheed caught the eye of his cousin Thistle. They both stared at Lieutenant Kov, as did many of the other warriors, waiting for him to reveal his gifts. *What is going on here?* Rasheed was confused, and slightly concerned.

Does ManCohalith have something up his sleeve? General Murn was on edge as he scanned Lieutenant Kov intensely, one eye on ManCohalith.

The wind started to howl, almost to shriek.

Lieutenant Kov took a step back but was blocked by the rest of the men. His eyes were wide with fear as he made sharp movements, trying to find a crack through the warriors to escape, but failing at each turn. His breathing was ragged, and his hands shook.

"ManCohalith, I–I haven't been able to use my gift. Not ever since ..."

"No man ever loses his divine gift regardless of the trauma suffered. Seize him," ManCohalith ordered, and the Generals swiftly grabbed Lieutenant Kov where he stood. General Velio and General Lakin held Kov, keeping him in place while General Murn stood in front of ManCohalith, his weapons drawn.

The Ruler stepped off his throne and approached Lieutenant Kov. The back of ManCohalith's hand tauntingly dragged against Lieutenant Kov's face. With one fluid motion, he grabbed roughly at the skin of Kov's chin and pulled. To everyone's shock, ManCohalith peeled a thin filament off Lieutenant Kov's face, revealing the face of someone they didn't recognize. His eyes were gray and cold, and his hair was a sleek silver color. Other than those features, he could have been mistaken as any other Zaed.

"A Delion," General Murn exclaimed, his hand tightening around the hilt of his drawn sword.

"You Zaeds are weak!" the Delion exclaimed. The spy knew that there was no hope for him. "Kov is dead! The Delions will defeat you and the soils of Sirius will be soaked in Zaed blood! We will ..." The spy stopped, gasping for air, choking on nothing.

"Where is my niece?" ManCohalith held his hand out, pulling the air slowly out of the spy's lungs. "How many warriors are the Delions training to fight the Goddesses?"

ManCohalith stopped, letting the spy take a deep breath.

"I will not tell you."

Once again, ManCohalith started extracting the air from him. "Where are the Delions training them?"

He let the spy breathe, but the spy shook his head, refusing to speak. "What information have you given to your compatriots? What do the Delions know that they didn't before?"

Again, the leader of the Zaeds received no answer. The spy glared at ManCohalith with hate in his eyes but spoke not a single word.

Blahom

This lasted for hours. There were moments when Rasheed thought that the Delion spy's eyes were going to pop out of his head from the lack of oxygen; moments where he could swear that he heard ribs cracking, as the air was pulled from his lungs. Blood dribbled from the spy's lips and yet, to Rasheed's horrified surprise, he did not utter another word. Rasheed shuddered as nausea washed over him. *No, I can't, not in front of everyone here. Not in front of the Generals.* He covered his mouth and breathed heavily.

When pulling the air out of the spy's throat wasn't working, ManCohalith resorted to cutting off fingers. The warriors watched. Rasheed had seen gore before but nothing like the torture ManCohalith was inflecting on the spy. It took everything he had not to vomit at the sight of someone enduring such agony. The long fingers didn't slice cleanly off and ManCohalith slowly pulled at the finger to tear off the remaining flesh, causing the spy to scream out in agony. Blood dripped onto the floor, staining ManCohalith's shoes.

"Answer my questions and I will put an end to your suffering!" ManCohalith exclaimed and the spy chuckled between pained breaths.

"You will never find your dear Daniella. Whatever you do to me won't stop the inevitable from happening. Your Goddess Blahom will give us children and then she will die a slow and painful death, and your baby girl will become our puppet. We will make sure that you will watch as they scream their very last breaths."

The wind outside whizzed through the air like a knife and ManCohalith's face contorted with pure wrath.

"I will not have anyone ever speak about my children dying!" ManCohalith drove his knife down, severing the last two fingers. His men watched on in silent horror. No one had ever seen ManCohalith lose his composure, but now, in this moment ... This was personal. This was about his daughters and this silent rage fueled his brutal interrogation.

Out of fingers, ManCohalith called for a torch.

"There is no point in prolonging your death! How many warriors are the Delions training to fight the Goddesses? What information did you leak to the Delions? What are you planning?" ManCohalith stared down at the spy. The Delion remained mute, already half dead. ManCohalith drove the burning torch against his ear. He knew that he wasn't going to get any information but, fueled by rage, he needed something to direct it towards.

"Where are the Delions training their warriors!" Silence from the Delion. Screaming in agony, ManCohalith pulled at his own hair, shaking his head. Rasheed and the other warriors watched as ManCohalith raged, as if his two daughters were already dead. He pulled the air out of the spy's lungs again, then let him breath. He looked to General Murn. "Kill him."

General Murn drew his blade across the spy's throat. Blood splattered as the head lolled to the side, hanging on only by a few tendons. Frustration boiled within Murn and he slashed his sword down, fully decapitating the corpse and then stabbed the body several times.

ManCohalith made no move to stop him. He felt his fingertips prickle as anger continued to burn in the pit of his stomach. This spy had infiltrated their ranks and put everything he cared about at risk, especially his children. An entire elite group of warriors was being trained to attack his daughters. *Why? They are still new to their training, why train an entire group just for them? What to the Delions know that I don't?*

ManCohalith strove to calm himself. When he discovered that this spy had actively work to harm his daughters, he had lost all restraint. He was glad Vasco, though he knew his father as a powerful and ruthless warrior, had not seen his father as a torturer. He would hear about it, of course, but ManCohalith was glad Vasco had been spared witnessing the ordeal.

ManCohalith's mind went to Mother Hutra. He would tell her about the spy, because word would get around, and better she hear it from him then some Lady Sister. She would be horrified to know about such a spy. ManCohalith pondered how to best calm his wife when she learned her two daughters were in more danger than they previously imagined. His anger started to rise again as he realized that the Delions might have a deadly amount of private information now, stolen by the fake Lieutenant Kov.

ManCohalith thought of Mother Hutra's loving eyes. He had gone into these kinds of rampages before and she never approved, trying her best to settle him and bring him back to earth. He knew that if she were in the room, she would be worried but would want him to remain calm. He took in a deep breath, feeling how his own emotions were affecting the weather unknowingly.

Everyone in the room was silent and the wind outside started to subside.

"Throw this worthless spy's corpse into the ocean," General Murn said to Brakkus and Lakin. It was hardly a body now, but a mangled bloody agglomeration of flesh and bones. General Brakkus picked up the spy's head and General Lakin dragged his body, leaving a bloody trail behind him.

Rasheed watched his father drag out the spy's head then his eyes settled back on ManCohalith. The leader was completely composed as he sat back onto his throne, was unfazed by the blood and fingertips sullying the Throne Room's floors. Rasheed heaved onto the Throne Room floor.

Chapter Eleven

The two Goddesses had finished their dance, breathing heavily while Mother Hutra looked on. Usually when going from training to rehearsal, Blahom and Katyana were so exhausted that even the easiest dance moves posed a challenge. Their training with Vasco yesterday was not as strenuous as their typical combat training, and both sisters were happy that they had energy to fully concentrate on their movements with the rest of the ensemble.

Blahom's lean stature allowed for more flexibility, and she had gained greater definition in her legs since training so that her muscles rippled through her calves when she performed. Katyana was picking up muscle mass, her offensive combat training building up her shoulders and arms and helping her to float with more ease during dance rehearsal.

Rehearsal concluded, a few of the ensemble of Lady Sisters dancers murmured amongst themselves, glancing sidelong at Blahom and Kat. Blahom feigned disinterest, but Katyana did not bother to hide her awareness.

Frustrated, she walked up to Mother Hutra, standing by herself.

"Did something happen while Blahom and I were out with Vasco? They are whispering about us. Things feel ... different."

Mother Hutra pursed her lips together, pausing to mull over the question. Blahom had seen the moment Kat lost her composure, walking briskly to question their mom. She calmly joined the two after seeing her mother's face, a face that Blahom had seen a handful of times before; the face of trying to figure out if it were better to lie or tell the truth.

"Mother," Katyana said sternly. "I don't want any more lies. One of the fishermen at the docks told us that there was a spy in the palace, and we saw Lita's mother at the marketplace. She said that Father tortured someone. Tell us the truth."

Blahom was surprised by how firm Katyana sounded in front of their mother, and even more surprised by how perceptive her little sister was becoming when it came to reading their mother's face. Despite how serious Katyana sounded, all Mother Hutra did was give her daughter a sweet smile before turning her attention to Blahom.

"You danced beautifully today, Blahom. Well done," Mother Hutra said. Blahom smiled broadly, proud of her and Katyana's fluid movements during rehearsal.

"Thank you, Mother. It's all thanks to Vasco," Blahom said.

"Vasco?" Mother Hutra was surprised.

"Yes, his training yesterday was enlightening. He stressed how important motivation was not just on the battlefield, but in every aspect in life." Blahom laughed softly. "I never knew him as such a good teacher. He's really grown into his role as a Lieutenant."

Mother Hutra smiled hearing Blahom praise her brother. Like most mothers, she had a soft spot for her son. *My Vasco*, she thought with pride. *I remember when he was small and fragile, his hand barely wrapping around my thumb, but he had a tight grip. And when he went to train ... I couldn't bear to see how bruised and battered he was when he returned. But his Transition made him stronger, and now, he's a Lieutenant. My beautiful baby boy. The love I have for him is tenfold.*

"Your brother is a fine Lieutenant."

"Surely. The way he was talking during our training, I wouldn't be surprised if he becomes as respected on and off the battlefield as Father."

Mother Hutra tilted her head, looking at Blahom with surprise.

"All this from one training session with your brother?"

"Well, I haven't seen him in months, and now being trained by him in his element is eye opening. He really is meant to be a leader."

Mother Hutra smiled, pleased.

"I'll be sure to tell your father about how much you enjoyed the training. Maybe he will even schedule Vasco to train you and Katyana more often."

"That would be wonderful," Blahom beamed. In her mind, that sealed it. Praise for Vasco would reach ManCohalith's ears, and Mother Hutra was bound to put flourishes on what Blahom told her. After all, Vasco was her favorite son. She turned her attention to her sister. Kat knew that their mother was ignoring her, silently indicating she would not be moved by her daughter's outburst. Mother Hutra always demonstrated composure and control.

But Blahom too was bothered by the whispers in the marketplace after they returned from training with Vasco. The marksmen hadn't acknowledged the sisters, the woman at the fruit stand whispered to other Zaeds of which Blahom heard "death" and "ManCohalith," and the baker gave the Goddesses questionable looks. This was far from their typical, friendly encounters at the market.

Blahom had tried to shake it off, even after seeing Lita's mother. Surely the whisperings were nothing, just gossip that would fade and pass. Her focus was ensuring Vasco's plan succeeded, so she could go back to her normal life, and perhaps back to Jhapalle or on to Rasheed or … But the whispers were everywhere.

Katyana had had waited long enough. "How did I dance, Mother? Was it good?" she asked in a small, almost childlike, voice. Mother Hutra softly smiled at her daughter.

"You did not allow me the opportunity to compliment you, dear, and I was not going to lie. I was trying to think of the right words on how to break terrible news."

"So, something did happen while we were away," Blahom said. Mother Hutra nodded, her smile fading.

"Yes. We were all fooled by Lieutenant Kov."

Katyana and Blahom stared at their mother in confusion.

"How could we be fooled by Lieutenant Kov? He's a skilled warrior but I never thought him much of a strategist," Blahom said, and Mother Hutra shook her head.

"Our Kov, who we love and respect, is dead and has been dead now for months. The one in his place was a Delion spy."

"So, they were right, there was a spy?" Katyana was shocked. Mother Hutra nodded slowly.

"I had spoken to him before but ... How ... how could ..." Katyana's mind spun, trying to wrap her head around the situation. *What could she mean Lieutenant Kov is a Delion? How is that possible? We clearly saw Lieutenant Kov.*

"The Delion's technology has advanced at a rapid pace," Mother Hutra continued. "It is terrifying what they can manipulate now. The spy was dressed in a sort of suit and appeared just as Kov. This is something unheard of. Your father tried to get as much information as possible, but the imposter died rather than tell us anything."

"So, what happens now?" Blahom's heart pounded in her chest. *Will this throw off Vasco's plans? Does Vasco even know this happened? Where is Rasheed? Is he alright? Was he there when the spy was revealed? I need to see him.*

"Now? Now we continue as we have always done," Mother Hutra said. "We will not let a Delion spy crush our spirit. We keep praying and dancing for gifts and revelations. For all we know he couldn't divulge anything of use to his companions. He is dead and there is nothing to worry about."

"But ..." Katyana began to argue but Mother Hutra gave her a piercing look.

"Your Father said there was nothing to worry about. I trust the

Alpha God and I trust him. This is not a time to let fear guide us." Mother Hutra spoke like the ruler she was, though her hands were shaking.

Blahom grabbed her mother's hand. "We believe and agree with you." Regardless of how alarming the news was, she knew that it was their role as Goddesses to trust the Alpha God, reassure the Zaeds, and remain calm. She took Kat's hand as well and gave them both a squeeze. "As Father would say, a war cannot be won if one side is infected with paranoia and fear. We will trust, be strong and courageous, just as you have taught us to be, Mother."

Mother Hutra's face softened. She turned to Kat. "My daughter, you danced beautifully. I'm proud of seeing your improvement," she said, and kissed each daughter on the forehead before she walked away.

As they exited the rehearsal room, they found Rasheed outside the door. His dark eyes bore into Blahom's and she could feel her heart thud louder in her chest. She noticed his beard, fuller than before and wished that he could hold her for a moment, and pull her aside somewhere, just the two of them. Kat walked on.

"Hello Goddess Blahom." He had a goofy but alluring smile.

"Rasheed, what are you doing here?" she inquired, looking around for Lady Mother Clara or Chi.

"I ..." Rasheed paused. "I heard you were back rehearsing and I wanted – had to see you, and make sure you were safe."

Blahom's heart melted at the thought of Rasheed rushing over to see her, even if just for a moment. She gave a small smile as she looked down and blushed. Despite the romantic tension, neither dared embrace the other, for fear someone would see.

"Rasheed ..." and then Lady Mother Clara was by her side, ever the mindful and diligent shadow.

"Good evening, Rasheed," Lady Mother Clara smiled. Rasheed bowed respectfully. "Have you forgotten, ManCohalith and Mother Hutra strongly encourage distraction-free environments for Blahom as she is now a Warrior Goddess." Even the most powerful warriors were put in their place time and time again by Lady Mothers Clara and Chi.

Blahom was surprised to hear herself called her a "warrior goddess." It felt good and heightened her sense of responsibility to her destiny. Looking back at Rasheed, her eyes told him that she appreciated his efforts, but it was time to leave.

"Good evening, Lady Mother Clara. My apologies. I didn't mean to take away the Goddess' time. As a natural protector, I only wish to make sure she is doing well after all the news regarding the Delion spy." Blahom was impressed. *Protector? Speaking confidently, are we? Everyone seems to be in a growth state now. Kat was right – things are different. But I like it.*

"Please forgive me." Rasheed's voice was respectful and he had already taken a step back, knowing that he should not have tried to interfere with the Goddess' schedule, even just for a short talk.

Lady Mother Clara looked at him. "Thank you for your concern, but she and her sister have a strict schedule to adhere to and should already be on to their educational classes. They are strong warriors and stronger Goddesses. A spy is nothing to rattle their spirit. However, the lack of focus is a different story."

Just like that, Blahom found herself whisked away. *Once again smothered*, she thought bitterly. *The "watch over" mandate, the "distraction free" statute. I am seventeen years old, and they treat me like I'm a child. No other Zaed female has this sort of life. I am a Goddess, a Warrior Goddess at that. It feels like a gift and a curse. Perhaps this the double-edged sword Mother talks about.* She still fumed internally. *And why shouldn't I embrace Rasheed? What's to stop me? I am a Warrior Goddess, and I will kiss who I wish. I won't let that happen again.*

Later that night, Blahom settled in her bed and tried to push Rasheed out of her mind and focus on more pressing matters. She had accomplished her part of the plan and now it was up to Vasco. All she could do was pray that the news about Lieutenant Kov didn't undermine everything.

"Do you really think we have nothing to worry about when it comes to the Delion spy?" Katyana inquired from her own bed, breaking into Blahom's thoughts.

"I think everyone should stay calm. If we're calm, hopefully they will follow," Blahom said softly.

"I feel like there's more than what Mother is telling us," Katyana said, and Blahom raised an eyebrow at her sister.

"What would she be keeping from us?"

"I heard some whispers from people. Something about elite warriors that the Delions were training."

"You can't believe everything you hear whispered in the halls. It's probably just embellishments to make the spy story more enticing," Blahom shrugged, but Katyana shook her head.

"It's not like it would be the first-time things were kept secret," she said bitterly.

"Katyana," Blahom gave her sister a stern look. "After all that Mother divulged to us, I think she's done with keeping secrets. Plus, what good would keeping a secret like the Delions having elite warriors do?"

"Maybe you're right," Kat sighed. "Still, I don't like any of the Kov situation. I wish we had our Transition gifts now. Then maybe we could do something about it," Kat grumbled.

"You know we are still far from being able to Transition. We have so much more training to go." Just the thought of more training made Blahom want to groan. "Once we get our gifts, we won't be the same, Kat."

Kat leaned forward on her bed. "How so?"

"Well, think about the other Warriors. When they received their gifts, the families had to adjust their whole schedule, their place of living, everything they once knew had to change. I once saw a Transitioned Warrior blow up his house on accident after receiving his Gift. We won't be the same women, either." Blahom shuddered as she remembered the burning wood and the shaking Warrior standing in the center of his destroyed house.

Blahom

"Are you saying that we could ... change, emotionally?" Katyana was surprised but holding onto every word Blahom said.

Blahom had a grave look on her face. "Vasco used to say that some Warriors didn't remember their Transition fully, or they came back a different man. Some were more violent, and some ... some were darker in who they were. It scared everyone around them."

Katyana was in deep thought, and a silence filled the room, save for the soft whistle of the wind through an open bedroom window.

"What do you think your gift will be when you Transition?" Katyana asked, trying to change the subject. Blahom shrugged.

"Honestly I haven't thought about it much."

Being too young to remember Vasco's Transition, Kat inquired, "What was Vasco's Transition like?"

"Well, Mother Hutra told me that he was going to the ocean to Transition. I just thought that he was going to jump into the water and then immediately swim to the surface and have his gift. Several days passed and I asked Mother where Vasco was, she told me that he was still underwater, and I remember crying for days because I thought he had drowned."

"But it's a Transition, it always takes several days," Kat said, looking at Blahom as if she was stupid.

"Well, I know that now, but I was much younger than you. It didn't make any sense to me. I thought he was dead, and no one was telling me. Anyway, two weeks later he came out of the ocean and back home and was different. It was like he went from my normal big brother to this man radiating with power."

"Did he make a massive tidal wave when he came out of the ocean?" Kat asked and Blahom wasn't at all surprised that her sister wanted to hear stories about their brother's power. Power that the two of them might have one day.

"Well, he used tidal waves when fighting Delions, and I heard some Warriors say that he once had a tidal wave so large, that it darkened the sky until it crashed down on an entire army. When he was alone with me, Vasco used to make little water bird figures fly around in the air. They were so dainty and beautiful, almost like moving glass. I think he got a kick out of watching me be enthralled," Blahom said smiling.

"Oh yeah, I think I kind of remember him doing that when I was really little," Katyana said, but Blahom was already moving forward, excited to recount more stories about her brother.

"There are stories I've heard where Vasco has drowned Delions where they stood on the battlefield. I even heard General Brakkus once say that Vasco concentrated hard enough to manipulate the blood in a Delion. He controlled the Delion like a puppet, using the Delion as a shield as he attacked others."

"That's amazing!" Katyana exclaimed, trying to imagine manipulating somebody's blood.

"So, maybe both of us will be gifted with the ability of water like Vasco," Blahom suggested. She was out of Vasco war stories and feeling tired.

"That would be boring if all of us had the same gift. Even Mother and Father have different gifts," Katyana said.

"Then what gift do you think you will get when you Transition?" Blahom asked and Katyana hummed, thinking.

"Maybe I'll be like General Velio. I'll be able to move the ground beneath people's feet. I could create massive landslides and destroy an entire fleet of Delions in an instant. I'll be able to crush any Delion like they were a bug."

"You certainly spend a lot of time with General Velio," Blahom chuckled, trying not to be too concerned about her sister's bloodlust.

"Because he is amazing. He was the one who trained Vasco, so he has been giving me pointers whenever I ask." Katyana grinned with excitement. "Anyway, other than water, what do you think your gift will be?" Blahom paused, wracking her mind for a possible gift that she would like.

"Maybe I'll be able to fly." *If I could fly, I could go anywhere I wanted to.* Blahom smiled at the thought. *I could help my people if they were stuck somewhere, and I could take Rasheed somewhere hidden, somewhere we would only know about.*

"Fly?" Katyana had been gazing at the ceiling, but at Blahom's words, she looked at her sister. "What good would that be in battle?"

"It would make transportation easier. Plus, I would be able to scope ahead and let our forces know what formation the Delion troops would be in," Blahom answered with certainty.

"I suppose that would be a little useful. Kind of boring though," Katyana frowned and Blahom chuckled.

"You and Vasco can have the outwardly dangerous gifts while I can have a subdued one that can still help. Besides, imagine what I would be able to do if I could use my gift to dance in the air. Wouldn't that be beautiful?" Blahom's thoughts turned to being able to perform the Dietrickt dance in the sky. She herself could be like a bird, flying around while dancing gracefully. She was jolted out of her thoughts by Katyana's laughter.

"Air dancing? If you air dance, then I'll never catch up with you."

"Don't worry, I'd pull you up into the air with me so we could dance together," Blahom smiled, turning in bed to look at her sister and their eyes met.

"But I'm afraid of heights and you know it!" Kat laughed and threw a pillow playfully at her sister.

"That sounds like something you need to talk to General Velio about. I'm sure he's not afraid of heights," Blahom teased.

"I guess you're right. It isn't very warrior-like to be afraid of things," Katyana said, her laughter dimming as she thought of her fears. Blahom didn't want Kat to focus on fear as a negative.

"I think it's normal to be afraid of something," said Blahom. The moonlight from outside illuminated the sisters' faces. "After all, I'm pretty sure Vasco is still afraid of bugs."

Both girls giggled at countless memories of Vasco shrieking and running away from insects that got too close.

"I guess that's true," Katyana laughed. She let out a contented sigh. "Just think, Blahom. After we Transition, we'll be the strongest warriors on the battlefield. You will be flying all around, and I will be causing crazy earthquakes." She let out a long yawn.

"Maybe," Blahom shrugged, unable to hold back her own yawn. "Or maybe we won't even have to fight."

"Why bring that up?" Katyana's voice went from kind to bitter in an instant. "We are going to be warriors. Why can't you just accept that?"

"Because it's not what I want, Kat," Blahom said gently, trying to disarm her little sister, but Kat shook her head, turning her back to Blahom in her bed.

"Well, it's what I want. Besides, at the end of the day it doesn't matter what either of us want."

Blahom sighed, turning around in her bed. She was tired of arguing, but she didn't want to end their conversation on how neither of them would get what they wanted. She turned her head, her body still facing away from Kat.

"Well, Vasco can get what he wants," Blahom said, and Kat glared at her.

"Why say that?"

"Because we are going to be aunts, Kat."

Blahom soaked in the silence, Katyana not knowing what to say. Finally, her sister spoke.

"Vasco ... he's going to be a father?"

"Yes. He'll be marrying Zya soon." She then turned to face Katyana. "And I know you hate secrets, but can you keep this one? It will be revealed soon enough by Vasco anyway."

Katyana nodded her head.

"This is a good secret." she smiled, but then grew serious. "Let's both work to become the best warriors we can be so that Vasco's child can be born into a beautiful world free of fear."

Blahom didn't want to fight Delions, but she did want what was best for her soon to be niece or nephew. "We will work together to give our new family member the best Sirius there can be."

With that, both sisters relaxed into their beds.

Blahom

The dance slippers hanging on the wall swayed in the soft breeze coming from the window. Blahom thought of the last time she had used the window to go see Jhapalle. It was also the time she got caught.

As the sisters drifted towards sleep, Blahom's mind returned to her brother. If Vasco's plan worked, then she and Kat wouldn't have to worry about Transitioning. They would not be warriors, and Kat would forget that she even wanted to fight. They would dance and, perhaps, Blahom would be allowed to be happy. She could see herself bouncing Vasco's baby on her lap joyfully while maybe even Rasheed could be sitting next to her.

The thought put a smile on Blahom's face, and sleep came sweetly.

Chapter Twelve

Vasco watched on as his sisters stood on a beach, adorned in their Goddess attire and painted faces. His view was blurry, but he could see that they both were illuminated by the glowing sun. Something gnawed at his heart while he stared at his sisters. He couldn't put his finger on it, but something was wrong.

After several seconds, Vasco's surroundings came into focus, and he fought back a scream. His sisters were covered in blood and surrounded by corpses of both Zaeds and Delions.

Katyana looked like she was trying to be strong, her face trying to mirror the stoicism of their father, but both girls were shaking uncontrollably. Blahom was shattered. Both had tears in their eyes that mixed with the blood that was splattered on their faces.

There was something else on the beach and his vision became blurred again. He felt he had to look somewhere else, away from his sisters. That something else was wrong. However, through his blurred vision all he could see were obscured visions of Zaed and Delion corpses.

"No!" Vasco exclaimed, sitting up in his bed. He never was able to see what he felt like he was supposed to, but after his sister's haunted faces, he couldn't bear to see anymore.

Vasco's heart pounded in his chest as his eyes took in the familiar room around him. He could see beams of light from the sunrise streaming through the orange curtains. His eyes went to his bookshelf that housed volumes and volumes of war strategies. He took in the sight of his red sheets, red as deep as blood, but calmed when he saw Zya's soft purple robe. Her various articles of clothing were strewn across a grey bench, and a small baby hat lay on the dresser, an early gift she had made for their unborn child.

He reminded himself that it was just a dream despite how real it felt; reminded himself that he was no Mother Hutra. His dreams were just dreams, not prophecies.

"Beloved?"

Vasco felt soothing hands wrapping around his shoulders. He looked over at Zya, her hair large and tousled from the night before, and her dark eyes bore deep into his. Could she read his mind with just a glance?

"Another nightmare?" she asked, gently kissing him on his back

"Yes. It was disturbing," he answered, and Zya continued gently kissing him down his spine.

"How can I help?" she climbed on top of him and kissed his cheek. "A massage? A dance?" she kissed him on the cheek again then smirked at him. "Something else?"

She started kissing down his chest and made her way back up to his face.

Vasco closed his eyes and let his guard down. He gave her a passionate kiss while he ran his hands down her curvy body, allowing his mind to be fully invested in her.

The two loved each other fully and passionately. Vasco held her close. Both could have fallen asleep fully content, but Vasco jolted up. He had things he needed to accomplish.

"I should head out to do some training," Vasco said, but Zya quickly pinned him down.

"Do you have to, my love?" Zya whispered in his ear, and Vasco tried to control his thoughts, but she was very convincing.

"You only head out with the intent to train when something is weighing on your mind. Did I not do enough to relieve you?" Once again, she saw right through him.

"Well, I also have a meeting later with ManCohalith. I feel like I talk to him better after a good training session, so if you could get off me ..." Vasco said playfully as he tickled Zya's sides. She laughed and let out a soft squeal as he pinned her down and gave her a kiss on the forehead before he rolled out of the bed and made his way to his closet for his clothes.

"I'm disappointed that you're so eager to leave me behind," Zya said with a pout, but Vasco knew she was teasing. Zya knew how much Vasco valued his duty and that she couldn't sway him to stay.

"You know that I'm not eager to leave, beloved," Vasco said as he threw on his shirt.

"I can count on you to be eager to return though, am I right?" she said playfully. "After all, you didn't return to me yesterday."

Vasco rolled his eyes. "As long as I can return to you, I will always be eager," he said as he leaned in to where she sat on the bed. Zya leaned in as well, her lips close to touching his. However, she quickly stood to her feet, avoiding the kiss.

"Well then, I should prepare for the day as well." Zya was picking out her outfit for the day and Vasco couldn't help but smile looking at her enticing body. Her curves beckoned him to run his fingers over her hips and breasts. She took her time, picking an outfit and then even more slowly putting the dress on.

"You're so cruel," he said, and Zya chuckled.

"Only because you love it when I'm mean," she said with a smirk. "Now, don't you have some training to do?"

"You're right, of course." Vasco pulled Zya in close to him, giving her a deep kiss. Zya pushed him back, breaking the kiss. "I'm serious," she said, a hint of attitude in her voice. Vasco was slightly surprised. "What's wrong, my love?" he asked, reaching out to touch her.

Zya moved away from him. "Why didn't you come home?"

Vasco moved closer to her. "I was training, Zya. You know this by now."

Zya rolled her eyes, but Vasco quickly grabbed her by the waist and gave her two kisses, one on each cheek. "Everything will be alright."

Zya thought for a moment, giving Vasco an unconvincing look, but she nodded anyway.

Vasco smiled, placing a strong hand over her belly. In months, he would be a father, with Zya as his wife. The very thought of being able to hold his child made him want to laugh out loud.

"I will be back after sunset," Vasco said, giving Zya a long kiss and removing his hand from her belly. He gave a sly smile and smacked Zya's butt.

"And we will be here waiting for your return," she smiled, placing her own hand on her stomach. And with that image burned into his mind, Vasco was out the door.

Vasco made it to the training arena, and ran several hand-to-hand combat practices with a training bag. He noticed other warriors practicing as well, but opted to train alone.

Zya, my love, always so eager to keep me away from my duties, Vasco thought as he continued to spar with the training bag. *Our child will have her insistence and determination, and I will train him to be the greatest warrior Sirius has ever known. I'll murder any- and everyone that tries to harm my sisters, my family. Anyone. I'll do anything to protect my family. Anything.*

Vasco, not one to do things halfway, attacked the training bag, his mind still haunted by the dream he had earlier. *Why did I see such an awful thing? What's my brain trying to tell me?* He tried to push the questions out of his mind to focus on the training bag in front of him, a training bag that represented a Delion on the battlefield, one with the intent to harm everyone he loved.

Taking a deep breath, Vasco forced himself to take a moment. He reached for a drink and the cold water soothed his dry throat and he coughed when he pulled his flask away. When he was stressed, he often pushed himself harder during training, and he most definitely was stressed about his upcoming meeting with ManCohalith and the horrible nightmare he couldn't seem to shake even after punching the bag until he felt as if he bruised his knuckles.

His mind wandered to Blahom. He hoped she had been able to talk to Mother Hutra and make his mother think of him as a strong leader and talk him up to ManCohalith. If Blahom had done her part of the plan, his meeting with ManCohalith should go well.

Vasco's train of thought was interrupted by shouting reverberating throughout the training space. Tensions were high in the training camp after the death of the spy posing as Kov and public outbursts seemed to be more frequent than usual.

"After everything with Kov, who's to say you're not a Delion! Perhaps that is why you did not want me there," shouted a Zaed warrior, angry he had not been asked to attend the torturing of the imposter, and opting to blame Jakk.

"How dare you even imply that!" Jakk exclaimed.

"Are you scared that I'm revealing you for who you really are?"

"You know I have no authority to summon anyone to a meeting in the Throne Room. How do I know you're not a Delion, trying to create a problem out of nothing?" Jakk was getting heated.

Low morale and tension among the Zaeds was often healed through the CCDC ceremony, but the next one was still days away; days until some semblance of calm was reclaimed. Until then, everyone would be on edge.

Vasco wondered if he should intervene. He knew both warriors and they could both be reasoned with, but now he saw blood pour from a cut on one man's forehead. It was uncommon for Zaeds to fight each other, but to draw blood was especially taboo. The moment blood was drawn, the matter between the two parties became a personal one. The last time Vasco could remember an incident like this, the two Zaeds removed themselves from any prying eyes and were gone for two days. Once the matter was done and over with, both had returned, and nobody asked any questions.

Unfortunately, the two men here continued to argue out in the open, creating discomfort in the training grounds, with onlookers watching and waiting for the soldiers' next move. As a superior officer, Vasco knew that he needed to interfere.

"Soldier Jakk! Soldier Majus!" Vasco raised his voice. The warriors paused, recognizing him immediately. "Be warriors of respect and don't contaminate the other Zaeds. Take your petty personal gripes away from the training grounds and come back once you've come to your resolution."

The two Zaeds limped away still arguing under their breaths. Vasco hoped that by the next day they would return, back to their normal, less-paranoid selves. The next CCDC ceremony could not come too soon. It was abundantly clear that the Zaeds needed to be healed.

"You're one to talk," one of the warriors nearby grunted. Vasco looked over to see General Levin's son, warrior Burris staring at him with his arms crossed. He was a large man, about two years younger than Vasco. With his strength and youth also came arrogance, a trait shared by many young warriors.

"Who do you think you're talking to, Soldier Burris?" Burris' voice held a venom that Vasco instantly found insulting, especially as he was a superior officer.

"I think I'm talking to a murderer," Burris' said, and Vasco raised an eyebrow.

"A murderer? I've slaughtered countless Delions on the battlefield, is that what you're talking about? I don't see why you would have such a problem with that."

"I'm talking about your own aunt. The one you so publicly hate and decry," Burris said, and Vasco stared at the young warrior, beginning to feel more confused than offended.

"Our Aunt Lorraine? What are you talking about?" Vasco demanded and Burris laughed bitterly.

"Don't play dumb, General," Burris practically spat Vasco's title. "It's not a good look for you."

"Again, I have no idea what you're talking about," Vasco spoke calmly, so as not to escalate the situation and trying to understand what Lorraine had to do with anything.

"Do you need me to jog your memory?" Burris asked with a sneer. "She's been missing since yesterday morning. And after you've talked so much about how much you've hated her, it's all a bit of an odd coincidence, isn't it?" Vasco glared at the warrior.

"Are you implying that I murdered Lorraine?" He shook his head. "I hate her, but I wouldn't kill her. Killing her does nothing for me. She's probably off meditating somewhere."

"You think she left her daughter alone in the house just to meditate? She is gone! No one can find her. No one could find you last night either, Lieutenant Vasco." Burris pressed and Vasco crossed his arms.

"She's a foolish woman, thinking she can interpret dreams. Who's to say she wouldn't wander off somewhere to meditate."

"So, you're not saying that you wouldn't kill her? After all that noise you made. With her out of the way, maybe you think you can reverse her dream interpretations."

"You're putting words into my mouth," Vasco said. "Once she returns from whatever meditative journey she went on, you're going to look like a fool for accusing me of murder," Vasco said, and walked away from Burris, not wanting to hear another word. Burris let him go.

Leaving the training area and mounting his horse, Vasco headed to the fortress. Something about Lorraine missing was nagging in the back of his mind. As he passed through the marketplace, a couple of fishermen hardly acknowledged him, and a shop owner whispered to another before giving him a terrified look, as if afraid Vasco would murder them on the spot. *Everyone knows. How could I be so foolish to have been missing last night out of every possible night?* Vasco thought on his love affair last night. He did not make it home to Zya because he was curled up in the arms of another Lady Sister. *I have a lot of explaining to do. Could everyone think that I murdered my aunt?* Vasco knew trouble followed him and today seemed to be no exception. Riding hard, he arrived at his destination faster than expected.

Entering the Battle Strategy Hall, Vasco could see ManCohalith waiting, a map of the planet spread out on the table.

"If you're not early, you're late." ManCohalith clapped a large hand on Vasco's shoulder approvingly then quickly shifted to business. He was not a man for pleasantries and Vasco, taking after his father, didn't mind.

Vasco stared down at the map in front of him.

"You said that you had some important information?" prompted ManCohalith, and Vasco nodded obediently.

"Yes. From what I've gathered, most of the Delions are congregating here and here," Vasco was pointing to two locations on the map highlighted in red.

"Where do you think the transportation device might be located?" ManCohalith inquired.

"From what we have been able to find out, there is a high likelihood that it's in their second location, closer to the mountains," Vasco moved his finger to point at the destination. "It would make sense that the Delions had the transportation device there, where it's harder to launch for any type of surprise attack,"

"So that is where we will strike," ManCohalith nodded, his voice final as he turned to look out the window, but Vasco interjected.

"I actually have another idea."

ManCohalith turned, his piercing eyes stared down at his son. "What is this idea?" Vasco tried to relax, wanting to prove to his father that he had thoroughly and meticulously thought this strategy through and that his plan was one worth taking a chance on.

"We should send our top General towards the first location, to draw as many Delions as possible there. While the Delions are distracted, I will take several of my men over the mountain to the second location, take them by surprise, and attack their flank," Vasco explained, trying to speak slowly and confidently.

"You want to take on this device by yourself with only a few other men?" ManCohalith was invested, but not too much.

"I do. This is too dangerous for any of our other Generals to take on, and I have been surveilling it for months now. I think it should be I who destroys the device."

ManCohalith thought to himself for a moment. *Vasco is correct,* he thought, *but he's being too rash. I know the threat against the Zaed women is important, but splitting our forces ... Is it worth taking the chance?*

"It might be risky having you split your forces," hummed ManCohalith.

"The secret base camp is filled with unarmed scientists and minimum guards." Vasco responded, consolidating research he had spent months accumulating.

ManCohalith paced the room and Vasco knew not to interrupt. "And it might be even more risky for you to come over the mountain side," ManCohalith continued, still walking back and forth. Vasco held his breath; he felt good about his homework. ManCohalith looked up, clasped his hands together and prayed. Finally, he stopped his pacing and looked his son in the eye.

"I see why you believe that this plan would work. A complete unexpected ambush would blindside the Delions effectively and even lead to a major victory for us. Make no mistake though, your plan would have to go into effect perfectly. If not, the death of you and all under your command is assured. Are you prepared to have that blood on your hands? Trekking up the side of a mountain is no easy feat. Have you considered the stamina needed by your warriors and yourself? After climbing the mountain, you would need to ensure your warriors still have the energy to fight an entire battle. If your best troops are going to the first location, will the troops that you have with you be able to shoulder the task that you are putting on them? Have you taken all of this into consideration, son?"

Blahom

ManCohalith piled on question after question, interested to see how his son would respond.

Vasco, confident, responded, "I have. I know that this battle will not be easily won, and the possibility of failure is high. Nonetheless, I know my warriors and I know myself. With the Alpha God's help, we will win."

Again, ManCohalith paced the floor. Vasco held his breath in anticipation. Finally, ManCohalith placed a hand on Vasco's shoulder.

"I'm proud of you, Vasco. We will bless this plan in the upcoming CCDC ceremony. I trust that you will lead us to victory."

"I will." Vasco smiled.

"Good. Let us go over your plan more fully. However, before we do, have you heard from your aunt recently?"

The taste of victory soured in Vasco's mouth. Once again, Lorraine was being brought up.

"No. I haven't." Vasco said stiffly. "I heard that she was missing this morning. Is that true?"

"Yesterday morning Trinity was crying, saying that she hadn't seen her mother, so a small group of us went to investigate. We kept it quiet, but searched for her, with no sign. Trinity is currently staying with General Lakin's family and Rasheed and Velio are continuing the search. I'm hoping Lorraine will turn up soon, but in light of everything, I'm concerned." ManCohalith had returned to pacing the room.

"In light of what?" Vasco asked, his voice tight, feeling as if his cousin Burris was in his face all over again. ManCohalith stopped his pacing and stared at his son.

"In light of the spy." he said, then looked out the window, over his kingdom. "Tension is permeating in every corner and shadow in this kingdom. The last thing we need after a spy infiltrating our ranks, is for a royal family member to go missing."

After a pause, ManCohalith turned his attention away from the window and back to his son. "Where were you yesterday?"

Vasco stiffened slightly. The last thing he wanted to do was be accused by his own father for a deed he had no part in.

"Why didn't you respond for the meeting in the Throne Room?"

An uncomfortable silence fell between the two men.

"Father," Vasco spoke up. "I was far from any of this. I was out," Vasco cleared his throat. "I was out laying with a Lady Sister." His father looked up at him. "It was not Zya so I would appreciate it if this was not revealed to anyone."

ManCohalith placed a hand on his son's shoulder. "Don't let this weigh on you. I was just wondering if you had heard anything. Now, let us further discuss your plan."

"Thank you, Father. One more thing, if I may, Father?" Vasco continued, "I must advise you that both my sisters did great during their warrior training. However, as you know Blahom is blossoming into a young woman. Father, as her brother, I am in awe of her, though I don't let her see." Vasco let a small laugh.

"What is it son?" ManCohalith was ready to hear what Vasco had to say.

"I ask that you consider lessening the "watch over" mandate and "distraction free statute" and allow her some time to be alone with her own thoughts or travel to the marketplace and socialize with the Zaed community. A little grace might benefit her, what with the rigorous schedule and current events that seem to occur every day." Vasco tried to keep his face neutral as he knew his father was a wise man.

ManCohalith looked at his son and turned to walk away. "Is that so? You are excused to focus on your plan of attack, Lieutenant Vasco." ManCohalith was clearly in no doubt about the siblings' colluding efforts.

Chapter Thirteen

Stiff muscles and joints popped as Blahom stretched in her bed. She had woken up early, but was too excited to go back to sleep. They were going to perform a CCDC ceremony, and everyone was long overdue for one. She would never admit it out loud, but she was also excited to be able to see Rasheed again. As a member of the royal dynasty, he had a seat close to the dance and she would be able to catch his eye during her solo and just the thought of him watching her made Blahom's heart flutter.

She could not stay in bed a second longer. Rolling out of bed to look out the window at the sunrise, Blahom felt all the tension from the past several weeks melt away. The sky was illuminated in stunning colors of purples, pinks, oranges, and yellows.

There's nothing like being able to start the day on a beautiful sunrise, Blahom thought to herself, giving a quick prayer. *Thank you for this.*

"Why are you up?" Katyana groaned from her bed, snapping Blahom's attention away from the window.

"Because I'm excited. I feel like we haven't been able to perform in a ceremony for ages." Katyana rolled her eyes and flipped over in her bed to lay on her stomach.

"You're so dramatic, it hasn't been that long," Katyana said, clearly not ready to get up yet.

"Even if it hasn't, it certainly feels like it. Anyway, this should be fun. This will be our first time dancing together where we both have solo dances," Blahom smiled, walking closer to her sister's bed. The ceremony today was taking place during a solar eclipse.

"That's true," Katyana said with a shrug. "But that doesn't mean we need to get up now. This is the first day in forever that we don't have training bright and early. Let's enjoy it by sleeping in."

"Fine, you do have a point," Blahom sighed, walking over and flopping back onto her own bed with a soft thud. She shifted back and forth, trying to get comfortable, but as much as she tried, she couldn't get to sleep. Her mind kept pulling up images of the handsome Rasheed and how he might look today watching her as she danced. The thought of him only made Blahom more restless, wishing that he were in front of her that very moment.

"You are tossing and turning, and it is keeping me from sleeping," Katyana groaned.

"I just can't get comfortable."

"Can you at least be quiet about it?" Katyana grumbled into her pillow. At this point, Blahom was fully awake and having fun annoying her little sister.

"Kat, I don't think I'll be able to go back to sleep."

"That's not my problem," Katyana said.

"How can you sleep so easily?"

"I won't be able to sleep if you keep talking."

"Come on Kat, what's your secret?" Blahom asked, though she clearly didn't expect an actual answer.

"Shut up, will you!"

"But Kaaaat," Blahom whined, and it was now obvious to Kat that Blahom was trying to annoy her.

Katyana chucked a pillow at Blahom's face, and she quickly

returned fire. Katyana buried herself into the blankets of her bed, not ready to "play fight." Blahom kept throwing little things at her sister.

There was a knock at the door and Blahom laughed and threw another pillow and Katyana shot her a deadly glare. There was a second knock and reluctantly Kat sat up in her bed. She looked around for something to retaliate with, her eyes settled on a shoe, which she swiftly threw at her sister. Blahom dodged and finally Kat, giving in, couldn't hold back a laugh.

A third knock sounded, louder this time, alerting the sisters to the presence outside their door.

"Come in." Blahom said, trying to compose herself.

Lady Mother Clara and Lady Mother Chi entered, ready to help the Goddesses with their garb and ceremonial makeup.

"What are you two doing? You both look disheveled," Lady Mother Chi asked and both sisters looked at each other, then back at her.

"We were just shaking off our nerves for the upcoming ceremony," Blahom answered.

"I'm sure that's what you were doing," Lady Mother Clara said dryly, eyeing the disarray in the room. She decided against chiding the two Goddesses as if they were children, despite the evidence on the floor. "But no matter, it's time to get ready for the ceremony."

Both Lady Mothers were swift in dressing the Goddesses, making sure that their garb hung perfectly on their frames. Blahom and Kat were adorned in every imaginable shade of gold, the fabrics sure to make them glow in the unique light of the eclipse.

Katyana's dress emphasized her lithe frame and strong arms, while Blahom's dress accentuated her hips, and a slit ran down the side to show off her strong legs. Both Goddesses had always appeared radiant, but with their warrior training, they now appeared fiercely strong.

Once their dresses fit perfectly, the Lady Mothers focused on hair and makeup. Lady Mother Chi hummed as she braided

Katyana's hair and Lady Mother Clara rocked back and forth to Chi's song.

Blahom relaxed into the morning routine. She looked at herself in the mirror, lost in thought, her brows furrowing over her eyes. This was how things used to be before she and Kat had started training to be warriors. If Vasco's plan worked and he ended the war, then calm mornings preparing for Ceremonies could be the norm once again. She hoped that she was successful in her part of the plan and that Mother Hutra talked Vasco up enough to ManCohalith. She had not seen Vasco since the training on the vessel, so she was left in suspense.

"I know that face. Are you plotting something?" Lady Mother Clara inquired as she painted Blahom's face with a steady hand.

"Of course not," Blahom said, but when Lady Mother Clara looked unswayed, she added, "I just missed this. It's been so long since the last CCDC ceremony."

"I've missed this too," Lady Mother Clara said gently. Even someone as strong as Lady Mother Clara couldn't escape the tension that existed everywhere since the unmasking of the spy. "I am blessed to be able to see you perform today," she said with a smile.

When the Goddesses were ready, the four women walked down the halls of their home and entered the dance rehearsal room where the other Lady Mothers and Lady Sisters were gathering. Mother Hutra was talking with Zya, giving her words of encouragement about the ceremony. Lita and Allysia ran up to Blahom and Katyana in excitement.

"You both look so gorgeous!" Lita squealed, careful not to smudge Blahom's paint as she hugged her. Allysia exchanged a sly look with Kat. "Are you ready to perfect your solo?"

Kat playfully stuck her tongue out at Allysia. "Are you going to remember all your steps?"

"That was one time," Allysia pouted as Katyana laughed.

"You two look more radiant with each passing day," Mother Hutra said proudly as she made her way to her daughters, Zya by her side. "I look forward to your dance. It will give our people such hope seeing you two together during these times." Mother Hutra looked away for a moment, and Blahom knew it was because she was thinking about the newest worry to befall their family.

Lorraine was still missing. The royal family was doing what they could to not to upset the Zaeds, but with gossip, this was not an easy task.

With the disappearance of Lorraine came skepticism about Vasco as well. Rumors were rife in the kingdom that how Vasco had murdered his own aunt. Some said Vasco killed Lorraine because of her dream interpretations about his sisters. Others said that Vasco killed his aunt because she had her own motives to make Trinity a Goddess by getting rid of Blahom and Katyana. Some of the rumors painted Vasco as a villain while others depicted him doing what he had to do to protect his family. Some of the Zaeds loved Vasco more for his vigor while others despised him for killing his own aunt in cold blood. And while opinion was divided as to his motive, most were certain that he was a murderer.

Each of these rumors reached Mother Hutra's ears. She would not believe her own son would murder her sister. Nevertheless, she was weighed down by the stress of the rumors of her missing sister and the disclosure of a spy. Now she looked forward to being spiritually cleansed. It wouldn't stop the rumors or show her where her sister went or even stop the war, but the CCDC ceremony would give her renewed energy to deal with everything to come.

Zya gave Mother Hutra a look of concern and love, forever admiring her strength and love towards her children. Zya had been hand chosen by Mother Hutra years ago to dance in the ceremonies and become a Lady Sister, which surprised her; she never felt that her skill level was on par with the other Lady Mothers and Sisters at the CCDC ceremonies. It was soon after she became a Lady Sister that Zya bumped into Vasco in the halls of the building. They would talk and flirt a little before she went into practice, and Vasco quickly started to make excuses as to why he was near the dance practice room so often.

During CCDC ceremonies, Zya would catch Vasco's eye in the front of the crowd while dancing, and Mother Hutra would watch on from the sideline knowingly. Zya wondered if Mother Hutra somehow knew that she and Vasco were fated to be together and did what she could to bring them together. If that were the truth or not, Zya felt indebted to Mother Hutra for taking her in as a Lady Sister.

Placing a hand on her stomach, Zya smiled softly. She only hoped that she would be as good a mother as Mother Hutra when the baby arrived.

"We look forward to performing, Mother," Katyana bowed her head in respect, then added, "especially Blahom."

"No one's surprised about that," chuckled Zya as she wrapped Katyana in a hug. "It's clear that Blahom's the happiest when she is dancing."

"And eating," added Lita. Katyana and the other women laughed at that, and Blahom couldn't help but laugh as well. Everyone was overjoyed to see each other and the sisterhood strengthened. To Blahom, it felt like a family reunion to be able to dance with these women once again.

"True happiness is dance and food," giggled Blahom.

"You can eat all you want after the ceremony. Let's start stretching. I cannot have any of my lovely dancers get injured during the performance," said Mother Hutra.

"You hear that, Allysia? No getting hurt," laughed Lita in a teasing voice. Allysia frowned, saying, "Will you let that go? I wasn't trying to trip anyone up."

"Then you should have stretched more," shrugged Lita. Allysia stomped her foot in frustration. "I did stretch!"

"Hush, hush," Mother Hutra scolded, and the two Lady Sisters quieted.

Stretching was a ritual, with the less experienced dancers

Blahom

watched the more seasoned dancers, trying to memorize their slow fluid motions even in warmups.

"Looks like you have an admirer," Lita leaned in and whispered to Blahom, and she looked over to see Allysia watching her movements, specifically her footwork.

After the group warmups, Blahom approached Allysia. "Do you need help with anything?" Blahom inquired. At first, Allysia hesitated to speak, but then she nodded, embarrassed.

"I think so. I really don't want to get hurt and mess up in front of everyone again," she whispered.

"Get that out of your head. You're more likely to get hurt if you think like that." Blahom said. "You'll do great. Here, just let your body feel the movement. Let your mind connect with the music and remember why we are performing. Think of the morale of the warriors and how we bring them joy before battle. Think about all the Zaeds and how your dance will bring them ease from whatever dreads they face throughout the day."

Blahom took Allysia's hands, going over some movements with her. Blahom was lifting her fellow sister up and Allysia started to feel her worries melt away under the older girl's tutelage. Blahom was a true Goddess through and through.

"There. No need to worry about anything. This will be a great ceremony." Allysia looked up at Blahom in awe, and Blahom added, "Plus, think of the food we'll have afterwards. All the fruits and meats that we could ever want."

"Thank you," Allysia said, laughing a little as she looked up at Blahom. "This will be a lovely dance today."

Mother Hutra's eyes glanced over at the windows, seeing the sun's placement in the cloudless sky. She glanced at Blahom. "Daughter, would you like to say some words to our women?"

Blahom was surprised. Her mother had only asked her to speak a few times, like when Katyana became a Lady Sister dancer or more recently, prior to the dream, when Mother Hutra was ill and Blahom had to stand in her stead. Blahom knew this request meant that she was maturing in her mother's eyes, and smiled. "Yes, Mother," she said, before directing her attention to the ensemble. "Everyone, circle up."

The group of women came together, and Blahom scanned the dancers to align energies. She noticed Lady Mother Kalis' blank expression. She made eye contact and Lady Mother Kalis rallied when Blahom spoke.

"First of all, I'm very proud of everyone. I miss you all so much, especially since Kat and I do not get to see you on a regular basis as in the past. I am sure I can speak for my sister when I say we have missed you sorely and we certainly did not forget you."

Kat was proud to be Blahom's little sister in moments like this. She was happy when Blahom spoke on their behalf. Whatever Blahom said, she agreed. Although she was a Warrior Goddess too, she never spoke to the Lady Mothers and Sisters and had no desire to speak in front of a crowd.

Blahom continued. "In the midst of all the turmoil and heartache, we have managed to remain strong, and full of heart. This ceremony, and our dance, is extremely vital to our spiritual culture, and it gives the Warriors strength and vitality. We must honor it with each step we take, each movement, for it brings forth life, power, and unity. May we go out and perform with passion and thanksgiving to our Zaeds and the Alpha God. As my sister and I join together for the first dual solo performance, may we use this symbolism to unite in thought and pray for revelation and the swift finding find my beloved Aunt Lorraine and cousin, our dearest Lady Sister dancer, Daniella." She bowed her head and swallowed the lump in her throat.

A few of the dancers fought back silent tears, and many murmured their approval. Mother Hutra clapped her hands together.

"With that, let's all get moving. We don't want to miss the beginning of the eclipse," she said. Exchanging final words of encouragement, the Lady Mothers and Lady Sisters made their way to the shore for the ceremony.

Blahom

* * *

The coming eclipse gave this evening's ceremony a particular relevance. The unmasking of the spy Kov had shaken the warriors and rumor and speculation had done their insidious job, undermining the army and sowing seeds of mistrust and tension. Tonight, lookouts were posted and discreet guards wandered the perimeter, while the majority of the warriors were given special dispensation to watch the celebration with their families. The Generals stood behind ManCohalith, grateful for the men who served so well and would now be restored by the dance and the music.

Blahom, Katyana, and the Lady Mothers and Sisters danced to the pulse of the drums, and the gathered Zaeds watched them with awe and reverence. The dancers' feet connected with the soft sand in time to the music as it became more and more intense. The sun and moon were about to cross, as were the two sisters, who had begun their duet.

Blahom's smile was radiant, truly in her element. She felt the beat of the drums in her bones and the salty smell of the ocean tickled her nose. The beats of the music drove her on. Her hips swayed and her feet slid sensually through the warm sand. She glanced up to see Rasheed watching with rapt attention. His burning eyes on her made her dance even more passionately.

Kat felt her body move to the rhythm with renewed purpose. She was fully focused on what this dance meant to her people. Since her training as a warrior, she began to appreciate the honor and understand the significance of the Dietrickt dance as a way for the people to renew their spirits, and how this ceremony was a moment of cleansing for all.

Zya moved in sync with the rest of the ensemble, feeling the music move through her body. She danced for her people; she danced for Vasco knowing about his upcoming mission; she danced for the baby growing in her belly. Her first child that she and Vasco were going to raise with all the love and care their hearts could give. Zya danced with a new ferocity as she looked into the audience and saw her love looking right at her. Vasco's eyes never left her.

The CCDC dancers were on the beach to the north as the sun and moon started to align behind them. Thousands of participants watched, and the spirit was powerful and moved through the crowd and even those who could not see the dancers felt touched by the ceremony.

At last, planet Sirius was bathed in a red glow of darkness as the moon completely covered the sun. The full totality of the eclipse would only last thirty seconds. Within those moments the music hit a crescendo, and the dancers were in complete submission to their calling. The Zaeds wept with joy, revitalized.

Zya during the Dietrickt dance

ManCohalith watched the ensemble of dancers. His eyes fell onto Lady Mother Kalis, going through the movements of the dance, but with dull eyes and a facial expression completely blank. It was as if she had no soul. Just as ManCohalith had noticed her, Kalis started dancing out of sync and a righteous anger filled the leader's veins. The fake dancer's eyes locked onto his.

In one fluid movement, she grabbed Zya.

"Seize the enemy!" ManCohalith exclaimed in a booming voice.

Everything came to a standstill. The drums halted and the dancers, wide eyed, ran. Some Zaeds sank to their knees to pray. Murmurs went through the crowd of those who could not see. Every person on the shore was frozen in place.

Before anyone could register what was happening, Kalis was holding a knife at Zya's throat. The warriors, instantly alert, would have gladly murdered the traitor where she stood, but with Zya held hostage, nobody moved.

In their silence, Kalis started laughing hysterically. At first, it started as a low giggle until it grew louder and louder and soon enough it was as if her laughter was drowning out the waves of the ocean.

Vasco met Zya eyes, and saw her fear. Vasco held himself back from sprinting to Zya's side, knowing the tragedy of one wrong move.

"Your ceremonies are nothing! Your worship is nothing! Technology is the answer to saving our planet. Not a dance!" Kalis pushed the blade against Zya's neck.

"We're coming to get what we desire, and we're coming for your precious women! Technology will rule Sirius. It will rule the world."

Zya opened her mouth to speak, but in one fluid motion, the Delion slit her throat and ran.

Blood poured from Zya's neck, and she crumpled onto the sands of the beach.

Chapter Fourteen

Chaos erupted amongst the Zaeds. Dancers screamed and ran inland, distancing themselves from the imposter. General Murn and other warriors sprinted to the fore, hampered now by the panicking crowds.

Vasco ran to Zya. Ignoring the fleeing Kalis and the threat she presented, he reached the dying mother of his unborn child and knelt at her side, holding her in his arms, entreating the gods that she could be healed. He placed a hand on her belly, sobbing, praying that she and their unborn child would live. Mustering what courage he had, he looked into Zya's eyes, hoping to see a spark of life. He was met by a blank stare in return. Zya took a breath and blood ran from the side of her mouth and eyeballs. The truth was undeniable. Zya was dead.

"Even on your most sacred of days, there will be loss of life. We are coming to take back the girl and anything else that belongs to us." The imposter's lips curled into a wicked smile. She had stopped running. She removed her dancer gloves and placed her fingers against her throat, revealing two fingers that were much longer than the others, a clear sign that she was of the Delion species. She slit her own throat, falling lifeless to the ground.

Blahom

General Murn and the others came through the crowd and finally approached Kalis' body. He grabbed her by the hair and tore away a mask, revealing her true face. A pale face with pointed ears and oval slanted eyes. The face of a Delion.

The horror of the moment set in, and wails rose from throughout the crowd. Mother Hutra looked at the dancers fleeing inland, Allysia and Lita among them. Lady Mother Clara stood at her side on high alert. Mother Hutra's eyes scanned those who remained on the beach, many frozen in shock or sobbing.

Among those still on the beach were both her daughters. Lady Mother Chi was already next to Katyana, coaxing her away from the beach, but Katyana refused to leave, sinking to her knees as she continued to cry. Mother Hutra ran towards them, gently cupped Katyana's cheek, and kissed her forehead.

"Head inland, away from here," she commanded, and Lady Mother Chi pushed Katyana to leave the area. Hearing her mother speak, Katyana regained her composure somewhat and followed Lady Mother Chi away. Mother Hutra continued to try to herd the few remaining dancers away from the beach, but lost sight of Blahom.

Rasheed had rushed to Blahom's side. "Blahom, we have to go," he urged, grasping her hand.

"But ... Zya ... I should've known ..." Blahom was frozen.

"Blahom, we don't know if there are more imposters or not. It's not safe for you here."

"But the baby ..." Blahom said. Rasheed shook his head in confusion.

"Blahom, my love," Rasheed swallowed his breath. "The baby is gone, and we have to go. Please, come with me further inland. We'll find your mother and ..."

"I need to find Vasco." Blahom said, pulling her hand away from Rasheed's. "Make sure my sister is safe. I need to be with Vasco right now."

Rasheed opened his mouth to argue but was stopped by the look in Blahom's eyes – regret, grief. He could deny her nothing in that moment. He nodded. "I will go with you."

The two ran back towards the murder scene.

Blahom scanned the beach, found Vasco, and ran towards him, oblivious to danger in her need to be with him. Her brother, blinded by tears, was clutching Zya's corpse. Blahom grabbed him from behind and embraced her brother, Enveloped in his own grief, he acted as if she wasn't there, completely stuck in his own agony, holding a bloody Zya and his unborn child within her. Blahom didn't care if Vasco acknowledged her or not. Tears ran down her cheek, aching to take away her brother's despair. Rasheed stood over them, scanning the area left to right, focused on their surroundings, nervous that other imposters might nearby. He saw Mother Hutra and waved her to them. Finally spotting them, Mother Hutra ran to her daughter and son. She knelt at her children's side, kissing both Blahom and Vasco on the forehead.

"We must move to safety. We don't know if there are more Delions," Mother Hutra whispered. Looking up, she saw ManCohalith's eyes on her. He and the Generals were on their horses, circling the area to create a safe perimeter. He nodded to his wife, and Mother Hutra knew that he would comfort their son while she tried to get Blahom inland.

Mother Hutra knew that her job was to return to the rest of the Lady Mothers and Sisters. They would need to be comforted after such a traumatic event.

"I can't leave him," Blahom said through gasps and tears. "The baby ..." Blahom trailed off and Mother Hutra's eyes widened and she took one last look at Zya. Now was not the time for this additional grief.

"Your father is the only one who can console your brother right now. Please, daughter, come with me," Mother Hutra said gently.

"I understand that you don't believe I am capable of being a warrior. But at least grant me the belief that I am capable of consoling my own brother. Mother." Blahom's eyes were fiery and for the first time she stood against the structure that she had so protected.

"Blahom, let's go," Rasheed said gently as he tried lifting her.

"She will come with me," Mother Hutra said. Blahom glared at her mother, furious. Before she could say a word, ManCohalith was with them.

"Blahom, you will in fact go with your mother and I will stay with Vasco and Zya. Rasheed, their safe arrival back is in your hands." Blahom gathered her anger as Mother Hutra gently took one hand and Rasheed the other, and they hastened away.

The Zaed culture was built on structure. The Generals and Lieutenants escorted the frightened and frenzied Zaeds inland, clearing the area swiftly and safely. Vasco and his father were left alone on the beach. Vasco had taken his shirt off and wrapped it over the gash in Zya's neck, trying to stop the bleeding. In his shock and disbelief, he rocked Zya in his arms, sobs shuddering through his body.

ManCohalith walked over to his son. "We cannot undo the past, only change the future," ManCohalith said, but his voice was filled with grief.

Vasco silently placed Zya onto the ground, closing her lifeless eyes. A last silent prayer and he stood and faced his father.

"I want to move out with my men tonight," Vasco said. His voice was calm and grave. "The Delions will regret ever attacking us on one of our sacred days."

ManCohalith nodded his head. "Level your head. Control your emotions. Go ... and show them no mercy."

There was no time to rest. It was time for action. Despite the tragedy, ManCohalith took moment to be grateful that Vasco had come to him earlier with his plan for attacking the Delions and taking their transportation device. Thanks to Vasco, the Zaeds had a plan on how to retaliate immediately.

* * *

Blahom sat on her bedroom floor, still in shock. Mother Hutra held her and tried to calm her daughter down. Rasheed had gotten them back safely and left them to be alone.

"It's my fault," Blahom murmured as a tear fell down her face. Mother Hutra shushed her.

"It's not your fault, Blahom," she said. "You wouldn't have known it was a Delion."

"I looked right at her ... I ..." Blahom trailed off as Mother Hutra continued to cradle her oldest daughter.

Blahom's mind was racing. *Why would they do that?* she thought. *They attacked an innocent woman and her unborn child. During our most sacred ceremony!* Dancing was of major significance to Blahom, and the fact that someone attacked during a CCDC ceremony, was a triple insult.

"Where is Katyana?" she asked, her mind flying to her sister.

"She is with Lady Mother Chi, somewhere in the palace," Mother Hutra said.

At that moment, Katyana's voice could be heard in the distance, and Blahom freed herself from her mother's embrace and ran from the room, desperate to know her sister was okay.

"Blahom!" Mother Hutra ran after her daughter.

Outside the Throne Room doors, Katyana and Vasco were in a heated exchange.

"This is no place for a trainee!" Vasco's voice boomed through the hallway. He had made his way back to the palace and Katyana had waited on her brother.

"But I am ready, WE are ready!" Katyana shouted back, "if you will give us a chance."

"This is a battle, not a training excursion, Katyana! I'm in no mood!" Vasco was clearly at the end of his tether. Blahom ran up and hugged Katyana fiercely.

"Are you alright?" Blahom's voice was filled with concern and worry, just like her mother.

Blahom

Katyana had a fire inside her. "I'm fine. Tell Vasco we should fight in this battle!"

Blahom was speechless for a moment. She had not wanted to fight, but after the blatant attack on her people, on Zya, she was done hiding. "Brother, we will fight with you." For the first time, Blahom was clear. She voiced what she wanted.

Vasco, adrenaline high, was not slowing down to talk or to listen to his sisters. He was in full General mode and called to his men. "Gather all the horses and armor from the campgrounds."

"Have you two lost your minds, you will not be fighting in this war!" Mother Hutra had run up and intercepted her daughters, her eyes fierce. "There is no reason you should be involved in this!"

"We are Warrior Goddesses!" Blahom shouted, clearly fed up. "We should be involved in everything regarding this war, the attack on our ceremony, and the murder of Zya! What I viewed as sacred has been tainted with Delion blood! I am SICK of people telling me how to live, and I want to decide my fate, my life as a WARRIOR GODDESS! I need you to stop being scared."

Everyone looked at Blahom, shocked that she would even say such a thing. Katyana was proud of her sister, though, and glad she had finally started to think like a warrior.

Vasco's stopped walking, his eyes narrowed. "You don't mean that."

"I do," Blahom said. Her heart was racing, and her chest was pounding. "Did you hear what the Delion said today? They're coming for Zaed women. They're coming for me, Kat, Mother – every woman we know and love. We've been training for months, and we're not about to be put on the sidelines."

"You spent one night in the forest and think you're a warrior?" Vasco said. "You haven't Transitioned yet!"

"Don't patronize me!" Blahom was inches away from Vasco's face. "It doesn't matter, Vasco, we will fight." Her green-gold eyes bore into his, unwilling to back down.

"Blahom, might I remind you that are a Goddess. You have no business ..."

"I am a Warrior Goddess!" Blahom interrupted. "Say it right! WE are Warrior Goddesses!" She gestured to Kat, standing behind her and ready to attack if necessary.

"Stop this! All of you!" Mother Hutra couldn't bear to see her children fight, not after recent events.

"You're upsetting Mother!" Vasco yelled at Blahom. "Won't you leave now and take Mother and Kat with you! Go check on the welfare of the other dancers." He turned his back and walked away, overcome with emotion. "I am going to meet Father. I suggest you two go back to your room. The love of my life and mother to my unborn child was just killed in front of our entire kingdom. Today is not a good day to challenge me."

Vasco turned his back and started to bark orders at his comrades.

"Zya was our friend first and a Lady Sister, Vasco, and if I want to fight for my Lady Sister and friend then you should put your pride aside and honor my request!" Blahom shouted. Everyone was silent. With his back turned, Vasco closed his eyes, and a tear fell down his face. His heart was crumbling, fully overcome with pain and rage.

A deep, uncomfortable silence followed, and Vasco took a deep breath. He didn't want to argue with his sister. He didn't want his mother to be hearing all this. He didn't want to have lost his unborn child. He didn't want Zya dead. He didn't want any of this.

"My sisters will not fight. Someone find Rasheed and tell him he will stand next to me and fight in Blahom's stead. We leave soon."

With that, Vasco walked into the Battle Strategy Hall and the doors closed, leaving Blahom, Katyana, and Mother Hutra alone where they stood.

* * *

The wind howled as Vasco marched with his men up the side of the mountain. Rage and anguish pumped through his veins as he pushed himself to move faster. Rasheed struggled to keep up, even armed with lighter weapons than the other warriors. Vasco knew Rasheed was inexperienced and he needed to keep Rasheed as far away from the danger as possible, under the circumstances.

After such an attack on a sacred day, Lorraine missing, Daniella still nowhere to be found, Lieutenant Kov and Lady Sister Kalis dead, Vasco's fellow warriors rallied behind him. Rumors about his link to Lorraine's disappearance declined, while confusion and fear was accelerating. This attack was more important than the sister of one of their rulers. The Delions would pay for their transgressions during the CCDC ceremony.

As Vasco continued his march, he couldn't shake what remained in his mind. Zya's lifeless eyes stared back at him. As the wind rustled through the trees on the mountain, he was haunted by the sound of her laughter. Every so often he could swear that he could hear the echoes of a baby crying. A baby that would never be born.

Blinking back tears, he pushed away memories, and tried to keep his mind focused on the present. "Kill them before they kill us," he murmured to himself. It was something that General Lakin had told him when he was younger. Those six words were so simple, but it was what Vasco needed to hear before a battle. Once the fighting began, killing them before they killed you was the only goal.

Glancing behind him, Vasco saw the small group of one hundred warriors following as they made their arduous trek up the side of the mountain. This group was small, but they were known for being strong and powerful, some of the best warriors, hand selected by ManCohalith himself.

"Keep up the pace!" Vasco exclaimed, and picked up his own stride. His warriors followed their general dutifully.

Vasco and his men had only one day to reach the top of the mountain where they would rest and regain the strength they needed. Even in the best conditions, it typically was a two-day hike. Sunrise was their goal, and they had no time to squander if they wanted to be fully rested in order to attack.

Chills ran down Vasco's spine and he tried not to let the frigid temperatures hinder his movements. The cold winds were relentless, and the snow was deep enough making each step a struggle. Not only were they contending with the elements, but also the thinning air. Panting as he climbed, Vasco felt his lungs ache with each breath.

Vasco tried to remind himself of the countless days and nights he spent training with General Murn through mountainous terrain and thinning air. He had trained and prepared for a moment like this. If he and his men were able to make it up this mountain, they could turn the tide of the war in an instant. Zya and his unborn child would not have died in vain.

Two of his warriors lost consciousness from the lack of oxygen and others carried them. No Zaed was to be left behind. They needed every warrior for the upcoming attack.

"We will rest once we reach the top of the mountain," Vasco said sternly, trying to encourage his warriors to move faster and inspiring hope of rest as their lungs and muscles ached.

Vasco knew that the Delions would never suspect a Zaed attack on the secret base. The mountains were treacherous and the Delions would think themselves safe. Vasco's mind kept going over the plan, fighting down his anxiety. It would be a massacre or a major victory. There was no third option and no room for error.

Hours passed as the group trekked up the mountain and, as night began to fall, the only light was from the moon. Vasco's heart pounded in his chest as he pushed himself to continue marching, inspiring his men to follow suit.

"We have to keep going!" Vasco talked more to himself than to his warriors.

At last, the group reached the top of the mountain. Walking onto the plateau, Vasco's eyes watered, and his pace slowed. Relief flooded over the men, but they knew the hardest part was yet to come.

Composing himself, Vasco looked at the sky. There were only about three hours until the planned sunrise attack. Vasco, ManCo-halith, and the Generals had determined to time their attacks on both

Delion campsites to coincide with sunrise, knowing that timing was the most crucial part to victory.

Haggard and weary faces stared at their leader. None of them were ready for a battle after the climb, Vasco included. Knowing that this would be a suicide mission if his warriors did not rest, Vasco grappled with how much time they needed to recoup. He wondered how his father would lead in this situation.

"We will rest here no more than two hours," Vasco said, and his warriors cheered at the prospect. "After we rest, we will prepare for battle. We will go down the mountain and destroy the guards and any other Delion unfortunate enough to stand in our path. I know this mission has been a trying one, but this attack and successfully seizing their device will be vital in winning the war. We will be victorious!"

Rasheed was out of breath, yet despite their fatigue, he and the other warriors cheered again. They had faith that their General would lead them to victory.

General Murn knew that the murder of a Lady Sister during a Dietrickt dance was an invitation to battle. To be attacked so intimately on such a sacred day reverberated painfully throughout every Zaed community. Furthermore, it fueled the warriors for battle. The CCDC ceremony was meant to heal the Zaeds and now all that tension was unresolved and would be harnessed into a ruthless, hate-driven battle. This battle wouldn't just be for Zaed victory: it would be fought for revenge.

On his horse, General Murn led his forces onward in the middle of the night, the moon obscured now by thick dark clouds. Rage burned in the pit of his stomach. He would bleed dry every Delion in his path, forcing them to regret their actions.

Attacking the Delions' main base placed the Zaeds at a severe disadvantage. The upcoming battle would be brutal and casualties on the Zaed side would be immense. Because of this, the strategy was to be swift. General Murn was anticipating a signal from Vasco to retreat as soon as possible. Every second that passed meant the loss of Zaed life. Their army was skilled but far too small to last long against the much-larger Delion forces. If this battle lasted for anywhere close to an hour, they would be wiped out.

The Zaeds marched in rigid formation, while the Generals and ManCohalith rode on horses in the first line, prepared for a full-frontal assault. To Murn's left was his brother, General Brakkus. To his immediate right was ManCohalith, and beyond him, General Velio and General Lakin. The five of them were a deadly force in their own right and Murn prayed that their men last until Vasco gave them the signal to retreat.

"You look stiff, big brother," General Brakkus' usual loud voice coming out as a low grumble. General Murn knew the nickname only came out when he had let his emotions bleed onto his face. General Brakkus only called General Murn big brother when Murn was lusting to spill Delion blood or when he showed obvious concern.

"Of course, I'm stiff," General Murn grunted, keeping his horse trotting at an even pace. "Aren't you?"

"Stiff? No," General Brakkus chuckled as he shook his head. "I'm ready for a fight. My arms are limber and prepared to swing my swords through Delion flesh as if I was cutting through a slice of bread. You, on the other hand, look like a marble statue." General Brakkus gave his older brother a hard, cautious look. "I don't want to watch you shatter."

"You won't," General Murn said. "I'm only worrying about Vasco giving the signal in a timely matter."

"You focus too much on things you can't control," said General Murn after taking a large swig of wine from his flask. He wasn't supposed to have it on the battlefield, but nobody had the heart – or the guts – to tell him.

"There is no controlling what Vasco does now," General Brakkus continued. "The only thing you can control right now are your own movements. We are going in to fight first and run away second. One thing at a time."

General Murn saw the value in his younger brother's words, but he'd never admit that out loud. "You're too simple minded," General Murn said with a ghost of a smirk on his lips. Brakkus knew his brother well and chuckled.

"And you overcomplicate things," Brakkus said, then added, "I'm happy to see that you're not as stiff now."

General Murn didn't respond, focusing ahead. Sometimes all it took was his younger brother to remind him what was important.

From their position high on the mountain, Vasco could see the Delion base faintly in the distance.

An hour had passed and, sitting in front of a small fire, Vasco kept a watchful eye on his sleeping warriors. Rasheed was next to him, snoring. Sleep was starting to tug at Vasco, but he fought it, hoping adrenaline would get him through the upcoming hours. *I'll sleep when the mission is done. No sooner, no later.*

The wind whistled against the trees and, in the quiet of the mountaintop, Vasco's mind drifted. The wind continued to howl, and Vasco could swear he could hear Zya's voice. Shaking his head, he tried to focus on something physical and real. Vasco stared down at his hands, watching as his fingertips twitched.

Again he thought he heard the sweet song of Zya's voice, and the shrill cries of a baby taking its first breaths in the world.

Vasco gave himself a shake and started doing multiplication tables in his mind. *I must keep my brain busy or it taunt me with the ghosts of those I loved.*

A chill ran down Vasco's spine, and he rubbed his hands together over the fire, blinked his eyes, and stared down at the fire. Zya's corpse stared back up at him. Gasping, Vasco jumped to his feet, eyes transfixed on Zya's dead body in the flames.

"Lieutenant Vasco? General Vasco!" Rasheed grabbed Vasco's arm, jerking him from his trance.

Looking over at the Rasheed and then back to the crackling fire, Vasco felt his blood run cold. It was just a fire, eating away at old twigs and logs. There was no Zya.

"General ..."

"I'm fine." Vasco said curtly. "I'm adjusting to the thin air."

Rasheed didn't press him and sat back down. "You are like a brother to me. I am glad you have me here. Even if it's only for moral support."

Vasco took in a deep breath, trying to calm his erratic heart, going over the plan yet again. Any hope of sleep was gone.

The sky began to tinge a deep purple, signaling that hour before sunrise. The Zaeds woke, rested and restored, ready to seize the Delion's secret base.

Anchoring long thick ropes, the warriors prepared themselves for the sprint down the side of the mountain.

Vasco searched in vain for words to spur his warriors on to victory. Raising his sword, Vasco shouted, "For the Zaeds!"

"For the Zaeds!" His warriors repeated and they sprinted down the side of the mountain like a deadly avalanche.

Chapter Fifteen

The sun was starting to ascend above the horizon and the Zaed army marched towards the Delions' main base, fully prepared for battle. At first, the Delions appeared like ants on the landscapes, but as the Zaeds moved closer, the ants became a massive fleet of Delions, making the Zaed army appear like a small scouting group. Nevertheless, the Zaeds had their divine gifts and were brutally trained warriors with tall unique physiques and wide backs, their bones strengthened from repeated strikes incurred in training. They were built solidly. They too were prepared for pitched battle.

The gap between the two armies began to close.

The Delion army tightened their formation and the Zaeds continued to march, bracing themselves for the Delions' first move.

With a fierce gesture, the Delion General commanded his men to charge. His forces did not hesitate, sprinting at full speed towards the small Zaed army.

ManCohalith saw the glorious sunshine and felt the power surge in him. Deep breath in and breathing out slowly, he knew it was time. Looking up to the sky, ManCohalith asked for protection.

Then, with a strong and steady hand, ManCohalith he gave a signal to halt his fearless kingdom defenders in their tracks. The Zaed army stood still while the Delions continued with their charge.

The Zaeds felt adrenaline pumping through their veins as the Delions stampeded towards them, closer and closer. They felt the ground shaking from the thundering of the enemies' charge.

ManCohalith patiently waited until he could see the whites of the Delions' eyes. With a flick of his fingers, he commanded the wind to pick up speed, creating a powerful tornado. He summoned the tunnel to rampage across the front line of the Delions. With a sweeping gesture of his arm, the vortex sucked the Delions into the deadly wind, and flung their bodies into the air miles away.

ManCohalith was in complete control, and hundreds of Delions died on impact when they hit the ground. The tornado continued to decimate the Delion army, and those behind the first line scattered in fear at this sign of ManCohalith's control over nature.

ManCohalith had cleared the path.

"That power is truly something to be behold," General Brakkus whispered to himself, having seen ManCohalith in action often, but still awed each time.

The Zaeds charged forward through the casualties of the first formation of Delions on the ground. The next battalion of Delions was the second of the three closer to the main base. This was the critical area where the Zaeds would fight until they needed to retreat. To minimize their casualties, the Zaeds would press no further.

General Velio followed ManCohalith's wind attack, unleashing his gift. The earth trembled and the ground slid beneath the next line of Delions' feet, causing them to fall. This was the opportune moment.

ManCohalith gave the order to attack, and the Zaed warriors ran with a vengeance.

"This is where the fun begins," General Brakkus said with a smirk to General Murn.

"Fun and foolish are two different things," General Murn said to his brother.

"Don't be so stiff, big brother," General Brakkus laughed, then went barreling into battle. General Murn, though never a fan of his brother's method of attacking, took in a breath, and followed, charging into battle.

General Murn immediately beheaded a fallen Delion with the blade of his sword while trampling over enemy warriors. A young Delion on the ground managed to grab his sword and sliced the leg of the General's horse, causing the creature to fall with General Murn still on top. The seasoned general tumbled off, rolled back to his feet, and continued his assault as untamable rage surged through his veins.

*　*　*

The rising sun illuminated the Delion's secret base. Vasco and his warriors would breach the site and seize any technology within. Rasheed's job was to find and store any files when they were successfully inside. If they found Daniella or Lorraine, then Rasheed would tend to the women and make sure they traveled back to safety.

As they ran down the mountain and approached the base, Vasco fixed his eyes on one of the guards along the perimeter. As the guard made his rounds, he paused, noticing movement heading towards him, but unable to tell what it was. Adjusting his eyes, the guard stared in shock and his face paled in horror at the force of the Zaeds stampeding his way.

"Zaeds are here, go ..." The guard attempting to call out was unable to finish his warning.

Wasting no time, his hands flowing in a circular motion, Vasco collected moisture from the air. He flung the water forward, manipulating it to fill the Delion's nose and mouth. The Delion guard fell to his knees and choked on the rest of his words. Vasco ran up and slit the Delion's throat.

Alerted by the melee, a handful of Delion guards ran to form a barricade between the Zaeds and the base, but they stood no chance. Slashing their swords brutally, the Zaed warriors eliminated the guards in minutes. Rasheed watched Vasco drive a dagger across a Delion's throat, and his mind flew to Blahom, hoping that she was safely tucked away in the castle. The Zaeds moved on, searching for the room that housed the Delion's advanced technology. Rasheed followed closely, shocked at the quick massacre. His stomach roiled and he struggled to fathom someone's husband, son, brother, friend dead in the blink of an eye.

The murder of one of their own on such a sacred day fed the Zaeds' vengeance as they sprinted inside the secret compound, kicking down doors and searching room after room for Daniella, Lorraine, and the teleportation device while disemboweling any Delion in their path.

The next door revealed a room full of Delions slightly older than Rasheed. One jumped off a table where it appeared he had been having sex with an unconscious naked woman. There was row of unconscious pregnant women laying on heavy metal beds. A few unarmed scientists cowered in the corner with their hands raised in surrender.

"Check for Daniella and Lorraine," Vasco ordered Rasheed.

Looking at the women one by one, Rasheed was perplexed. "I'm not sure any of these women are Zaeds. I'm not sure any of these women are alive."

"Sure, they are alive. They are pregnant." *Pregnant.* The word stuck in his throat. *My Zya.* His eyes twitched and Vasco strove to find his way back to the moment. Looking down at the Delions he was holding at bay, he demanded "What are you all doing here? Who are these women?"

The scientists were shaking like children. They were not fighters; not even trained warriors. "Answer me now!" Vasco yelled.

A lone Delion stood up. "They are not what you think. We made them." He dropped his head.

"What do you mean you made them?" Vasco strode up to the young Delion.

"Our technology has created life." The Delion was holding his composure much better than his peers.

"Why? Tell me why?" Looking at the unconscious women and each of their plump pregnant bellies, Vasco thought about his Zya's bloody corpse. His mind flashed to holding her in his arms and kissing her belly. "Who has done this to them?" Vasco saw the naked Delion in the corner and turned on him. "I'm going to ask once more. Who is responsible for this?"

Shaking in fear, the naked Delion spoke, "We all have ... We all have given the dead life."

"Where are our Zaed women? Daniella. Where is she?"

"I do not know anyone."

"I am sure you all know that she is the daughter of one of our most respected Generals. Where is she?" Vasco was losing patience in this room of pregnant lab women.

"There are no women here," the Delion said, his voice cracked and shaken. "That is not our responsibility. We create here. The more experienced scientists have the real women."

Vasco herded the Delions into a corner, onto their knees. "Where are the women?

"They are down the hall," one answered, hoping his forthrightness might save their lives.

Vasco smiled grimly. Breaking the young Delions was easier than anticipated and he knew he was getting close. "Where is the teleportation device? It is also down the hall? I will ask once more – where are the Zaed women, Daniella and Lorraine?"

"I don't know."

Vasco pulled his out his sword and slit his throat.

Looking at another Delion, he asked, "Do you know?"

The boy's eyes widened. "The General's daughter was down the hall for some time. They may have moved her through the device. I do not know about the others."

Looking at his men, Vasco said, "Daniella and Lorraine are not here. Let's move on to the next room." He skewering his sword through the Delions' skulls one by one, and showed no mercy to their pleas. He wiped splattered blood from his face and left the room.

She is gone, Daniella is lost, Rasheed thought to himself. He followed behind his leader. Shaken.

Adrenaline still pumped through Vasco's veins. He did not care how many Delions he needed to slaughter to find what they were here for. Perhaps Daniella and his aunt had been sent away; perhaps they would not be found today. At minimum, he was determined to recover the device – the device that wouldn't bring Zya and his unborn child back, but might help his people and to atone somewhat for their death.

He turned to see Rasheed in front of him. "Have you no mercy? Those boys were younger than me. Perhaps if you had not murdered them, we would be able to retrieve our loved ones."

Vasco saw the shock on his cousin's face, but there was no time for softness now. "And have you no discernment? Those 'boys' are the brains behind the technology calculated to bring about our demise and the demise of our women. Daniella is gone. We may be lucky to find Lorraine – if finding her does equal luck." He continued his search.

Room after room and still no sign of living women or the device. Vasco and his Zaed warriors continued, annihilating any Delion they came across. The Zaeds left each room with more blood staining their swords and clothes, but the device kept eluding them. They knew they were fighting time; knew that their army was fighting at the main base. The longer it took to find the Daniella and Lorraine or the device, the more of their fellow warriors would die.

* * *

The air smelt like blood. The whirling wind blended with the screams of dying Delion scientists, heard even inside the secret room housing the coveted technology. The heavy footsteps of the Zaed warriors thundered throughout the hallways, coming closer, and the

Delion's secret lab

Chief scientist knew that his remaining researchers didn't stand a chance against the revenge-driven warriors. The only option was to escape into the device themselves.

The young researchers were terrified. They used coats to muffle their cries, trying to hold back heavy sobs, and tears streaked their faces. The youngest of the group hid under a desk, rocking back and forth and muttering words of prayer. The Chief scientist gritted his teeth.

"Come now, my son!" An older scientist, panic in his voice, grabbed the hands of one of the crying youths. Before the Chief could do anything, the two ran to the transportation device, saving themselves. The elder of the two pushed the button to activate the device and disappeared into its humming center, sending them to Earth in an instant.

The footsteps of the Zaeds came closer and closer.

Seeing the way to escape death, the other researchers and scientists started to rush towards the machine, anxiety and fear putting all other thoughts out of their heads.

"Stop!" shouted the Chief. "The Zaeds can't get their hands on our work. They will use the technology against us, and our entire civilization will be destroyed. We must leave them nothing." He could feel his own fear, but knew he needed to remain strong as the leader. "We are Delions! Do you want the guilt of your sisters, mothers, and daughters being murdered because of your cowardice?"

Disbelief permeated the room. The scientist had poured their lives into innovation and creation. Now they were being asked to tear down all they had built.

"We destroy everything, then we escape through the device," the Chief said.

Realizing the severity of the situation, the older scientists sprang into action; running through the room, tearing apart confidential paperwork, and devouring scraps of information. The room was filled with the sound of ripping paper, smashing glass, and the gags of Delions trying to eat their work lest it be found by the Zaeds.

The Chief rummaged through the cabinets of his desk erratically, searching for a specific file. His hands shook as he grasped the manilla envelope he needed – *OPERATION IMPOSTOR; Case File 001 Kov.*

File in hand, the Chief sprinted towards the machine, ready to usher the rest of his team through. The large transportation device that they had worked so hard on was to be their salvation. It stood there, humming, gleaming like a treasure under the fluorescent lights.

The Chief felt his stomach drop as a wave of nausea hit him. Once they had made their escape, the device would be a gift for the Zaeds, and the demise of their families and all they loved would be inevitable.

The device needed to be destroyed.

"Xandar, come here," the Chief commanded, pointing to the youngest researcher, already following close behind. Xander was scared but ready to obey his leader. The Chief shoved his files into Xander's hand then pushed him into the machine.

"You go through first. Tell the leaders on planet Earth that we have been compromised. We're right behind you."

Vasco and his Zaed forces could be heard pounding on the door. It had been barricaded, but they were moments away from pushing through.

Wide eyed, the youth ran through the device to safety.

With the sounds of death on the other side of the door, once again the scientists stampeded towards the machine. The Chief stood at the opening with his arms wide to hold them back.

"Everyone! We can't let the Zaeds get their hands on the device. It must be destroyed!"

"But without it we'll die!" one screamed trying to shove his way past the Chief.

"Yes!" The Chief had tears on his face. "We die but we save our families and the Delion people!"

"I'll worry about that later on Earth!" the other scientist rebelled, "now get out of my way!" and he shoved his way through, and ran into the machine.

The Chief had no time to debate with anyone else and ran to grab a crowbar to begin to dismantle the device.

"He's right! We must save our families!" another scientist exclaimed, moving swiftly to grab a hammer.

"Get the youths through! Everyone else grab a tool!" shouted one of the older scientists.

In seconds, the young researchers were corralled together. "Your young minds are our future," the Chief said, looking at the Delions that stood before him. "Go!" And then they were gone.

The Chief and remaining Delion scientists knew what had to be done. As soon as the young researchers were through, the Chief and the others started tearing at the metal, attempting to get at the wiring that powered the device.

Just then, the door to the large laboratory was battered down, and the huge room was flooded with Zaed warriors.

The Delions had succeeded broken in nearly obliterating their knowledge. What greeted the invading Zaeds was the sight of overturned furniture, broken technology boards, and shreds of paper on the floor. At the furthest end of the lab, the Delions were still attacking their massive machine. The blue energy doorway of the device flickered and crackled, slowly changing to a deeper purple. The scientists took their final moments trying to get to the wiring, even as the Zaed army advanced on them. The sound of metal clanging onto the ground rang through the air as the Delions frantically jerked on paneling and pulled hunks of wiring out of the machine.

The machine went black.

Relief and sadness swept over the Delion scientists. Their job was complete, and they turned to see the Zaeds only feet away, swords in hand. As one, the scientists fell to their knees and glanced at one another one last time. Grabbing the sharp paneling from the ground, without taking a breath, the Chief slit his own throat and, with the assured knowledge of their deaths, the rest of the Delions followed suit.

Vasco, Rasheed, and the other Zaeds froze in their steps, looking at the corpses bleeding on the floor. Their eyes scanned the room for any sign of living women. There was no one, and no other rooms to search. Before them was the tower transportation device. The device that was said to be what would turn the tide of the war.

For a second, time stood still. Surrounded by blood, shattered glass, corpses, and torn papers, the Zaeds let out a collective breath, too exhausted to cheer, unsettled by the chaos. Memories flooded back for Rasheed and the loss of his birth father who had also died in battle when he was an infant was brought home to him again. Rasheed knew that this was a victory. He took deep, heavy breaths, satisfied that this was possibly the end.

Vasco wanted to bask in their glow of victory, but one job still needed to be done. He turned to Rasheed commanding, "Your job is done, go quickly and return home with the files. The path is clear." Without hesitation, Rasheed quickly organize the materials as best as possible and left.

He sprinted from the building and headed for the stream.

Inhaling and filling his battle-wearied body with air, he held that breath and calmed his mind, focusing on nothing but the rushing water. He could feel it flowing the same as he felt the blood in his veins. Moving his hands in a fluid motion around his chest, he conjured the water to rise into the air. Vasco's feet were planted firmly on the ground as he gritted his teeth, trying not to let the weight of the water flood his mind. The water rippled and pulled and lifted from the stream, obeying the command of Vasco's will. Finally, blowing out the air, Vasco focused his energy and with the raising of his hands, threw the water into the sky.

ManCohalith saw the massive geyser that his son's divine gift had created, knowing that meant Vasco was successful. No longer needing to push any further towards the Delion's main base camp, the Zaed forces could withdraw now that the secret base camp had been seized.

"Retreat!" ManCohalith exclaimed through the screams of fighting and the Zaeds were quick to obey.

General Murn started to fall back when his eyes locked onto his brother, still fighting as if he hadn't heard the call to retreat.

"Brakkus ..." he started – and the world slowed down. In an instant, General Murn was watching everything in slow motion. A Delion had taken Brakkus by surprise and succeeded where all others had failed. Blood sputtered and poured out of Brakkus' neck as he hit the ground, his haggard breathing garbled by his own blood seeping out of his sliced throat.

Charging at the Delion responsible, General Murn focused all of his rage on plunging his sword through the creature's skull. The Delion was dead instantly, and General Murn knelt next to his baby brother on the ground.

General Murn looked into Brakkus' open eyes. *He's laughing at me. I'm sick of his pranks.* For a moment, he had lost reality. Memories flooded back and he remembered how his baby brother would always love to pull ridiculous pranks. Mother Hutra was never amused by them, and Murn would always chide Brakkus for being so lighthearted, something Murn secretly admired him for. He shed a tear, the past overwhelming him. *Memories.* Of kneeling on the bed, powerless to help as his wife died. Of hoping to hear his newborn cry as the doula tried to save him. There was no cry. Both were gone. General Murn had stayed in that room for two days, his dead newborn in his hand and his wife's body on the bed. Brakkus was the only one he allowed to enter the room; Brakkus who finally grabbed the dead baby and the hand of his brother and led him out. How could this be happening now? General Murn wanted to weep and wait for General Brakkus to get back up, as he always had.

Then, in a split second, sense came crashing in like a splash of cold water. General Murn knew not to be swallowed by disbelief during any tragedy. He knew that his brother was dead. Death was the only truth of life and, for warriors, it often came faster than for others. This was a reality ingrained in them and it grounded him now.

General Murn knew that he needed to go, and there was no reality in which he would leave his brother's corpse on a battlefield. Wrapping his arms around Brakkus, General Murn swiftly lifted the slain general up, careful not to open the wound in his neck. Hauling Brakkus' corpse onto his back, General Murn sprinted after his fellow Zaeds in retreat to their Zaed land.

Chapter Sixteen

The Zaeds were hit by simultaneous waves of joy and grief when ManCohalith and what remained of his warriors returned. They marched through the streets, and musicians played along the way. Trumpets vied with the sound of Zaeds cheering in celebration of the victory. In other pockets of the city, somber melodies underscored the weeping at the memory of missing family members. While their deaths were honorable, it was still a blow to the Zaeds to lose any warriors, especially a General as powerful as Brakkus.

In contrast, there were murmurs of happiness and pride that Vasco had succeeded in his mission to attack the secret base, and rumors about Vasco and Lorraine were largely stilled.

After every battle, Blahom, Katyana, and Mother Hutra would gather in the Throne Room to see ManCohalith and Vasco and to be told the news about the deaths on from the battlefield. They would wear black today, a sign of mourning. Even if their army had been victorious, they were sensitive to the loss of precious life.

Today there was no Blahom.

ManCohalith entered the Throne Room, flanked by General

Murn, Velio, and Lakin. He stopped – "Where is my daughter?" – looked anxiously for Blahom.

"She has been gone since last night. We are not able to find her," Kat spoke up quickly, worried about her sister.

ManCohalith paled. "What do you mean?"

Mother Hutra quickly intervened. "After your troops left, Blahom left to retrieve Trinity from her lessons and did not return.

"Katyana, dear, you did not know this yet, but I am happy to tell you both now. Shortly after the arrival of our warriors marching back home, our beloved Blahom returned to me. Shaken but marching bravely, not with her ... her sister in her arms. It was another child." Mother Hutra took a deep breath. She had made peace with Lorraine, and knew that ManCohalith's romantic entanglements were the price she paid as his wife. But she had not easily extended the term *sister* to Trinity. "Blahom saved a young Zaed girl from being taken. She will tell us more in due time. She is safe; the young girl is safe; Trinity is safe. She is getting cleaned up and will arrive here shortly."

Katyana's relief at the sight of her father and the knowledge that he survived the battle and that her sister was safe brought stinging tears to her eyes. She blinked them back. Both she and Mother Hutra had already heard of the victory of Vasco's leadership, and they were ready to lay eyes on their family.

ManCohalith strode quickly towards Mother Hutra, gave her a strong hug and a kiss, and turned to embrace his daughter. Holding back tears, Katyana hugged him back.

Blahom walked through the door, Trinity and the Lady Mothers in tow. She appeared dressed in a makeshift garment, meant to represent both her warrior and Goddess roles. Lady Mother Clara locked eyes with Mother Hutra, tilted her head, and shrugged her shoulders as if to say the wardrobe change had been out of her control.

"Father!" Blahom ran to ManCohalith and her sister and gave embraced each in turn. "I love you, sister." Her emotions were obvious. Something had fueled a new energy in her.

Blahom

Ignoring Blahom's new wardrobe, ManCohalith said, "Tell us what has happened my daughter. Your mother says that you are a hero."

"Father, I am no hero. The heroes are you and brother and the Generals who faced death to protect us and the Zaed people. The truth is I disobeyed the mandates, and I wandered off alone. For that I am sorry. Outside the city, I heard a child weeping. I saw three men, though their faces were covered by their hoods. They had captured a child and placed her in a cage near a tree. She was asking them to please let her go home to her mother, and I recognized her voice. It was the same young girl who came up to me during our Dietrickt dance ceremony the night Mother's dream was revealed. I don't know where she had been, or how she was captured, but I could not leave her there. I camped out all night praying and asking for Alpha God to tell me what to do. My heart was pounding. I could not quiet myself. I continued in prayer, trying to recall the lessons I had learned in training. I didn't know if there were more men, and I was afraid. I stayed awake and watched closely. No one else came, and, by morning, it was still just the three men.

"Father, I had my small knife given to us during training. I pulled it out as we have been taught, and I stood up and faced them. I summoned my courage, as you have shown me, and yelled out, 'Your Zaed Warrior Goddess comes to you through the power of Alpha God. Show your face and release the girl.' I could hardly believe how strong my voice sounded in the cold air, with the sun rising behind me.

"They took off fleeing. I ran up and cut the lock and got the girl and we left quickly, before the men could recover themselves and return. Her name is Kamila Welch. She is shaken, but she is safe, Father. I'm sorry I did not see the faces of those who committed the crime. They ran off, their hoods still on." Blahom's heart rapidly raced as she panted heavily reliving the story. "Father, I did hear them speak. They spoke like us. Perhaps they were Zaeds?"

"Or perhaps an imposter, or three new imposters! This taking of our women is out of control!" ManCohalith blurted out, furious. "I will not take this moment from you, Daughter. You have done a courageous thing. You are brave. You are becoming exactly who you were destined to be – a Warrior Goddess." He took a deep breath and Blahom's relief vanished. Something else was wrong.

"Today we mourn a great loss ..." he continued, and only now did Mother Hutra take a second look at the room.

"General Brakkus was slain in battle." ManCohalith looked at his wife, his powerful voice full of remorse.

"I buried him," General Murn said quietly. "His body wasn't ... he needed to be buried quickly. I picked a spot beneath one of his favorite trees."

The room was silent. Without warning, Mother Hutra fled to her room, sobbing in grief for the loss of her younger brother. The Generals took their cue to depart; Lakin and Velio to drink away the horror of battle and find their families. General Murn slowly returned home alone, knowing Mother Hutra could not share her grief with him.

Blahom looked at her father and frowned. If it weren't for his clothes, she would have mistaken him for a common Zaed. It had not struck her before how weary he appeared after battle, that even someone as powerful as he could look so fragile.

"Blahom, I need you to talk to your Aunt Melissa and Rasheed. I would myself, but I need to comfort your mother." ManCohalith clutched Blahom's hands, gently looking her in the eye. "I know your heart has a special place for Rasheed and this is not an easy task, my daughter, but I can trust you with this."

It was customary for a warrior's next of kin to officially deliver news of the death of a warrior in battle to the family. Blahom was honored with the assignment.

"Of course, Father, and I will be careful and stay on the cobbled road and I will go alone," Blahom said solemnly. Lady Mother Clara looked to ManCohalith to intervene, but he did not speak. Blahom turned on her heel and left the Throne Room.

"I'm coming with you," Katyana followed close behind, her countenance heavy with grief, shaken by the death of General Brakkus, but ready to be by her sister's side, as much to supply support as to not be alone while mourning her uncle.

"No. There will be a lot more pain and tears. Aren't you tired of seeing that? Just ..." Blahom shook her head, frustrated, angry, and looking for the right words. "Just stay here. Where it's safe. There's a point where you don't want someone crowding your space all the time."

Kat was taken back by Blahom's harsh words, and deeply hurt. Much had happened that she felt she was not privy to. Had she crowded Blahom's space? Now, she wasn't sure.

Blahom turned to Lady Mother Clara. "I told my father I will go alone. I want to do this alone."

"Blahom, I am not to leave you. It's much ..." Lady Mother Clara began but Katyana interrupted.

"Alright sister, if that's what you want." Katyana struggled with each word, wanting to give her sister space, but equally did not want Lady Mother Clara to go if she could not.

"It is what I want. I don't need my shadow to accompany me for this," Blahom's words were sharp, and Lady Mother Clara heard the depth of emotions her young charge struggled to contain. Blahom knew she was wrong; her eyes begged Clara to understand. "I'll be fine. This is something that I need to do on my own."

Lady Mother Clara gave Blahom space and grace. She gently kissed Blahom on the forehead but didn't say another word. Kat stalked off.

Alone at last, Blahom threw on a cloak and left the castle, breathing to clear her head. She debated taking a horse, but it was not far and the horse would make her conspicuous at a time when she yearned to feel her feet on the road and to soak in the few moments of solitude.

She walked down the cobbled streets, mind and heart in a swirl. Even with Lady Mother Clara and Katyana gone, she still felt surrounded. Several Zaeds noticed her and gave her a reverent bow. She acknowledged them with a nod, but wished that her cloak better hid who she was.

Blahom's mind drifted with each step. In the eyes of most, she was a perfect Goddess who upheld every duty given to her, meant to be a shining example to all female Zaeds. She was a Goddess among a people in a never-ending war. A war in which, if not soon ended, she was determined to fight. She knew she was not ready, but the expectation that she put an end to the war felt destined. She thought of her role as warrior; her role as Goddess. She thought of Kamila and what she had been through and how to teach the child to dance. Guilt welled up as she thought how she had not retrieved her own sister Trinity for her dance rehearsal as she had been supposed to do – her mother had left that detail out of the story. It was all so much pressure and Blahom felt like she was going to collapse under the microscope.

Blahom's destination appeared in front of her and she steadied her thoughts. The house was quiet, and Blahom wondered if Rasheed and her aunt were even home. Knocking quickly on the door, she stood stiffly on the doorstep waiting to deliver the dreadful news.

She felt herself freeze. She had been so consumed in her own thoughts that she hadn't figured out what she was going to say. Her mind panicked as she tried to remember what ManCohalith said to families in mourning. *And Rasheed was on the battlefield with Vasco.* Thoughts swirling now. *Is Rasheed, okay? Was he injured? Am I to not honor his victory while delivering the news about General Brakkus?*

Rasheed swung the door open and he striking eyes looked down at Blahom. His kind face, still dirty from battle, was what Blahom had wanted to see, but now, she hesitated to look him in the eye.

"Blahom, please come in," he said solemnly. Usually, Rasheed had a smile on his face, but he was almost unrecognizable, any remnants of laugh lines gone from his face, dark circles underneath his eyes, and cuts on his cheeks. Standing before Blahom wasn't the jovial Rasheed she was used to, but instead, a weary warrior back from the battlefield, waiting to hear whether or not his father had survived.

Blahom entered and saw her aunt sitting in a chair, staring blankly at the wall. Rasheed softly cleared his throat, and the woman locked eyes with Blahom.

"The rumors about my husband are true then," she said somberly, know what a visit from the Goddess meant. Before Blahom could find any words of comfort, Melissa burst into tears, her shoulder shuddering as she wept.

"He always loved us being together," she said, through her tears. "He talked and talked about family gatherings. He was excited for everyone to see each other. He'd hug his brother Murn tightly and he'd make his sister laugh until she snorted. ManCohalith was always so stern but even he couldn't help but laugh at Brakkus' jokes. He wanted us all to be happy and for what? He's just ... I can't believe ..."

"Mother, let me guide you to your room. I'll come back and see you out Blahom," Rasheed said gently, taking his mother's arm and leading her away.

Blahom watched as the two disappeared deeper into their home. She stood awkwardly in the main room and wondered if she could slip away without having to look Rasheed in the eye again, but then scolded herself. It would be rude to leave after Rasheed said that he would return and now was no time to be a coward.

Rasheed's heavy footsteps preceded him into the room. His tunic was stained by his mother's tears, but he gave Blahom a weary smile.

"Thank you, my Goddess, for delivering the news of my warrior father to us," Rasheed said in earnest. He rarely called her "goddess" and when he did, it was an attempt not to let his emotions show. "As you know, my birth father was killed when I was an infant and several years later my mother remarried Brakkus, who treated me like his own flesh and blood."

Rasheed's voice was stiff, trying to maintain the formality between them and show how grateful he was that the Blahom had come to deliver the news herself, much as he wished that she hadn't had come to at all; that he could continue to live in his naive bliss that his father would come barreling through the door and laughing about some sort of broken arm he sustained. Hearing his thanks made Blahom's stomach churn. *To lose two fathers to war!* "Please, don't thank me," she said.

"My mother heard the rumors that my father had died on the battlefield, but no one had confirmed it officially. The fact that you, his family, were able to bring the news, put her soul at ease," he explained, his voice quiet and emotionless. He was not the gentle soul who adored Blahom at this moment. Between war and the lifeless bodies he saw following Vasco and the warriors to seize the devise and now news of his father, Rasheed had lost a piece of himself.

"You will be honored as a warrior in the CCDC ceremony." Blahom bowed reverently to Rasheed as the women were trained to do for all warriors who had returned home. "You have brought us victory and we are grateful. We will dance in your honor." Blahom lifted her head and stood up slowly. "General Murn buried your father. Sometime soon I'm sure he can take you ... and your mother ..." Blahom's words dried in her throat. When she looked up at Rasheed, she noticed tears pricking the corner of his own eyes.

Not only had a wife lost a husband, but a son had lost a father.

Ignoring all regal protocol, Blahom wrapped her arms around Rasheed. He was solid in her arms but holding him, allowing his grief, he appeared sapped of any strength left him.

Blahom remembered when they were young, before she was constantly followed by her Lady Mother and was allowed to be a child. She remembered how gentle Rasheed was, even then. Once, he had taken her aside and given her a flower. Under the flower was a mess of roots and dirt and Blahom had looked at him, confused.

"Why does the flower still have its roots?" Rasheed looked down, bashful and embarrassed, and told her that he wanted to give her a flower, but hadn't the heart to kill a flower by picking it and he wanted her to quickly plant it so it would grow.

Blahom was always moved by that memory. In a world where most boys his age were being taught to be ruthless warriors, Rasheed was still sweet and caring, even to things as simple as a flower.

Rasheed wrapped his arms around Blahom for a moment, and steadied his breathing. "Thank you, Goddess," he said softly, his voice weak and tired. His words brought Blahom back from her memories.

"You do not need to call me Goddess. I am your Blahom." Blahom paused and grabbed both his hands and looked at him.

"Tell me," she said, through her own tears. "Tell me about your father, so that he may live on."

Rasheed was silent for a moment. "Follow me, let me show you something."

Rasheed's room was plain with very little decoration. Swords leaned against the wall, but, other than the weapons, nothing else was in plain view. Rasheed closed the door behind them, opened his closet, and pulled out a green bottle of wine.

"This was my father's favorite. He gave it to me to hold onto for him, so we could share it once we got back from the battle," Rasheed frowned. "I'd like you to share this with me, Blahom."

Nodding her head, Blahom smiled at Rasheed, trying not to look so somber. "It would be an honor."

Rasheed left the room to grab two goblets, proclaiming that Brakkus himself would have drunk the wine right from the bottle. He poured two glasses and he and Blahom sat on his bed. Blahom took his hand and looked at him.

"To General Brakkus," Blahom said, and Rasheed raised his glass. "To my father."

The two clinked their glasses together and took a sip. Tasting the wine, Blahom coughed and then laughed. "My uncle liked the bitter, dry stuff, huh?"

Rasheed grinned, wincing at the taste of the wine as well. "Yes. I don't know if I'll ever completely understand why. With the way he liked his desserts, you'd think he would enjoy the sweeter wines."

Despite the taste, the two continued to sip, sitting peacefully together.

"You know, Uncle Brakkus was the one who gave me my first taste of wine." Blahom whispered the secret to Rasheed. "I remember looking at how he drank it so happily during a family dinner. When no one was looking, he asked me if I wanted a sip, and I said I did."

"Oh no," Rasheed laughed.

"Yes! He let me take a sip and I gagged and coughed, swearing it was the most disgusting thing that I tasted. Of course, me coughing like that made my mother look over and she quickly figured out what happened. Both Uncle Brakkus and I got such a scolding."

Rasheed chuckled. "That sounds like something he'd do. I can only imagine the look on his face being yelled at by Mother Hutra though."

"He tried blaming the whole thing on me and Mother kept shouting. 'She's only ten! You're the adult here!'" Blahom and Rasheed laughed in unison.

One glass became three and the two were laughing, sharing old stories of General Brakkus. While it was bitter and dry, the wine made Blahom feel light and airy, and her vision spun.

"Blahom, why didn't you follow me that day on the shore?" Rasheed inquired, breaking the lighthearted moment with a deep, dark question. It took a moment for Blahom to understand.

"You mean when Zya was murdered?" she asked. Rasheed nodded.

"I couldn't leave. Vasco needed me," Blahom answered, honestly, trying her hardest not to slur her words.

"But you could have been killed. Doesn't that scare you? Knowing that the Delions want you dead?" Rasheed asked. Blahom rolled her eyes.

"The Delions want all of us Zaeds dead. I'm not so special," she said with a slightly serious tone, swirling the wine glass with her

Blahom

fingers as she had seen done many times before. "Besides, I couldn't let my brother be alone on the shore like that. He had just lost so much so quickly. I couldn't just leave him to sit there alone."

"I love you. I want to protect you the way you wish to protect others. You truly are a Goddess," Rasheed whispered.

Despite the sadness of the situation, this was the first time Blahom felt completely at ease. There was nobody standing by her side to remind her of her duties. No Lady Mother to scold if she spilled wine on her dress, though she put the goblet down, just in case.

Feeling Rasheed staring at her, Blahom locked eyes with him, completely ensnared by his gaze. It took her a moment to realize they both had stopped speaking.

Blahom put her hands to his face, and Rasheed closed his eyes for a moment. "I should get you a cloth for your face," Blahom whispered as she felt the heat emit from him.

Rasheed opened his eyes and put his hands on Blahom's, their eyes lost in each other. "Please, allow me, Goddess," he said, as he got up to fetch a wet cloth from his washroom.

As he ran the cloth under hot water, Blahom took notice of his defined muscles as they rippled under his tunic. Even exhausted with grief, he remained strong and fit. Blahom inhaled deeply, her heart racing.

When Rasheed returned, he handed the cloth to Blahom, letting out a small hiss as the cloth met the cuts on his face. Blahom pulled away, but Rasheed stroked her arm gently.

The feel of his fingertips sent an electric shot through Blahom's spine, sparking feelings she hadn't known she had. Her heart pounded in her chest like thunder before a storm, and her hairs raised at the feel of his gentle, callused hand. For months, she had wanted nothing more than to spend time with this sweet soulful warrior, and now he was in front of her, staring into her eyes intently, and she stared back at him.

Something inside Blahom broke. Her entire body was on fire.

Suddenly, she was no longer a Goddess. She was only a young woman wanting to lose herself to a young man. This decision was hers and hers alone. Blahom leaned in, lips grazing his.

Rasheed welcomed her advances, and, threading his fingers through her hair, kissed her with a fiery passion. Through their grief, love, and sadness, they carried a deep affection for one another, and in this moment, those feelings could heal them.

Sadness had shuttered Blahom's heart at the loss of her uncle, however other emotions crept in as well. While she was mourning the loss of Brakkus, she was also feeling the joy of newfound freedom and a genuine connection. Breaking the long kiss to look at Rasheed, she never wanted to leave his side.

Blahom entangled herself in Rasheed's arms, and the two continued to immerse themselves in their love. She knew she would not make it back home.

Chapter Seventeen

Morning came and the beginning rays of the sunrise crept into Rasheed's room. Blahom woke with a jolt, though Rasheed was still soundly asleep. She stared down at his kind face and gently caressed his soft cheek. She wanted to stay curled up next to him and go back to sleep, but knew she had to return home.

Moving silently, Blahom slid her garments back on and left. Rasheed would miss seeing her when he woke up, but it was safer this way, and her aunt was less likely to see her leave.

Walking through the streets, Blahom felt her heart buzzing with joy. Early mornings were a time when the city was awake and bustling with activity. Children were shouting and playing, while vendors peddled their goods. Among the Zaeds, chatter had begun with news that Vasco and his men were spotted nearby and would be arriving any moment with the transportation device in tow. The early risers were joyous about the major victory and Vasco was being hailed as the next war hero. A lavish celebration was already in preparation in Vasco's honor and women were out shopping for the finest garments, hoping to catch his eye.

Blahom overheard the excited chatter of a mother and daughter discussing the news of Vasco's arrival with the device and that the Zaeds had practically won the war. Excitement shot through Blahom at the thought of seeing her brother.

Not long ago, the Zaeds had whispered about Vasco as a murderer. Now that thought was all but buried. After such a tremendous battle, no Zaed would dare to attempt to slander Vasco's name. Blahom knew that Vasco wouldn't have killed their aunt, but it was a relief to be able to hear her brother's name lauded in public again. *Mother will be so proud hearing such words of praise for her son.*

Gladdened, but knowing Lady Mother Clara would be angry and worried, Blahom hurried home. She opened the door to her room and there stood a troubled and boiling Lady Mother Clara.

"Well, you didn't save Trinity from being taken because she has been here all night," Lady Mother Clara spoke clearly and sarcastically. "You chose to put down your crown and be a whore last night." Each word a scathing fire, indicative of Lady Mother Clara's sense of disappointment and betrayal.

Why is she looking at me like that? Blahom wondered, anger and embarrassment swirling in the pit of her stomach. *I was safe – she knew I was safe. What I did is nothing to be ashamed of. Besides, what does she even know? She wasn't there.*

Before Blahom could get out a word, Lady Mother Clara continued. "As you know, your schedule is different today. We will be mourning your uncle's death, and Mother Hutra needs all the support of family. Also, not sure if you heard while you were off playing a harlot, but your warrior brother has returned. Our marvelous Zaed warriors have accomplished a great triumph and we are going to be celebrating the victory of your brother's devised plan at tonight's CCDC ceremony. However, our first stop is to greet him in the Throne Room where ManCohalith will inform him about the casualties. Your mother has asked that you dress in your Goddess attire."

After the murder of Zya, Blahom yearned to represent both her

Blahom

warrior and Goddess elements. She knew, though, that this was not the time for rebellion. "Of course. It is important that Mother feel supported and happy."

Lady Mother Clara ushered Blahom into her room to get dressed for the long day. Blahom's embarrassment was reinforced by Katyana, who had clearly overheard Lady Mother Clara's scolding.

"Did you get the space that you needed?"

"I was delivering the news of Brakkus' death," Blahom said, wondered if they knew what had happened between her and Rasheed. "Let's remember it was per Father's instructions."

Lady Mother Clara was indifferent to Blahom's story. What mattered was that she had not come back last night, even given the magnitude of the danger. Lady Mother Clara, caught between her loyalty to Blahom and her loyalty to Mother Hutra, seethed in anger, and made no attempt to be gentle while doing Blahom's hair.

Elsewhere, the crowded streets parted as Lieutenant Vasco and his warriors arrived with the transportation device in tow. Vasco looked like a giant, holding himself atop his horse with dignity and strength. The crowd cheered, proud of their future ruler. Despite their fatigue, the cheers of the Zaeds bolstered the warriors' spirits. The liveliness and applause of the Zaeds confirmed to Vasco that his father was alive, and thankfulness swept over him.

Looking out into the crowd, Vasco saw Zya staring back at him, cheering his name. His heart raced and he almost jumped off his horse to run to her, only to blink and find, of course, that she wasn't there.

"Look! We're almost at your home!" one of his Captains exclaimed, leaning on his horse to talk to Vasco.

Vasco tore his mind back to the present. Soon he would embrace his mother and sisters, ManCohalith, grateful to see him, and his brave General uncles, safe after such a dangerous battle. He knew his father would debrief him on what happened at the Delions' primary base camp. Vasco was eager to discuss about what he found at the secret base camp of the Delions.

Dismounting his horse, Vasco and his warriors strode through the hallways towards the Throne Room, and the Zaeds who saw them bowed in reverence. Vasco was only mildly surprised to see that some who bowed were the very Zaeds who had whispered about him killing his own aunt. *Ah, the hypocrisy*, Vasco thought, silently laughing to himself. *It never fails that one battle can change people's minds so quickly.*

They pushed open the Throne Room doors, and Vasco and his men stepped forward to greet their rulers.

Standing next to Mother Hutra's throne were Katyana and Blahom, smiling at their brother's triumphant arrival. Vasco's heart leapt with joy seeing his sisters. He looked up at Blahom, and gave her a victorious smile and she looked back at him, vibrating with happiness that their plan that day on the vessel had worked.

Vasco and his warriors knelt before ManCohalith and Mother Hutra.

"Vasco!" Mother Hutra jumped from her seat. Formal etiquette required she remain seated, but the sight of her son after such a dangerous battle overcame protocol. Vasco rose from his bow and Mother Hutra wrapped her arms tightly around him.

"I am so happy you have returned safely to us, my son," she said warmly as she embraced him and kissed his face. Mother Hutra took his arm and led him closer to the thrones. ManCohalith rose to his feet.

"I commend you and your warriors on the successful attack of the secret base. Thanks to your plan, we now have the coveted Delion technology. A celebration is already being prepared for you and your warrior's return. We will also honor the brave Zaed warriors that executed the plan of attack on the Delions' primary base as a distraction. Job well done, my son." ManCohalith spoke with pride in his voice, and then embraced Vasco. The warriors' cheers and applause echoed through the room.

"Thank you, ManCohalith. Your leadership and courage led us to this victory. All the brave warriors have earned this celebration.

There is no place like home," Vasco said happily, looking back at his fellow Zaeds with pride.

"Unfortunately, I have tragic news to deliver," ManCohalith said, and a hush fell across the room. Vasco looked to his father, dread rising in his heart.

"Even in victory, casualties in war are inevitable," ManCohalith said, his voice somber and grave. "We lost many brave warriors during our battle. Among the fallen, was your uncle, General Brakkus."

Vasco stiffened at the statement, feeling his entire body going numb. He had watched General Brakkus fight on the battlefield time and time again, ruthless and powerful, seemingly invincible against any attack. It was his uncle who taught Vasco that off the battlefield there was time for laughter and joy. This news felt like a cruel lie.

Vasco's eyes turned to his mother, the news of Brakkus' death still fresh for her, too. He opened his arms, pulled her close, and held her while she sobbed. The watching warriors bowed their heads in respect, dealing with their own feelings of shock and loss. ManCohalith looked out at his men, bowing his head as well in memory of General Brakkus. Katyana wept openly. Blahom had no more tears to shed.

Vasco's anger only grew. *No more death! First Zya and the baby, then my uncle, and if I can't end this war Blahom and Katyana could be next. They cannot – will not – die on the battlefield.*

"Know that our brave warriors' deaths were not in vain," ManCohalith said, new strength in his voice. "Securing the machine and attacking the Delion base assures us better footing in this war. We would never have made these advances without General Brakkus and the others who were lost in battle. The Zaeds are more powerful than ever, and we will put an end to this bloodshed once and for all. Tonight, Lieutenant Vasco will be made General Vasco!"

The assembled warriors cheered with renewed vigor, but Vasco remained silent, holding his mother.

"Unless there is more to speak of, you are all excused. Everyone, return home to your families and rest before tonight's festivities,"

ManCohalith said, smiling at his warriors. They bowed before him respectfully, and made their way out of the room until it was only Vasco standing before his family.

Blahom wanted to grab his hand and pull him out into the hallway, eager to catch up with him, but she noticed the grave look on his face.

"ManCohalith, I wish to speak with you in the Battle Strategy Hall," Vasco said, his voice grave.

"Of course, my son. Let us waste no time."

As ManCohalith left with Vasco, Blahom and Katyana wrapped comforting arms around their mother, knowing she would need their strength now. Blahom cast a last quick look after her brother and her father, tension building in her stomach. No time for that now.

In the Battle Strategy Hall, completely alone, ManCohalith settled his gaze on his son.

"Vasco, I want to tell you again how proud I am of you. This victory is because of your plan, and we would not be here today were it not for your clever and focused thinking." ManCohalith stared at Vasco's face. It was clear his son wasn't listening. ManCohalith took a step forward. "What is on my son's mind now that must be spoken away from your mother and sisters?"

After a moment of silence, Vasco found his voice. "While this fight was considered a victory, I cannot fully celebrate. We were able to retrieve the device, but it was damaged in the battle. I'm hoping that our own scientists can restore it to its original power." Vasco said, but struggled to look at his father as he spoke.

"Why is there a need to restore it? The Delions can no longer use it, and that was our goal." ManCohalith studied his son's face yet again. "There is more you wish to tell me. Do not continue to swallow your words."

Vasco looked up at his father. "With your permission, the machine needs to be fixed because I want to go through it."

ManCohalith's eyes widened.

Vasco continued. "There were Delions on the secret base who

made it through the device before it was dismantled. They have for certain taken Daniella and perhaps Aunt Lorraine. They will be bound to dedicate all possible resources to eradicating the Zaeds after witnessing our attack. If I go through, then I can discover where the device is teleporting them, and better understand what they're planning. We might find Daniella."

"What do you mean 'for certain they have taken Daniella'?" ManCohalith was at full attention.

"We saw a room full of young boys impregnating what looked to be women created through their technology. Father, I do not know about those women. That is far beyond the technology we as a people can even fathom. Before we destroyed them, they told me Daniella had been taken through the device. They were not certain about anyone else." Vasco was still in shock about all that he had seen.

"With the state of the machine you brought back, something can easily go wrong, even if we could make it operable again," ManCohalith said, his voice was steady, not giving away his own feelings.

"I don't care about the possibility of something going wrong ..."

"You should care about something going wrong!" ManCohalith snapped, cutting Vasco off before he could continue. "The risks of doing something like this are insurmountable. How do you suggest you would get back to Sirius after going through this device?"

"From what we've seen from this device, it is like a doorway. Once fixed, if I can go in, I would be able to come back out," Vasco explained but ManCohalith shook his head.

"You don't know that. Nobody does! You have no idea where the machine would take you or what to expect or how to prepare. And even if we could get this doorway to work, what is your plan once you get to the other side?" ManCohalith let out a long breath, trying to calm his emotions.

"Son, we have trained generation after generation for war here on Sirius. We battle on the strength of our divine gifts. We know nothing of this other planet and if our gifts would work there. There are too many unknown variables for us to take a gamble on your life."

"Father, if it is a chance that we will finally be able to end this war with the Delions, then it is a chance I'll take. I understand that there are risks, but that is why I want to do this alone. There will be no other Zaed in danger but me," Vasco said, his voice unwavering.

"I'm not going to lose you to a suicide mission with next to nothing to gain." ManCohalith was firm.

"Have I ever failed you, Father?" Vasco asked. ManCohalith was silent. "I have been blessed and, with my divine gifts and blessing, I will make our people and family safe again. I will go through the machine and communicate with Mother through the dream realm. I will kill the remaining Delions and return through the doorway with Daniella. The Delions will be taken by surprise, and I will be there and back in a matter of weeks."

ManCohalith heard his foolish son's words and gritted his teeth. "This mission is needlessly dangerous and makes no sense strategically."

Vasco tried again. "Father, let me be a General and do this. For you, for our family, and for the future of every Zaed man, woman, and child." Vasco paused for a moment, then said reluctantly, "But I will not go without your blessing."

There was silence. ManCohalith knew that Vasco's plan was foolhardy and ill-considered, and he could not let his only son undertake an impractical suicide mission.

After what felt – to Vasco – like an eternity, ManCohalith spoke. "You are my son and have the spirit of my courage in you. When I was your age, I was similar, stubborn in my ways, thinking that I alone could save the entire kingdom. However, I had to learn when the time was right for me to act, when to ask for assistance, and when to realize that some risks weren't worth taking. I know that this request is coming from a place of strength, I do. Though your bravery is commendable, I will not give you my blessing."

Vasco's heart dropped. Once his father's mind was made up, there would be no changing it.

"I understand, Father," he said, looking down at the floor.

Blahom

ManCohalith placed a hand on Vasco's shoulder. He empathized with his son's need to win the war and appreciated his tenacity, but to lose a son to such a mission ... He had lost too much in this war already.

"Come, let us prepare for the ceremony. It's time for us to live in the moment rather than dwell on the future. Tonight, we bestow you the honorable and well-deserved title of General," ManCohalith said, with one of his rare small smiles.

Vasco nodded, not speaking, struggling to subdue the voices in his head. Screams. Screams of agony. Screams that came from Zya and his unborn child. Some that came from Blahom and Katyana; others from his mother and father. Despite trying to drown out the voices with wine and a small prayer, he couldn't block out the screaming.

He knew there was only one way to win this war and protect those who were left of the ones he cherished.

Chapter Eighteen

After so much sadness, the Zaeds were relieved to celebrate their warriors at the CCDC festivity. So much had been building up and the Zaeds were long overdue for the release and joy of a proper ceremony.

Katyana and Blahom were getting dressed into their ceremonial garb for the victory dance they would be performing. Lady Mother Clara worked diligently on Blahom's hair, tugging and smoothing it into place, making Blahom's head ache. However, this was her punishment, and Blahom endured the process without whimpering.

The room was fraught with tension. Blahom knew that Katyana was upset with her from the night before. Blahom also worried about Vasco's behavior. What could be so important that Vasco walked away from their mother in her grief? Blahom quelled her worrying thoughts, certain Vasco would explain soon enough. She turned her focus to more pleasant memories.

Lady Mother Clara moved on from Blahom's hair and started applying golden paint to young Goddess' lips. A small smile quivered at the edge of Blahom's lips, as she replayed last night's adventures with Rasheed. His gentle caresses and their passionate kisses.

Blahom

"You look like a true Goddess, Blahom," Lady Mother Clara said with a nod, completing Blahom's makeup. "Please, remember to act like one."

"Yes, Lady Mother Clara," Blahom said quietly, feeling the sting in her words. It would take some time before Lady Mother Clara forgave Blahom for her late-night escapade.

"Come, sister. Let's stretch in the rehearsal room," Katyana said, trying to ease the tension and leading Blahom out of the room. The Lady Mothers followed at a distance like shadows.

"Ever since last night, you haven't been acting like yourself," Kat said, poking at her sister hoping to get the details.

"What are you talking about? Nothing has changed. I'm the same as ever," Blahom said defensively, and Katyana rolled her eyes.

"That's a lie. You've been weirdly giddy even with Lady Mother Clara mad at you. And have you thought about Mother? She has been distraught ever since hearing about Uncle Brakkus and yet here you are, all smiles and giggles."

"Lady Mother Clara has nothing to worry about and I am certainly comforting mother. Did you forget I was next to you when we consoled her in the Throne Room? Besides, am I not allowed to be happy occasionally? Vasco's back, we had a victory in a battle, and we're celebrating tonight. We should all be somewhat happy," Blahom said as she continued to walk down the hall at a quick pace.

"You know that's not what I mean," Katyana snapped. "And Vasco's acting weird too."

"I love you, sis." Blahom knew her sister just wanted to feel included. "You know exactly what happened, though I will not tell you any more." Blahom gave her sister a sly smile.

"Whatever. I definitely want to hear more after tonight's ceremony," Katyana said, proud they were having a sister moment.

The two Goddesses reached the rehearsal room and started to stretch – leaning down, touching their toes, then the floor. They moved to sit on the ground, reaching over their outstretched legs.

Usually, stretching felt like meditation to Blahom, breathing into a stretch as her body relaxed and her tensions melted away. Now, however, something was different.

Both Lady Mothers sat in the room, keeping an ever-vigilant eye, and frustration rose in Blahom as she sensed their eyes on her. Never had she felt so bothered by their presence, but since her time alone with Rasheed, everything felt pronounced. Blahom yearned to have that freedom again.

There was a knock on the door, and Lady Mother Chi opened it, clearly about to chide whoever was interrupting rehearsal, though she was silent when she saw who stood there.

"Vasco!" Katyana smiled, running over.

"Sorry for not visiting my dear sisters sooner. I had some boring battle things to discuss with ManCohalith," he said with a light-hearted laugh.

"Are you here to watch us practice?" Katyana smiled, asking sarcastically.

"No, my silly sweet darling sister," Vasco said with a returned air of sarcasm, "I wish to talk to Blahom. It's something that has to do with Zya," he said, growing somber. Always the older brother, it was hard enough for Vasco to accept Blahom growing up; Kat would be his baby sister for a while yet.

"Yes, of course, brother." Blahom headed towards the door, her mind racing with questions.

"I'm coming too." Katyana offered, but Vasco placed a hand on her shoulder, halting her.

"I'm sorry, my love, but this is about things you don't understand yet," Vasco said, his voice grave.

Kat crossed her arms and stomped her foot, eyebrows furrowing in anger at his tone. "Whatever. I understand plenty."

"Kat, you are a beautiful and smart Warrior Goddess, but this conversation is for Blahom and me."

"Anything you can tell Blahom, you can tell me," Kat said with a glare and Vasco sighed.

"I am discussing something incredibly depressing with Blahom.

We just lost General Brakkus, and I don't want you feeling more pain than you need to." Vasco tried to be gentle, but Kat saw through him.

"So Blahom gets to share the pain? I'm not a kid anymore, I'm a warrior! I've been training for pain!"

"Kat, I don't want to hear about you being a warrior." Vasco shot his youngest sister a stern look – a look that Katyana had seen on ManCohalith, and she saw the resemblance now. "In another year or two I will come to you with things like this, but not now."

"Okay, fine. Whatever." Pretending to be unbothered, Kat turned her back and continued to stretch.

Vasco led Blahom out of the rehearsal room to a private space. He was one of the few people that Blahom could be alone with, and they both appreciated it now.

The two siblings embraced in a tight hug. "What is it that you need to tell me about Zya?" Blahom asked and Vasco sighed.

"Unfortunately, I had to lie to get the two of us alone," Vasco said with a frown and Blahom looked at him in confusion.

"What is it?" she inquired. Vasco gently grabbed his sister's hands.

"You helped me convince our father to go with my plan to take over the Delion secret base and seize the transportation device. And it worked beautifully. That was the plan of the century, and you helped pull it off. You are a hero as much as I am and one day in history books, they will be praising your name for helping me." Vasco slowed and took a deep breath. "I need your help again, sister, but this is going to be a lot more difficult than my last plan."

Blahom could tell that he was struggling with what he was about to ask her.

"Vasco, you're my brother and we're a team. You know that I'll always help you however I can."

"You're not going to like my plan," Vasco's voice was laced with guilt.

"Well, what is it?" Vasco's hands started to fidget in his sisters.

Vasco's eyes shot around the room, as if to make certain there was no one else there.

"I've been speaking with Father. I just left some of my trusted men working on fixing the transportation device. They will be done by the start of the ceremony. The damage was largely mechanical and we are certain it can be repaired, however they're unsure of how long the device will stay powered on." Blahom could hardly understand the words coming out of Vasco's mouth.

"Why do you want to fix the device?" Blahom asked.

"Because I need to go through it and get to the other side. I saw the Delions leaving through the device. They have Daniella. They are going somewhere, and I need to follow." Vasco's eyes were wide as he continued to speak. "I won't allow this war to be dragged out any longer for you and Kat to fight in it. This is ludicrous! You are not meant for battle and Katyana is a child!"

"Vasco – what do you mean they have Daniella?"

"Please, Blahom. I need your help during the ceremony. Give me time to slip through the device. They have sent Daniella through and maybe Aunt Lorraine as well."

"You want me to help you run away?" Blahom asked angrily.

"I'm hardly running away," Vasco laughed, giving her a reassuring smile. "I'm going to save all of the Zaeds and my sisters."

"Going to the other side to god knows where? That sounds like a suicide mission!" Blahom yelled. She didn't care how charismatic Vasco sounded; she knew better than to let him leave to do something so dangerous.

"It's not a suicide mission! Why do I feel like I am the only one who sees them taking our women and murdering us as a threat?" Vasco's voice raised in frustration as he paced back and forth. "Do you remember the technology the Delions created to disguise themselves as Lieutenant Kov and his sister? Not to mention they murdered my Zya and our unborn child on the beach during the CCDC ceremony. Her blood stained my hands and will forever be in my mind. Do you know I can still hear our child's cries despite it never being born? I can't let the Delions continue to develop technology like that to someday return and possibly kill my entire family. I lost Zya and the baby and Uncle Brakkus, but I refuse to lose anyone else! If there is a chance to find our cousin Daniella, I have to take it."

Blahom wanted to cry, not knowing how she could possibly share the burden that he was feeling.

"How long will you be on this other side?" Blahom asked in a quiet voice. Vasco was silent for a moment.

"I honestly don't know."

"This wasn't part of the plan," she said, trying to suppress tears.

"Things change, Blahom."

Blahom stared at her brother. *Can't things to go back to normal? Can't we be could be a peaceful happy family?* Her thoughts raced as the world shattered around her. Her brother should be reveling in victory, letting the machine stay broken; rejoicing that the war was practically won, and he was now a General. *Instead, he's running away to continue chasing the enemy.*

Blahom ran away through the halls, and Vasco chased after her.

"Blahom, wait!"

She ran past the closed training room door, to her bedroom, and slammed the door shut. Leaning against the door, Blahom sank to the floor, breathing.

"Blahom, let me in!" Vasco demanded, pounding on the door.

She was silent, still on the ground. Tears welled up in her eyes until she couldn't hold them back.

"Blahom, let me in!"

Blahom didn't move from where she sat on the floor, crying.

"Please, Blahom," he said quietly. "I love you, my dear sister. I know you'll do the right thing." With those words, Vasco walked away from the door.

It took Blahom several minutes to pull herself together, and she returned to the rehearsal room where Katyana was still stretching, the Lady Mothers still in attendance, waiting for Blahom's return.

"Blahom! Your makeup for the ceremony!" Lady Mother Clara scolded.

"I'm sorry. Remembering Zya and hearing what Vasco had to say ..." Blahom trailed off.

Lady Mother Clara's face softened. "Come here, my Goddess. We still have time for me to redo it," she said gently and Blahom followed her back to the mirror. Her reflection did not show her turmoil over Vasco's request.

* * *

Blahom's heart was beat loudly in her chest as she got into position.

As usual, the CCDC ceremony brought everybody out. After the tragedy at the eclipse celebration, ManCohalith had instituted a standing order that security be enhanced for all future CCDC events, and warriors were in evidence everywhere, alert and standing guard, offering an increased feeling of security to what was already an exciting day. A sea of Zaeds gathered on the beach, expanding to the surrounding cliffs, vying for position to see the dance. The air buzzed with anticipation and joy.

Scanning the crowd, Blahom, the soloist for tonight, let her eyes settle on Rasheed, seated in his late father's place next to the other Generals. Rasheed had been staring at her from the moment the dancers arrived and now gave her a slight smile and a warm wink. She was the only one he wanted to see, and that thought made Blahom's heart race even more. Her heart fluttered and she ached to relive the memories of their night, but knew there were more pressing matters.

She tore her gaze away and found Vasco. He was smiling as he sat next to Mother Hutra and held her hand, the two apparently in a lighthearted discussion. ManCohalith was seated on the other side of Mother Hutra, quiet but enjoying the smile on his wife's face, welcome after so much sadness.

Blahom knew her mother was trying to keep herself in the

present and celebrate rather than dwell on the sorrow of her brother's death. Trying to keep her face neutral, Blahom started her dance with the other women. Inside, her stomach burned with sadness and frustration. It broke her heart that Vasco was going to leave while their mother was so fragile and run off without their father's blessing. It pained her more that she was going to help.

Will I be forgiven for doing this? Blahom asked, her eyes looking up to the sky. *By helping my brother, I will be hurting my family, especially my mother. Is everything worth it? Is this the right choice?* Blahom knew her questions were futile. Nothing was going to stop Vasco from doing what he needed to do.

Her movements were graceful and flawless, the crowd entranced as she went into her solo dance. She was focused and committed, using all her pain and emotion to fuel the passion in her dance.

I will remember to be thankful for all the seasons of life. I am thankful for all the warriors who made it home. I am thankful for those who had the courage to lay their lives down for us. I am thankful for my family and my brother. I know and trust he will return to us safely. I am thankful for it all.

Blahom's arms moved elegantly in praise to the music. Her dancing was like water, fluid and natural. She set up to prepare for a twirl that the Zaeds knew well, likening it to that of a whirlpool. Rising to the point of her toes, Blahom purposely shifted all the weight of her body to her right ankle, the weakest.

The burn of muscles, her tendons pulled as her ankle rolled, and her foot twisted beneath her. With a scream, she fell onto the sands of the beach as gasps erupted throughout the crowd. The Zaeds had never seen her make such a mistake, especially during a CCDC ceremony.

Mother Hutra jumped from her seat and ran towards her daughter, Lady Mother Clara and Lady Mother Chi alongside. Katyana, out of her position, knelt next to her sister, her eyes wide in shock.

Blahom's ankle was beginning to swell and bruise.

Looking out into the crowd, Blahom could see all eyes glued to her, concerned and anxious. ManCohalith remained in his seat, radiating dismay. Rasheed rose – and paused – longing to be by her side, but not wanting to reveal their relationship.

Blahom's eyes took in her mother, her father, Katyana, then Lady Mother Clara, and Rasheed and ... Vasco was nowhere in sight. Her heart sank, and she fought for breath around the lump in her throat. *Vasco. Gone!?* Her brother, who, under any other circumstances, would have been by her side, had left.

Blahom remembered the first time she had twisted an ankle. The pain was so great they had called for a doctor. Vasco had heard about his little sister's injury and was immediately by her side. Now, instead, he had chosen to vanish into the crowd.

"Blahom, relax. Breath, daughter. You need to slow your breathing down," Mother Hutra said gently.

Blahom didn't hear a word from her mother. Her emotions churned and grew until she felt she was drowning in sadness, guilt, love, loyalty, fear, and anger. The world grew dark at the edges.

"Blahom, snap out of it!" Katyana's concern bled through her voice. Her words didn't reach her sister either. All Blahom heard was her own rapid breathing. Tears streaked her cheeks as her ankle pulsed and her heart broke.

Blahom prayed her brother would return. *Safely. Soon. Within the week, had he said? A week of not knowing* ... And then it too was all much to bear and she passed out on the sand, her last thought that when she came to, Vasco would be on another world.

Later, she knew she had been foolish. She should never have let him leave.

The End

Acknowledgments

To my writing consulting team, thank you for being my superheroes.
   Rita L. Hubbard
   Olivia Dallas Johnson
   Ernest Dempsey

To my emotional support tribe, thank you for helping me keep my head off a swivel . I love you.
   Mina Starks
   Morvitz St. Clair Jordan

To my Family,
   Daddy, Mommy, Fenesa, Joy, Grandma...
   and all 100+ in my familial tribe. Your love is truly unconditional. Thank you. I love you.

To my beloved late WC Hunter,
   My most impactful and deepest memories come from your undeniable faith in God and leadership. Im forever grateful.

About the Author

April Q. Russell is passionate about all facets of the creative process. This is April's debut book.

April also founded and created RevHo, a private membership content and social house in Marietta Ga nestled on 7 acres.

She holds a BA in Mass Communication and Psychology from the University of Tennessee. She spends her time between Los Angeles, California and Atlanta, Georgia. April enjoys all things food, traveling, outdoors and is always up for a good creative and writing session. Visit April Q. Russell online at www.aprilqrussell.com